Perfect Lie

Perfect Lie

Claire Sheldon

Book 1 – Lisa Carter Files

Stories that inspire emotions!
www.rubyfiction.com

Published 2021 by Ruby Fiction
Penrose House, Crawley Drive, Camberley, Surrey GU15 2AB, UK
www.rubyfiction.com

A CIP catalogue record for this book is available from the British Library

ISBN: 978-1-91255-040-1

Printed and bound in Great Britain by Clays Ltd, Elcograf S.p.A.

For Karen Blackburn and my friends and colleagues past and present of Insolvency Risk Services. Without you none of this would have been possible.

Acknowledgements

Thanks to fellow authors Jeanette Hewitt, Louise Jensen, Rebecca Bradley, Cally Taylor, Angela Clarke, Roz Watkins, Lucy Mitchell and Darren Young for your ongoing support through my writing journey. Sean Coleman and Rachel Burton for their knowledge and guidance.

My Choc Lit and Ruby Fiction family and the Tasting Panel who I am forever indebted to. Special thanks to those Panel members who passed the manuscript and made publication possible: Hilary Brown, Jackie Blake, Shalini G, Lorna Baker, Jenny Kinsman, Alan Roberton, Ruth Nagele, Bee Master, Gillian Cox and Jo Osborne.

My editor for working her magic and, trust me, there was a lot needed!

My creative writing tutor John Gibson, who is missed greatly.

Jimmy Eat World for their continued inspiration when nothing makes sense.

My first readers: Julie G, Carol C, Julie S, Georgina G and Rhian J.

Special thanks go to my Nan, Grandad and Janice who used to let us stay up and watch *The Bill* during our summer visits down south. If only you knew what you were creating.

Lastly, my number one fans the real Alex and Melanie and of course Andrew for his continuous love, support and for putting up with me.

Prologue

Chloe

She never imagined it would end this way. Travelling to the unknown, bundled into the back of a van.

Her hands were bound behind her back. The more she struggled to free them, the more the rope cut off her circulation. It chafed against her skin, causing blisters to form.

She was close to dehydration, licking her lips in search of moisture. Her mouth felt as if it was full of cotton wool, stopping her from shouting for help. No one would hear her over the rumble of the engine and loud voices and laughter coming from the front of the van.

The strong smell of tobacco and weed stung her nose as she tried to get a sense of where they might be taking her. She'd lost track of how long she'd been lying there, drifting in and out of consciousness from the beating she had received, the blood long dried on her face.

She tried to kick out, shuffling towards the door in hope of making an escape but the pain from where she had been held down, beaten and raped both by the various men and a series of objects, was too much. She knew better than to just give up. She tried to remember her training; there were protocols for everything. But no one was coming to rescue her. She had screwed up big time.

Suddenly feeling cold and alone, she thought of Adam. Had she told him how much she loved him when she saw him last? Did she need to make her peace with God? Should she have paid more attention at Sunday school? Surely this wasn't the end?

The van came to a sudden halt and the laughter and talking stopped. The doors opened and the sound of the crunchy gravel replaced the drone of the engine. Her ears were filled with the sound of their footsteps in time to her racing heartbeat.

The door would open at any moment and she'd be in for the fight of her life. Was she ready? She would fight through the pain because, if she didn't, what was left would be much worse.

The doors opened and the back of the van filled with bright sunlight as someone grabbed her legs and dragged her out. As her body scraped along the floor of the vehicle she attempted to block out all the pain as she summoned all her strength, tensing her body. If she didn't fight back, this would be the end …

Chapter One

MONDAY
Jen Garner

Jen placed her mug down on the kitchen island as she watched the kids arguing over whose turn it was to have the Coco Pops out of the variety pack. She enjoyed moments like this stood in the house's stillness, observing the scene play out in front of her. The only distraction was the sound of the passing lorries taking their loads to the next destination. Suddenly her senses sparked as her husband, James, came up behind her, wrapped his arms around her waist and whispered into her ear, 'Come back to bed once you've dropped the kids at school.'

Jen laughed at the idea. James pressed closer into her, and she felt his erection underneath his dressing gown. She turned to look at him as thoughts of following him entered her mind.

'Shouldn't you be at work by now, Mr Garner?'

James leant over her and kissed her forehead. 'I was planning to take some time off and work from home but, seeing as you're not interested, I'd better get ready to go in.' Jen stood on her tiptoes to return the kiss, brushing her lips across his as she pulled away, teasing him.

'Sounds like you're fresh out of luck to me.' She laughed. 'Anyhow one of the mums wants to talk to me about the school play or something.' James was turning to head back out of the kitchen when he stopped.

'I'm meeting Harry for a couple of drinks tonight if that's okay? Jess has gone home to London, and he says he's lonely.'

Jen rolled her eyes. She knew there would be a reason for his affection. 'Just don't go getting yourself into any trouble, ay?'

'I don't know what you mean,' James responded with his knowing smile as he headed towards the stairs.

'Melanie, give Alex the Coco Pops,' Jen shouted, returning her attention to the scene playing out in front of her and noticing them both still arguing over whose turn it was. 'Right, come on you two. Let's at least make an attempt at getting to school on time,' she said as she cleared the surrounding table.

With the kids dressed and packed into the car, Jen headed towards the school. The weather wasn't inspiring her, and she really needed go to out for a run once she'd dropped them off. It was cold, dark and she wouldn't be surprised if it started raining before she made it home to change.

As they stopped at a set of lights, she noticed Jess's pink Beetle pull up next to the car. Jen turned to wave as Jess looked straight through her. She'd been on a double date with Jess and Harry several times and she'd always been met with the same frosty reception. Jess was a party girl, but Jen couldn't help but think that she seemed a little fake. The image Jess portrayed of herself was too perfect to be true. Jen made an effort for James' sake. After all, Harry was his best friend and if she didn't, she would no doubt get left at home with the kids.

Since the children started school, Jen had struggled to make friends with the other mums. She'd attempted to join the PTFA but found them all far too cliquey and she was too old for all the backstabbing and bitchiness that sometimes followed. She knew she needed to at least make some effort with Jess – at least they had something more in common than their kids, even if it was just Harry and James' friendship.

'Jennifer, I'm so glad that I've caught you,' Helen shouted from behind her when she got to the school.

'I got your message, where's the fire?'

'It's the school play. I wrote the sizes down wrong and now I need to get everyone's measurements again.'

'Okay, Helen. Who've you got so far?' Jen replied as she kissed both the kids goodbye and went over to help collect the measurements.

Disaster being averted and costumes organised, Jen returned home to find a package on her door step. As she opened the box she noticed that it contained a single red rose and six white lilies, but no card or invoice to say where they were from. She inhaled their scent as she pondered the strange combination. Had they been left at the wrong house? It was unlikely they were from James. He wasn't one for buying flowers at the best of times.

She placed them on the island in the middle of the kitchen. Switching on the kettle, she searched for a vase and her phone. Jen decided to settle for James' large drinking glass as a temporary home until she could locate a vase. She so rarely got flowers that the vases would no doubt be at the back of a cupboard somewhere. She located her phone just as the kettle boiled, then poured the hot water on the teabag and sent a message to James.

Thanks for the flowers??? Love you J.

She wouldn't get a reply until he was on his way home, given how busy he was at work. James was a technical manager for a big company, and there was always something or someone that needed fixing. She returned to her drink and held it with both hands, trying to harness some of its warmth. As she took a sip, her phone pinged.

What flowers?

The plot thickens, she thought. She finished her drink and contemplated her morning run. She needed to make sure she was still on track with her training schedule for the race through the streets of Nottingham that was coming up. As she headed upstairs to change, her phone beeped again, calling her back into the kitchen. Another text from James; maybe he wasn't as busy as he made out.

You've probably been out already, but apparently, they've found a dead body at the back of one of the supermarkets in town.

Bloody hell!!!! I'm about to head out now, I'll see what I can find out, ly x, she responded.

A body found in their home town? Nothing much ever happened in Long Eaton as it was, she thought to herself as she put on her running gear and tied her hair up, pulling it through the hole in her baseball cap. She was ready to leave. She opened the app on her phone and started her music. As she opened the front door she was hit full force by the cold wind *and* it was raining. She stepped outside and braced herself, hoping she would warm up soon enough.

She began her normal running route, hoping to improve her time. As her feet began to pound the pavement, the familiar beat settled her breathing and she concentrated on the run ahead. She wasn't racing anyone at Parkrun today, so she could just take it slow and steady.

As Jen ran towards the canal she thought about the unexpected flowers. Again, she pondered the strange combination. A red rose was a sign of love, but as for the lilies? She loved lilies, which is why she assumed they were from James. Who else would buy her flowers except for him?

The ground was wet as she ran through the puddles but she kept looking ahead, concentrating on her goal. The trees were already shedding their crispy leaves and turning golden as autumn took hold. She ran past the occasional dog walker, each one choosing whether to acknowledge her or not. She didn't mind. They were all only distractions to her. Her times were improving; she was getting faster and becoming stronger again. She would no longer be chasing the pack; the pack would be chasing her.

As she arrived at Sandiacre Lock, she passed the farmhouses and footbridge, reaching her pace. Straight on from there she headed down the canal towards Long Eaton. She liked Long Eaton. She'd moved here with James to start a family away from the hustle and bustle of the city ... but now a body had been found. Maybe it wasn't as safe as she'd thought? The canals made excellent running routes for her training. They were her sanctuary, her space to think and plan; organise her chaotic mind. The canal paths provided many answers to life's questions and motherly woes about her children and their lives at school. The tracks spelt freedom and always showed her the way home. With the ducks quacking as she ran past, she dodged more dog walkers along the same scenic route. Then she came off the canal and headed along the cycle track. There she would negotiate the puddles and potholes that filled the worn-down concrete, each having their own history and stories to tell.

She felt the cold temperature more here as the wind blew against her and the trees waved, cheering her on. Jen felt alive as the endorphins kicked in, and her heart raced. As she reached the end of the track, she turned and headed towards the town. She could run to the supermarket, or take the turning that would send her the other way along a less used route. As Jen ran down the slope, she noticed several police officers milling around at the gate.

'I'm afraid you can't come this way, miss,' one of the officers warned.

'Can I not get on the track further up?' she asked, trying to catch her breath.

'The route between here and the supermarket is closed. There's been an incident.'

This must be what James mentioned in his text, Jen thought, noticing two teenage girls standing at the gate giggling with one of the other officers.

'Can I go that way instead?' she asked, pointing towards the bridge. They all stood there for a moment, while the officer contacted his boss with the proposed new route. As Jen waited, she became aware of a conversation between the younger officer and the teenage girls.

'Have you got a tattoo?' they were asking.

'Go on, show us.' The other girl cackled at the officer's response.

Though Jen could only hear half of the conversation, it

took her mind away from the fact that she had now lost her pace. She smiled to herself as the young officer flirted with the young girls and they lapped up his attention.

'The body has an infinity symbol on her ankle?'

Her sense suddenly prickled as she heard the mention of the infinity symbol.

'I've not seen anyone with one of those ...' The girls giggled again.

'Miss.' The other officer was trying to regain Jen's attention.

'Sorry I was miles away,' Jen said, touching her right wrist.

'You should be okay to go that way.'

'Thank you,' Jen said as they stepped aside and let her past. She smiled at them both, and took a sip from her bottle before she began to run again. She'd lost her rhythm and her thoughts were now full of tattoos and their meanings.

As Jen ran across the bridge, she could see the police officers in white overalls searching the water below. She'd Google it when she got back home. She guessed the reporters would be at the other end. Or perhaps she had got there before the story broke nationally? The terrain had changed to muddy, wet grass. She kept going, but her mind was still distracted. She wished that she'd gone a different route and avoided the scene altogether, as her thoughts were now filled with questions.

Chapter Two

DI Chris Jackson

Chris felt exhausted despite having had a good night's sleep. Something wasn't quite right. He didn't like the feeling of being so tired, never mind the headaches and problems focusing. He couldn't help but think that it was all work related. The budget cuts had left fewer officers to do the same jobs, and his own job was also starting to change. He had less time to be out on the street solving crimes and bringing the bad guys in. His days were becoming full of spreadsheets and report writing. Maybe he needed his eyes checking? Perhaps he was spending too much time staring at over-colourful PowerPoint presentations on the same screen? Or maybe he just needed some time off, away from work and the pressures it brought?

He realised he needed to leave soon, otherwise he'd be late for the meetings that filled his day. As he turned and surveyed his flat, he couldn't miss the mess and realised he had no idea when the girls from 'Maid Madness' were due. They used to come weekly but, with him living alone, there was less and less for them to do. He'd made the mistake of asking them to change to monthly and he'd become complacent. He would make sure he'd at least made a start before their next visit.

Chris had been one of the detective inspectors working under the Special Ops unit for the past five years. As a child he'd always wanted to be like the cops on the television. He'd romanticised the job but had learnt the hard way that real policing wasn't as glamorous as it was on shows he'd enjoyed when he was younger. Working his way through the ranks at some speed in Nottingham, Chris had made the job he'd once day-dreamed about his own.

As he looked around the living room in search of his laptop cable, he noticed his cat, Fluff, on a pile of his freshly laundered clothes. Chris tried to bat her away, but she had other plans; she was comfy and the clothes were still warm from the dryer. Fluff was the only woman in his life; her white Persian cat hair always managed to get everywhere. There was always one hair that managed to evade capture and would appear on his work suit out of nowhere at the most inconvenient times.

Chris found his laptop cable and hung up his clean shirts. The hairs would have to wait until later when he wasn't in a rush and could sit there with the lint brush.

He was ready to go and about to head down to the car when his mobile phone rang.

'Detective Inspector Jackson speaking.'

'Morning, sir. Sorry to ring you before you've made it into the office but there's been a murder.'

Chris was taken aback for a second.

'There was a triple nine call at about seven-thirty,' the officer continued. 'They want you to be senior investigating officer seeing as Long Eaton is on your way in, sir.'

'I picked the short straw, huh? I'll grab my stuff and head over there now. Whereabouts in Long Eaton is it?'

'Just up the road from the Long Eaton police station, so park there and I'll get someone to meet you.'

'Who's in charge up there?'

'Sergeant Gillroy, sir.'

'Great. Well, tell him I shouldn't be more than half an hour depending on traffic.'

'I will do.'

Chris ended the call. It had been a long time since he'd heard those words before 9 a.m. Nottingham was more known for its drug problems and knife crime. Long Eaton was a small town on the outskirts of Nottingham and Derby where very little crime ever happened. Until now, it seemed.

'Bye Fluff,' Chris shouted as he left the flat and hurried towards his door and then on to the underground garage shared with his fellow residents.

As Chris headed towards Long Eaton and whatever horrors he'd be faced with, he found himself thinking about home. He couldn't remember exactly when he'd last been to see his parents. When he'd announced he'd joined the police force during his eighteenth birthday meal he'd been met with varying reactions. He'd never hidden his fascination with all things crime-related but still often wondered if his parents had expected him to go to university. He was an only child and had been pretty close to his parents, but there would be no chance of him popping over to see them anytime soon, having been assigned the SIO role in this latest investigation.

Chris had been so focused on progressing through the ranks of the police force and, having almost reached the top, he was beginning to pine for some female company. Someone to go home to at the end of a busy day and share his life with. Fluff wasn't the best at listening to his policing stories, so he tended to save them all up for his dad who lapped them up, while his mother would just stand there with that disapproving look on her face.

There *was* one other female in his life: his colleague, Detective Sergeant Julie Ryan. He often found himself partnering Julie out in the field, so she was always the first person he'd turn to when he needed help at a crime scene.

'Ring DS Ryan,' Chris instructed his car's hands-free phone.

'Morning, boss,' Julie answered on the third ring.

'Morning, Julie. Did you have a good evening?'

'I did, thanks. And yourself?'

'Yeah, same old, same old. I don't know if you've heard along the grapevine but there's been a suspected murder in Long Eaton. I'm on my way there now.'

'I'd heard whispers in the canteen.'

'Are you free to come and join me at the scene?'

'I'll grab a pool car and meet you there, boss.'

'Great, I'm about five minutes away. I've been told to park at the Long Eaton station and ask for Sergeant Gillroy, so I'll be around that area.'

'See you there shortly, boss.'

Chris had told Julie on more than one occasion that she should put in for her inspector exams, although she was happy as a Detective Sergeant. 'I'm in no rush for the increase of paperwork,' she would tell him. Thinking back, Chris wished someone had mentioned that to him when he was so keen to join the top flight. He might have thought twice about the leap from policing on the streets to the office amongst spreadsheets and report writing.

Chris found a parking spot easily and, as he climbed out of his car, he surveyed the area. The police station was located right next to a major supermarket. The management there would be the first people he needed to get on side.

'Morning,' Chris said as he approached an officer who he'd just seen talking to a member of the public. 'Detective Inspector Jackson,' he said, holding up his warrant card.

'One moment, sir,' the female officer responded as she excused herself from her previous conversation. 'Sergeant Gillroy has just gone into the station to speak to a witness. I'll radio him and tell him you've arrived.'

'Thank you …?'

'… Officer Hayward, sir. Nikki Hayward.'

'Nice to meet you, Nikki. Chris Jackson.' He held his hand to shake hers. 'Am I okay to take a walk up towards the scene?'

'Yes, I'll let the Sergeant know you've gone that way. I'll inform the officer on the cordon as well.'

'Thanks, Nikki.'

Chris started to walk away from the station and headed towards the outer cordon.

'Inspector Jackson,' Chris said, holding out his warrant card to the officer stationed at the cordon.

'Go straight on, sir. The forensic tent is just round the corner.'

'Thank you. My colleague Julie Ryan is making her way over so if you could let her through and point her in my direction that would be great.'

'Okay, not a problem.'

Chris took the short walk towards the back of the supermarket where the tent had been erected. They'd obviously already spoken to the management, which meant one less thing for him to organise.

'Detective Jackson,' Sergeant Gillroy greeted him as he approached from behind him. 'Not sure why they called the big guns in? We have everything under control here.'

'I've been asked to act as SIO, so if you could walk me through events so far …?'

'Of course. But like I said, I have it all under control.'

'It'll be a swift and clean handover then.'

Chris could tell that the Sergeant was in no rush to hand anything over, but he wasn't in the mood for a pissing contest. Certainly not here stood in the rain while there was a murder investigation that needed to get underway.

'When did the incident report come in?' Chris prompted him.

'We received the call from control at 7.33 a.m. I sent officers Curtis and Haywood to investigate. They found the dog walker who had called it in, visibly shaken by what he'd seen. Claims that in his thirty years of walking his dog in the mornings he has never come across something as horrifying as this.'

'I should hope not,' Chris answered, unsure if the Sergeant would get his humour.

'Officer Curtis is still with the body now, waiting to be cleared by the CSIs and Dr Walsh, the on-call pathologist.'

'Thank you, Sergeant. I'll be taking the lead from here. My colleague is on her way over and we'll decide from there our plan of action.'

'You'll be needing one of these.' A forensic suit was thrust into Chris's arms by the Sergeant.

Chris began to climb into the suit when Julie arrived with a polystyrene cup full of a steaming liquid. 'Ah, a woman after my heart,' he said as his cold hands wrapped around the cup.

'Yeah, I know what you're like without your morning coffee.'

Chris laughed. This would make things seem less gloomy. He took a sip and waited for the caffeine hit he craved. 'Julie, would you grab one of the officers who are familiar with the area and check the perimeter and make sure everything is secure?'

'Of course, boss. Need help with the suit?'

'No, I think I'm good,' Chris said as he looked sadly at the coffee, knowing he'd need to sacrifice it before he went any further.

Chris prepared to walk onto the scene. He wasn't sure what to expect after his brief update from Sergeant Gillroy, who seemed rather put out to have not been assigned the role of SIO himself. He rounded the corner and noticed a second tent that reached across the path towards the bridge that he assumed the body had been found under.

'Morning all,' Chris said as he entered the tent.

'And here's the man we've all been waiting for,' Dr Walsh greeted him.

Dr Amanda Walsh, one of Derby's best Home Office pathologists, had been with the pathology department since before Chris joined the team. He knew of her high standards but hadn't had the opportunity to work with her until now.

Chris looked round at the activity going on inside the tent. 'What have you got for me?' he asked the uniformed officer.

'We have an unidentified female, face down in a foot of water. I checked her pulse on arrival but nothing else,' the officer responded.

'Thank you, Officer Curtis. If you've been cleared by the CSIs, head back to the station and get yourself cleaned up. I'll catch you later.'

'Thank you,' he said as he made his way out of the tent.

'Chris, if you would,' Dr Walsh spoke, indicating towards the fence and the three-foot drop. 'I'm not sure how much forensic evidence we'll find in the water and around where the body has been dumped given this dismal weather,' she said, as she circled the body like it was her prey. 'Right, let's get her turned over and see what we've got,' Dr Walsh ordered as a couple of the CSIs came over to assist.

Chris made sure he was out of the way as the water seeped into his shoes.

The body was of a woman who looked to be in her thirties with dark hair matted around her pale face, her make-up smudged and her nose sat at a strange angle. Any signs of bleeding from the initial injuries had been washed away but the stench of bleach was unmissable.

'What a waste.' Chris sighed and thought back to the street girl who had been found dumped last year. They always said that every cop has that one case he never forgets, and Daisy was his.

'She looks like she'd taken a good beating. Though I suspect this would have happened some time prior to her death, judging by the colour of some of those bruises. Plus someone has tried to cover their tracks. I'm sure you can smell the bleach they've used in attempt to clean her.' Dr Walsh began her initial visual search.

'Do we have any idea of the time of death?' Chris asked, as he started to do the maths in his head.

'Not a hundred per cent sure. I'll have a better idea once I get her back to the lab. If I had to guess, I'd say late last night or early this morning, judging by the rigor mortis.'

'Do you have any thoughts on how she got here?' Chris questioned.

'I suspect she'd been dumped from around the back as it wouldn't have been easy to get over the fence,' Dr Walsh said, pointing towards the other end of the tunnel.

Chris walked through the shallow rainwater, thinking about his increasingly wet socks and the woman they'd just found. She'd been dressed like she'd been out clubbing, but as far as he knew there were no clubs left in Long Eaton. As he walked, he met more CSIs combing the water for evidence. He acknowledged them before heading back towards the body.

'Any ID?' he asked on his return.

'There wasn't any on her person, but the CSIs are searching the area.'

'Thank you, Dr Walsh. Will you be taking her to Derby Royal?' Chris asked, pulling up the schedule on his phone.

'Yes. Depending on what happened overnight and, with any luck, I'll have some results for you late today, early tomorrow.'

'Can I just check, the tattoo on her ankle … is that the infinity symbol?' asked Chris.

Dr Walsh looked over at the girl's ankle. 'Well spotted, Inspector. It looks like that, yes. I'll be able to confirm once I get her on the table.'

This was Chris's least favourite part of the job. Though the body had been dumped in the small town of Long Eaton, she was still someone's daughter, sister, wife or girlfriend. They would no doubt be waking up, wondering why she hadn't come home or hadn't been in touch recently. With no ID found on the victim, it meant that the woman's identification could take that bit longer. Though hopefully the tattoo would help.

That had been part of the reason that the death of the street girl, Daisy, still played on his mind. They had never found a next of kin and, with little being known about Daisy's family, someone out there was missing a daughter whose life had ended so violently. He just hoped that this case would end differently.

'Thank you, Dr Walsh. I'll get out of your way,' Chris said, climbing out of the ditch.

Chris left the tent deep in thought and went to get out of his overalls, which had started to become uncomfortable. It was probably because he wasn't used to wearing them, unlike the other guys processing the scene. He stepped out of them, almost losing his balance.

'Find anything useful?' Julie asked, as she watched him wobble.

'Not really. If we'd got to the scene earlier? Who knows?'

'The perimeter is secure, officers stationed at all possible entry points.'

'Thanks, Julie. Can you call the team and get them to meet us here? I'll go and inform Sergeant Gillroy that we're going to be here until the site is cleared.'

'On it, boss.'

Julie headed back to the station, leaving Chris rearranging his clothes. He wondered how long before the press got hold of the incident. Chris formed a plan of action in his head, ready to brief his team once he was back inside the warmth of the station. He began to think about the members of his team and how best to utilise them, knowing they'd all be keen to make a start. Right now, however, his first priorities were a hot drink, along with dry shoes and socks from the boot of his car, where he always carried spares.

'Good morning all, thank you for coming through to Long Eaton for this morning's briefing,' Chris addressed his team who were all crammed into a small room at the Long Eaton police station. It was certainly clear that Sergeant Gillroy was in no rush to help when he had showed Chris and Julie through to the incident room. Either that or the station wasn't equipped for cases of this scale, and this really *was* the biggest room they had to offer.

Chris's team was pretty small compared to others in the unit. They were used to investigating different incidents, but they all came together when there was a murder.

Detective Constable Greg Sanders was the father figure of the team, DC Sally Croft was always looking for her next step up the career ladder. Then there was DC Trudie Clarke, always a calming influence in any situation, and DC Colin Goodwin, the youngest team member who, on top of all the police work, had a family of his own to support. Detective Sergeant Julie Ryan was his right-hand woman.

'As you are no doubt aware by now, Julie and myself have been drafted in to investigate the death of a young female,' Chris said, pointing to the photo he had pinned to the wall. 'We have no identity information for her but what I can tell you all from my brief chat with Dr Walsh is that our victim was beaten badly. It's most likely she was dumped where she was found.'

'Boss, are there any witnesses?' Sally asked.

'The emergency call was made at seven-thirty this morning by a dog walker. He was accompanied home by a PC Nikki Haywood,' Chris said, looking at his notes.

'Did we get anything out of him prior to his departure?' Sally enquired.

'Our dog walker – a Mr Walker, would you believe? – was pretty distressed, so it was decided to get him home and we'd get a statement from him later,' Julie responded.

'Sally, will you grab Nikki and go and see if he's happy to give a statement? Now that he's hopefully more settled?' Chris asked.

'Of course, boss,' Sally responded.

'There's also possible CCTV from the supermarket next door which will need viewing and copies taken.'

'I'll head over there now, boss,' Colin responded.

'Great.' Chris looked around at his team. 'One thing we do have to go on, though, is our victim had this tattoo on her ankle.' Chris continued, holding up the photo. 'I'm told it's an infinity symbol. I need someone to contact local parlours and see if anyone remembers doing this design. Though this is likely to be a long shot if the girl wasn't local.' Chris took a short pause before beginning again. 'We all know how important the first forty-eight hours of a murder case is. Go out, speak to your contacts, see if you can find out anything about this girl.'

Chapter Three

Jen Garner

Jen was relieved to be back home after her run. She'd been distracted by not only the police presence but also by the mention of the infinity tattoo. As she stripped off and got into the shower, she ran her fingers over her faded tattoo on her left wrist. There was only one other person she knew that had a tattoo like hers, and they hadn't seen each other in years.

Her former best friend had been there the night she'd met James in a sweaty nightclub in London. James had been on a stag do with some friends and their eyes met across a crowded dancefloor. The rest was history.

Jen began to wonder if it had been Chloe's body in the ditch and, if so, what the hell she'd been doing in Long Eaton? Jen quickly dismissed the fear; there must be hundreds of people out there with the same tattoo in the same place as them. It had been bittersweet the last time she'd seen Chloe, when they'd said their goodbyes and parted ways.

They'd promised each other they would keep in touch, but this had been more difficult than she'd imagined. She'd set up a Facebook page, and in the beginning they used to post pictures to each other, letting each other know that all was okay. She'd check in on Chloe once she'd finished in the shower. Right now she was happy to relax as the jet streams washed over her.

Wrapped in a towel and her fluffy dressing-gown, Jen powered up her laptop. The more she thought about it, the more she missed Chloe. In all her time to Long Eaton she'd not met anyone else who came close to their friendship. The mums at the school gates and those she met at James' work dos were different. None of them had the same spark.

Scolding herself for being so silly she put on some clothes, moved the laptop to the living room table and logged into Facebook. It must have been a year since she'd posted and probably just as long since she'd checked it.

Logging in, she noticed that Chloe hadn't posted for the last six months either. She was met with the usual rabbit picture: their code that meant everything was okay. Rabbits with baby rabbits had been her calling card since the children had come along. Though no one knew about the page, Jen logged in and checked the messages, navigating towards the draft folder where they used to leave messages for each other that weren't public. She opened the last unsent message and was met with a picture of a man sat outside a cafe, possibly somewhere abroad, with a hint of blue sky in the surroundings.

Chloe had obviously met someone and was happy. It made Jen feel warm inside, knowing that Chloe had at last found someone to take care of her the way James took care of her. Satisfied that everything was okay with Chloe, Jen searched out a rabbit photo to post. While she had the computer on, she decided she might as well check the latest reports to see if there was any further news on the discovery.

Jen had been so engrossed in Googling and reading silly articles she soon lost track of time. 'Argh,' she scolded herself. She needed to make a move now or she would be late to pick the kids up.

'So who's been buying you flowers?' James asked as he entered the kitchen, dropping his backpack on the floor and removing his shoes.

Since arriving back from school with the kids, she'd completed the housework and dinner was bubbling away. Her tasks for the day were almost complete. 'They're definitely not from you then? They seem like such an odd combination, a single red rose mixed in with lilies.'

James shook his head as he walked over to the island and looked at the flowers. She watched him fight back a sneeze

as the fragrance hit. The pollen played hell wi...
which was part of the reason he avoided buying Je...

'No card?'

'No, they were left on the doorstep, I assumed someone
had delivered them and left them when they couldn't get an
answer. Or they are meant for someone else, but no one has
claimed them.'

James moved behind Jen as she stirred the casserole. 'Have
you got a secret admirer I need to worry about?'

Jen laughed, pushing him away before she was consumed
by his embrace and the scent of a man who'd had a hard day
at work.

'Did you see anything about the body when you were out
running?' James asked, releasing her.

'No, only a few police officers standing around chatting.
They let me pass to run along a different footpath, though. I
did see a couple of crime scene guys combing the river.'

'And the kids?' As James spoke the kids came running into
the kitchen

'Daddy, daddy!'

Her alone time with James was now up. Daddy was home
and that meant it must be playtime.

James scooped them up as they competed for the first hug.

'How are my two favourite little people?'

Melanie spoke excitedly about her school play, while Alex
told the same story over and over about his volcanic rock. Jen
wondered when they'd last been this excited to see her. She
couldn't imagine a world without them. Though life had its
woes and challenges, she felt indestructible with her family by
her side.

'Melanie, you manage to stay out of trouble today?' James
asked

Melanie looked at the floor, hoping to avert her dad's gaze.

'Alex, did you remember to bring home your spellings?'

Alex crossed his arms. 'Yeah, they're in my bag.'

...e kids helped Jen set the table. James
...e out of his suit into something easier to
...bit of sauce escaped his fork. They always
...gether for dinner; the one rule they always
...James worked late or there had been some
...ent, the kids took great pleasure in bargaining
...d on how he'd make up for missing the family
meal... ...atched as Alex pushed his dinner around his plate.
Any second now he'd ask, 'Can I leave this?'

After dinner, the kids argued over whose turn it was to load
the dishwasher and whose turn it was to read, as Jen searched
through their bags for the books. Once the arguments were
over and school books read, it was time for bed. The kids said
their good nights and the tooth-brushing routines and toilet
trips came to an end. Jen was looking forward to cuddling up
on the sofa and watching some rubbish on TV.

'You still okay if I go out and meet Harry?'

'There was me hoping you'd opt for cuddling up on the
sofa with me.'

James moved over and kissed her forehead.

'I won't be late back, I promise. Harry messaged me earlier
and said he's bored and lonely.'

'Please don't get too drunk. You've got work tomorrow.'

'I won't. We're just going out for a couple. I might go up to
the police station and see if I can see anything.'

'Why? Aren't you doing the one thing you always complain
about when you see a news report that someone has died?
Isn't it always you who moans about the whole circus that
follows from the press to the general nosey busybodies?'

'Love you,' James said as he kissed her again. 'Don't wait
up.'

Jen poured herself a large glass of wine, knowing he
wouldn't be back until closing time. As she wrapped herself
in the blanket, she checked her phone and began to plan
the week's activities; football to dance classes and her own

training. She was also sure there was a meal coming up with James' clients in the near future.

Suddenly the phone rang and Jen jumped to her feet. The last thing she needed was the kids being woken up. 'Hello.'

Silence. There was no one there. It was probably one of those stupid sales calls. She returned to the sofa and channel flicked for a while until sleep crept up on her. She found herself struggling to keep her eyes open and drifting off to nothingness.

Jen started to come round from dozing when she felt a breeze of cold air and the light touch of cold hands. She forced her eyes to open and she tried to focus on James as his blue eyes glistened from the cold air outside.

'Sorry, I didn't mean to wake you.' James swept her up in his strong arms, lifting her off the sofa.

Jen nuzzled into him and caught the scent of cigarettes and stale beer mixed with his aftershave. His chapped lips brushed her neck.

He carried her upstairs as if she was light as a feather and placed her gently down on the bed. She reached out to him, pulling him close again and felt his breath on her face. He smiled, kissed her neck and began unbuttoning her blouse. She inhaled sharply to let out a moan of anticipation as his lips reached her navel.

They made love with passion and lust. As they both came to a climax, they fell back on to the bed. James pulled the covers over them and whispered 'I love you' as they sank into a blissful sleep.

Chapter Four

Jen watched as Melanie and Alex walked a little way in front of her, and found herself feeling proud of the little people they were both becoming. She was also glad that the morning had gone without a hitch. Husband out of the door, kids ready for school and in the car all before eight forty-five. Now they were walking together with no arguments.

'Jennifer!' came the high-pitched voice from behind her.

'Helen.' Jen turned to greet one of the mothers she had helped the day before. 'Everything okay? Did you get everything sorted?'

'Oh yes, yes. I just wanted to catch up with you and say thank you for yesterday. You were a lifesaver.'

'Don't be silly, you'd have sorted it on your own. You just needed pointing in the right direction.'

'Look, do you want to grab a coffee or something? I can tell you all about my new pen-pal.'

'Pen-pal?'

'Yeah, I found this company online. I'm currently writing to a prisoner.'

'Sounds ... erm ... interesting. But I'm afraid I need to get back home. I've got so much stuff to get organised, and I need to make sure I go out for a run as well. Some other time, maybe next week?'

'Of course, and I still owe you big time.'

'Us mums need to stick together.'

'Anytime you need help with anything, just let me know.'

'Thank you. I'll bear that in mind.'

The kids had stopped at the school gate and waited for her before they crossed the threshold into the school.

'See you two later.' Jen dropped down on her knee to kiss both of them goodbye.

'We've left a note for you, Mummy,' Melanie piped up.

'I'll look forward to reading it, now off you go.' Jen stood again as her knees cracked and watched them both running into school, surrounded by their friends.

Home, coffee, run were her plans for the rest of the day, maybe with a bit of domestic goodness thrown into the mix.

The joys of motherhood. Jen had never experienced anything like it; of course there had been some challenging things she had faced. She was just glad she had chosen to settle down and have kids when she did. If only they had come with an instruction manual, though! Still, at least they seemed happy …

Her mind drifted back to the flowers and who they might be from. The odd combination was the most confusing part of it all. Why not just send her a bunch of lilies? Why stick the rose in as well? Had the florist made a mistake with the order? It wasn't like she could phone up and check, having no idea where they came from.

Jen had driven home in a strange sort of daze on autopilot. Now she set about making herself a cup of tea, finding her tablet and looking at whatever note the kids had left her. The kids often left little notes for her around the house. She was always grateful to receive them but still struggled to decipher the handwriting.

Mum, don't forget your going out tonight with daddy to one of those things he makes you go to.

She knew it was coming up; good job she hadn't gone for a coffee. She wasn't even sure she had anything suitable to wear, or at least something she hadn't already worn out multiple times before. She laughed to herself as she imagined the whispers of the fashion police, and then went back to reading the note.

Don't forget we want Jodie to babysit she brings us sweets!

That was something she didn't know. Melanie had always

said they had a secret that Jodie made them promise never to tell anyone. *Oops*. Though Jodie only lived next door Jen sent her a text, apologising for the short notice but she really had totally forgotten.

Jen was almost organised when she headed back downstairs to her cup of tea. It had become routine to drop the kids off, come home and have a cuppa before she decided what she was going to do for the rest of the day and when she was going to fit running in.

She was just finishing off her tea when she heard the letter box. Wishing there was a well-trained dog to go and pick up the mail, she jumped down off her stool and headed into the hall. Luckily she'd decided against sitting in the living room with her drink or she'd have been tempted to stay there for most of the day, achieving nothing.

She was bending down to pick up the usual small pile of letters when she noticed a cream envelope addressed to Mrs J Garner. Thinking nothing of it she ripped it open, revealing a sympathy card. She immediately dropped it on the floor when she noticed the picture on the front was of six lilies; just like the ones that had been delivered the day before. She stared at the card, not really knowing what was going on or why she had dropped it like it was some hot piece of coal.

Forgetting the rest of the mail she returned to her stool and opened the card, dreading what it might say inside.

Jennifer, my thoughts are with you and your family at this sad time.

She placed the card carefully, as if it was a dangerous substance, onto the counter. She picked up the envelope to try to study the postmark which in her rush to open, she had ripped through. As far as she could tell it was posted in Nottingham, but that didn't give her a clue who it was from.

Who'd died recently that she knew? Her parents were long gone. James' parents were both as fit as fiddles out in the Derbyshire Dales. Something wasn't right, but she couldn't put her finger on it. The flowers and now a card with a picture of almost identical flowers. And then she remembered the silent call …

She knew she was being silly; someone was just playing a prank on her, trying to get her upset and into a panic for no reason. Part of her wanted to bin the flowers which were currently elegantly displayed in her living room. As the silence of the house began to drown her, there was a short sharp knock at the door which made her jump and her heart race. Why was she so spooked by a card and a bunch of flowers?

'Are you okay? You look like you've seen a ghost,' Jodie asked as Jen opened the door.

'You made me jump, that's all. I was just sat reading the gossip sites and contemplating a run. Everything okay?'

'I just wanted to pop over about tonight.'

'Tonight?' Jen asked, puzzled as she tried to remember what was happening tonight.

'The text you sent about ten minutes ago?' The penny suddenly dropped, and Jen was back with it again.

'Oh yeah, looking after the kids while we go to this meal. You should've just texted.'

'I couldn't find my charger and with the battery running low I thought it would be quicker just to pop round and see you. Though I'm beginning to wonder if it would have been safer if I'd texted …'

'No, no, it's me. Head's all over the place. I need to run, clear my mind.'

'Okay, well, I won't hold you up any longer. About seven like normal?'

'Yeah, seven is good. Thanks Jodie.'

Jen waited until her neighbour was off the drive before closing the door and retreating back into the house. She scolded herself for being so silly and letting such a little thing scare her so much. She clearly needed that run more than she thought she did.

Jen decided she needed to plan her run this time, and not just go wherever the wind took her. She knew that her normal route was a no go, because of the cordons still being up in all likeliness. She needed to run a straight path that led to nowhere. Where she wouldn't be distracted.

As she changed, she couldn't shake the feeling of confusion and concern about the flowers and then the card. If these two events had happened on their own, she would have shrugged it off but, together with the silent phone call, something wasn't right. It was a bit far for someone to go just to play a prank on her.

She made sure the front door was locked and secure. Once she'd made it out of the house she stretched and was ready to go, but she still found herself racking her brain over who would go to these lengths to play a joke on her. Outside of her 'mummy' friends, there wasn't really anyone she socialised with unless she was at a client meal with James.

She picked up her pace as she reached the canal paths. She planned to run until she couldn't run any further, then work out a way of getting home later. She began to pick up the pace at the same time as she became aware that someone was behind her. Though whoever it was seemed to be keeping their distance, she couldn't shake off the feeling she was being followed.

She was used to other runners thinking they could keep pace with her, but this seemed different. Every time she slowed so did her follower; every time she sprinted they would too. She told herself that she was being silly, that her senses were heightened because of the flowers and the card. She tried to subtly look back at him; *all the gear and no idea* came to mind as she tried to study him without being obvious or running into someone coming the other way. Surely she would know if she was being followed, right?

Finally, after trying almost every way to lose him, she came to the canal bridge and an opportunity to change her route and run into Long Eaton presented itself. Jen had been planning on just running in a straight line. This would be a way to see if she really was being followed. She would be able to loop round so nothing would be lost.

Decision made, Jen turned and ran over the bridge away from the canal. Now she found herself faced with new obstacles as it appeared to be dustbin day that side of Long Eaton. She also now had factory workers to contend with as they came out for their cigarette breaks. Some jeered at her and wolf-whistled as she ran past them. Once she had navigated her way through, she dared herself to turn around and see if her follower was still behind her. Hopefully, if he had been following her, he'd have got lost somewhere between the bins and the factory.

Arriving into the town centre, she would now have a different sort of obstacle: more people. Jen found herself running towards the local police station and one of the main supermarkets in the town. The supermarket car park was filled with TV vans, radio broadcasting units and dozens of people. Part of her had hoped the cordon had been cleared so she could get back on a running route home.

'Any ideas when I'll be able to get through?' Jen asked a police officer, hoping it would be soon.

'Not sure. My Sergeant is just clearing the area then hopefully we'll be able to lift the cordon.'

People were suddenly surrounding her, listening in to the conversation she was having with the officer, trying to glean more information to post on their social media pages no doubt.

'Okay, great, thank you. Are the same cordons in place as yesterday?' Jen asked, trying to work out a route in her mind.

'Yes, miss. Is there anything I can help you with?'

'No, thank you. I was just trying to figure out a route back on to the canal so I could run home.'

'In that case, if you follow ...' the officer started to give her directions back towards the canal like she didn't know where she needed to go. She let him finish and thanked him, taking one more chance to survey the crowd for her follower before she was back in the zone running.

Jen had almost forgotten about the incident when she found herself face to face with her follower doing stretches against the canal lock.

'Afternoon,' she found herself saying to him.

'Afternoon,' he responded back. As Jen looked at him, she wondered if she recognised him but quickly batted the idea away. Why would she? He had obviously just come out of Runners World as he was dressed head to toe in the latest fashion. *All the gear and no idea*, she thought to herself again as she sped off home.

Once she was home, Jen ran herself a bath. Her run hadn't cleared her mind, just confused it even more. As she soaked in the bath, she lay there thinking about her mystery follower, trying to place him somewhere. She had come across lots of runners in her time. Had she just noticed him more today because of his outfit? Had the flowers and the card made her more suspicious?

With all this going on, she still needed to concentrate on being wife and mother of the year material. An hour or so sat getting ready to go out with James and his colleagues and she'd be good to go. She just hoped James' suit was clean and she could find a suitable dress that she hadn't worn last time they were all out.

Chapter Five

DI Chris Jackson

'Morning all,' Chris greeted his team. They all looked as tired as he felt. 'I know we've worked all night on this case. Grab a coffee and let's see where we are with things.' Chris longed to be back in his office in Nottingham; at least he had more space there, compared to the room they were all crammed in.

'Do you need me to write?' Julie asked as she handed him a cuppa. 'I know how bad your writing gets when you're tired.' Julie knew Chris too well.

'Okay team, what have you got for me?' Chris enquired once he noticed they were all back in their seats.

'As I have the pen, I'll start off,' Julie volunteered. 'Chris and I are heading to Derby Royal to meet up with Dr Walsh for the autopsy. Hopefully we'll get some news on our victim's identification.'

'Did anyone get anywhere with the tattoo?' Chris asked.

'I spoke to a couple of the parlours in Long Eaton boss, and phoned around a couple in Nottingham,' Greg responded. 'The infinity symbol is a very popular tattoo and as our victim just had the basic style on her ankle, she could have had it done by anyone.'

'So, no luck with identifying her based on her tattoo? Like I said, it was a long shot.'

'Boss, you might be interested to know that the tattoo has various meanings, though the universal meaning is something that never ends like love or friendship,' Greg added.

'So, the tattoo is likely to have its own unique meaning to the wearer.'

'Yes, boss.'

'Shame she isn't here to tell us then. Sally, anything from the witness statement?'

'Afraid not, boss. Mr Walker didn't see anything out of the ordinary. He walks his dog every day and night same time, same route. He always checks under the bridge out of habit if nothing else.'

'So, dozens of people could have walked past this girl, and no one noticed?' Chris asked, puzzled at how no one else could have spotted her.

'I don't think so boss, given how early she was found. Is it worth appealing for witnesses?' Sally asked.

'Let's wait until we've been to the autopsy and hopefully have a more definite time-frame.'

'The CCTV from the supermarket is pretty grainy. Their rear car park isn't really used as much anymore. Some staff do park there, but the quality of the footage isn't great,' Colin said, adding his findings.

'But did it show us anything?' Chris questioned.

'I've got someone trying to clean the image up as we speak.'

'Great, keep me informed. Anyone else got anything?'

'I did some research of the local area boss, and there are a couple of unused air-raid shelters in the area near where the body was found. I am awaiting a structural engineer and clearance from Network Rail before I venture any further into them,' chipped in Trudie.

'Let me know if I need to chase anyone up, Trudie.'

'Will do, boss.'

'Right, we've made a start. Let's meet up once Julie and I are back from the autopsy and we can reassess the situation. Thank you all.'

Right on cue, Chris' phone rang.

'It's the boss, he's probably ringing for an update. I'll meet you at the car,' Chris told Julie as he swiped to accept the call.

As they arrived at the hospital, a member of the reception staff guided them downstairs to the bereavement suite where the dead came to be dissected and scrutinised before they began their final journey, where the overpowering smell of cleaning agents clung to your clothing and dulled your senses.

Chris greeted the receptionist. 'Dr Walsh is expecting us.'

'Take a seat and I'll see if she's free,' the receptionist replied as she picked up her desk phone. As they both took their seats Chris was almost scared to look around at the people waiting in the reception area. He didn't want to catch anyone's eye, just in case it led to questions regarding their visit. Julie was less guarded as she smiled and said 'morning' to anyone who looked her way.

'Inspector Jackson,' Dr Walsh said as she pushed through the double doors into the main reception area. 'DS Ryan. Good to see you both again. If you'd both like to follow me.'

Chris and Julie both stood up and followed Dr Walsh as she swiped her card, letting them both through. 'I'm sorry I couldn't get to her sooner. We're currently working through a back log, so had to clear some of those first.'

Chris and Julie followed Dr Walsh through a series of corridors and down more flights of stairs to a viewing area that looked over the table where the mystery girl lay covered over with a black sheet.

'If I make a start and you can view from here. There's a speaker so you'll be able to hear me. I'll then take questions afterwards if that's okay?'

'Thank you, Dr Walsh,' Julie replied as Chris looked down below at the surroundings.

'I just need to scrub up and I'll be ready to begin,' Dr Walsh said, leaving the viewing area.

Chris could see several people working below, setting things up ready for the autopsy. Though they were behind a Perspex screen, they couldn't escape the clinical smell.

'When were you last at one of these?' Julie asked.

'In Derby itself it's been a while but, as for the Nottingham hospital, once every two weeks or so I'd say.'

Moments later Dr Walsh appeared below and began.

'For the record Dr Amanda Walsh and Lab Tech Riley Moss will be performing this autopsy on our Jane Doe number 003489 found in Long Eaton. It should also be noted that this autopsy is being witnessed by Detective Inspector Chris Jackson and Detective Sergeant Julie Ryan.' Dr Walsh removed the sheet from the victim. It was clear the body had previously been cleaned, as the woman's hair was wet and slicked back.

As Chris looked at the body, he once more saw the resemblance to Daisy. For a moment he thought that it was Daisy on the table.

'Julie do you remember Daisy, the hooker from last year?'

'Not really, I don't think I worked the case with you. Why?'

'There are similarities between the two dead girls.'

'You thinking our offender might be the same person?'

'I'm not sure.'

'Put in a request and get the files brought over. I'll have a look at it with you and see if I can spot anything.'

Before Chris had a chance to answer Dr Walsh began.

'From initial inspection, our Jane Doe was in her mid to late thirties, a well-nourished Caucasian female. During prep for this autopsy Riley noticed the escape of hair dye. I would say judging by her pubic hair she is naturally blonde and dyed her hair recently to this brown. Her eyes are blue.'

'My original measurements of Jane Doe are recorded as weight fifty kilos and height one hundred and sixty centimetres.' Riley spoke as Dr Walsh began to make her incisions.

'Ribs, right three and seven and left one and nine all show signs of breakages.' Chris flinched as Dr Walsh spoke. He'd broken a rib once and that was painful enough, but to have four all broken at once she must have been struggling to breathe.

Dr Walsh and her team carried on below as Chris and Julie looked on in fascination.

'Thank you for letting us witness the autopsy, Dr Walsh,' Chris said as he took his seat around the large circular table.

'Not a problem, now how can I help. Any questions?'

'What are your conclusions regarding the cause of death?' Julie asked.

'As you both witnessed, despite the number of broken bones this girl had along with other haemorrhaging, her actual cause of death was drowning. There was a substantial amount of water in her lungs, also given the position she was found in. I would take a guess that they held her head in the rainwater, making sure they had finished her off. Judging by her injuries, I doubt she would have been conscious, and if she was she'd have been in a lot of pain. I have asked that a sample of the water we found her in and the water in her lungs be sent for analysis.'

'Thank you, Dr Walsh. Did you manage to get any transferable DNA from her? I did notice the overpowering smell of bleach at the scene yesterday. So much so it got me thinking back to an older case, if I'm honest with you.'

'As we saw at the scene, it was obvious that she had been beaten. Once I got her on the table and completed a more visual exam, I noticed some tearing and bruising which indicated to me she had been brutally raped.' Chris' stomach muscles tightened as Dr Walsh spoke. How could someone do that to another person? He just didn't understand human nature sometimes.

'No sign of semen?' Julie queried.

'None of that either, I'm afraid.'

'Assuming she was transferred to the site in some sort of vehicle, did you find any transferable evidence?' Chris asked.

'Sadly anything that was there isn't any longer, whether that is due to the rain or the water she was left in.'

'They clearly knew what they were doing, to have made sure they left nothing behind.'

'There are some signs that she tried to fight back with various snapped false nails. Anything that was there has been removed. Any blood that soaked into her clothes is likely to have been hers and has been tainted by the rainwater so a clear result would be harder to obtain.'

'Anything more about her identity?' Chris asked, finally getting to the all-important question of who she was.

'All initial soft searches have been done, and we are still no closer to finding out who she is. I have inputted blood type, fingerprints and DNA into the system so your guys should be able to pick that up in Nottingham.'

'Have you been able to find anything regarding her tattoo?' Julie asked.

'My team and I have tried, but this is a pretty bog-standard infinity symbol and has no unique traits we can look into.'

'Our initial enquiries have found the same as well,' Julie responded.

'Have you been able to pin down a more precise time of death? Chris asked.

'There are a lot of variables, with her being found in water and the changeable weather. I've estimated the time of death between 1 a.m. and 4 a.m. Monday morning.'

Julie and Chris looked at each other and the notes they had scribbled down, Julie's being the more readable of the two.

'There would have been a lot of blood splatter wherever she was beaten. Find me that location and I might be able to tell you more. I'm afraid with the crime scene as it stands there isn't much more I can offer,' Dr Walsh explained.

'Thank you, Dr Walsh. Will you give us a shout if you get a hit on the identification?'

'Of course. We could be looking at tomorrow, though. I'll get Riley to give you a call if anything comes up.'

There wasn't much more to be said on the subject, as Julie drove Chris back to Long Eaton, where his team would be no doubt waiting. Though the sun was finally coming out, a girl had been brutally attacked and murdered. Worst of all, they had no idea who she was and someone would still be missing a daughter.

'Thanks, Julie. I'm just going to make a couple of calls and I'll be with you,' Chris told her as she tried to drive round the obstacle course that was the various media outlets and nosy parkers who were hoping to see or hear something.

'It looks like I'm going to have to park inside the station car park. Do you want dropping at the council grounds so you can try to avoid being spotted?'

'Thanks Julie, that'd be great.'

Chris arrived back at the station without alerting any of the waiting press. He wanted to check the files again for Daisy. This case had so many of the same hallmarks that he'd remembered from her case. If he could find a connection, maybe this would solve Daisy's mystery as well.

He'd give archives a call and then log into a station computer and search the Holmes database, which was supposed to spot similarities between cases that had been inputted. It would possibly mean a trip into the office before heading home, but it would be worth it.

'Afternoon all,' Chris greeted his team. 'I know you're probably all tired, so let's make this quick so we can all head home for a couple of hours' kip.' Chris began to fill his team in on the autopsy.

'So, no useful DNA or transferable evidence from the victim at all?' Greg asked.

'It seems like whoever dumped her made a pretty good job at cleaning her up beforehand.'

'With there being no transferable evidence at all on our victim, I think it would be safe to say this was done by a pro,' Sally offered.

'Which makes our job that bit harder,' Chris concluded.

'Could our victim be a call girl?' Colin asked.

'My gut feeling says no, because we would have expected her fingerprints to have pinged from any previous arrests.'

'Unless she's either completely new at the street game or been very lucky to have not been picked up?'

'Possibly Colin, but she didn't look like a call girl, which I know means nothing but ...' Chris didn't know what the answer was, with the correlation between her and Daisy. She could have well been a call girl, but right now he wanted to keep that avenue to himself. He quickly changed the subject. 'Trudie, how did you get on with the air-raid shelters?'

'They were built during World War Two to provide shelter for those who worked over at Toton Sidings. There have been several attempts to restore them over the years to make them available for educational use but this has been vetoed by the railway companies who own them.' Trudie moved over to the incident board and began to draw a diagram.

'The shelter is made up of two tunnels, which come from the north and south and meet in the middle. The building is structurally safe, though there is a lot of drug paraphernalia and evidence of rough sleepers down there.'

'Anything down there which could be connected to our murder?' Chris asked.

'It's hard to say. There were no signs of fresh blood in the surroundings. If we send forensics there, they are likely to find hundreds, if not thousands, of samples of DNA because of the rough sleepers. So it could turn out to be a very expensive, pointless exercise,' Trudie explained.

'A piss in the dark, then?' Chris was starting to get frustrated by the lack of progress.

'To be totally honest, yes. We've had clearance that it's safe for us to go down, but I don't think we'll find any evidence that relates to our unidentified female. If we do, it will probably be contaminated by whoever else has been down there since.'

Chris wondered which way to take this case; his team were all visibly exhausted and needed either a break or a break-through.

'Trudie, will you get hold of Dr Walsh and her team? Ask her to come down and check the shelter to see if there's anything you guys might have missed. Make sure you tell her there's no rush; it can wait until tomorrow morning. They aren't going anywhere if they've been there since World War Two. Colin, did you manage to get anywhere with the CCTV footage from the supermarket?'

'Yes and no, boss.' Colin moved to the front of the office. 'We managed to clear up the footage enough so we could see what looks like a white van, parked just in front of the cut-through.'

'Did you manage to get a full or partial number plate?' Chris asked.

'Afraid not, boss. It looks like an attempt had been made to conceal it. The blokes who got out of the van are equally unrecognisable.'

'No images of our victim?'

'No boss, the van was reversed up to the entrance. They were clearly prepared for the cameras and made sure they went out of their way to evade them.'

'Thank you, Colin.'

There was a knock, and they all turned round to see Sergeant Gillroy stood at the door. 'Sorry to interrupt. The supermarket management are asking for a time-frame for the cordons being lifted. They want to know whether they can have their car park back yet?'

'Team?' Chris asked, looking around. He had the sneaking suspicion that the supermarket hadn't asked about the car park and Sergeant Gillroy was just continuing to be his difficult self.

'I don't think anything would be lost by us lifting the outer cordon and returning the use of the car park,' Julie commented 'There isn't any evidence that could be lost or compromised.'

'Anyone else got any thoughts?' Chris asked. 'No? Okay, Sergeant Gillroy if you're happy to get your team to roll back the outer cordon, the supermarket can have their car park back.'

'Will do, boss,' Sergeant Gillroy responded with words dripping in sarcasm.

'Okay, the rest of you go home and get some kip. I want to see everyone bright and early tomorrow morning.'

'Yes, boss,' they all echoed, clearly happy to be heading home for the night.

As for Chris, he had some files to collect and a visit to the archives before he could go anywhere.

'Chris, before I go is there anything I can help with?'

'No Julie, you get off.'

'Thanks, boss. See you tomorrow.'

Chapter Six

Jen Garner

James arrived home from work early. Obviously the promise of a night out with a meal and drinks included had spurred everyone on to finish their work more quickly than normal.

Jen had been sat at the table helping Melanie with her homework when he'd arrived. Swooping in, he kissed both of them and asked how their day had been.

'Everything okay, Jen?' James asked, clearly noticing that there was something on her mind.

'Yeah, yeah … I got another random item through the post again.'

'Oh, anything of interest?' James enquired as he stood next to her.

'Melanie, I think that's enough for today. Why don't you put your homework away and go and watch TV with your brother?' Jen waited to make sure Melanie was out of earshot before she divulged anything to James. 'I've been sent a sympathy card.'

'Okay?' James looked puzzled as Jen got up from her seat and pulled a card from the drawer where she had hidden it from the kids.

'James, look at it,' Jen said, thrusting it towards him 'It has the same flowers that were delivered yesterday.'

'Was there any clue inside who it was from?'

'No, it just said "Jennifer, my thoughts are with you and your family at this sad time".'

'And you've got no idea who sent it?'

'No, it's the same as the flowers.'

'Guessing you've checked the postmark?'

'Of course!' Jen said as she stood up to look for the envelope, pushing it into his hand. 'James, I'm spooked. And I was followed on my run as well.'

James broke out in laughter, seemingly in disbelief. 'I doubt that very much, I've been running with you. No one can keep up with you, never mind follow you.'

Jen marched crossed the kitchen, barging into him on her way past.

'Jen …' he shouted after her 'Jen, I'm sorry. I just couldn't imagine someone being able to keep pace with you. I had visions of this person trying to keep up with you and it made me laugh.'

Jen stood on the bottom step of the stairs, making her the same height as him.

'Look, we can't do anything now at five-thirty on a Tuesday afternoon. Go and get ready, I'll sort the kids and we can talk about this tomorrow when I'm off work.' James moved closer and kissed her. 'Love you,' he whispered as she started to climb the stairs.

She walked into their room and sat down at the dressing table, staring into her mirror as if hoping it would magically transform her. Right now going to the meal was the last place she wanted to go. She tried to summon the enthusiasm to pick a dress.

Come on Jen, pull yourself together, she told herself as she felt a chill run down her spine. If somebody really was trying to scare her, then truth be known they were succeeding. Because something just didn't feel right about the whole situation; the symbolism of the flowers being carried over onto the card …

She had started to put her make-up on when James came upstairs.

'Right, that's the kids settled,' he said cheerily as he opened his side of the wardrobe. 'I'm really looking forward to seeing some of our clients tonight.' James continued to rabbit excitedly, but then he must have noticed Jen's expression. 'You okay?'

'Sorry,' Jen replied, snapping out of her trance. 'Yeah, I'm good. Just putting my make-up on.'

James came up behind where Jen was sat and rested his hands on her shoulders. 'I was going to wait for later, but I've brought you something.' Jen looked up at James in the mirror as he reached into his pocket. 'I picked it up on my lunch break,' James said as opened the box and fastened the necklace around Jen's neck. 'It's a diamond heart, with two smaller hearts that represent the kids.'

Jen reached and touched the necklace as James kissed her neck. 'James it's ...' Just as she was about to finish her sentence the doorbell rang.

'That'll be Jodie,' James said, rushing half-dressed down the stairs to get to the door before the kids.

Jen sat there and studied her reflection in the mirror, thinking about the card and flowers again. They really had rattled her more than she dared to admit.

'Right, the taxi is on its way. We good?' James asked, popping his head around the bedroom door, still only half dressed in his penguin suit.

Come on Jen. You can do this. 'Yeah, will be right with you,' she said, standing up, brushing herself down and reaching over to apply a final dusting of make-up.

'It's here!' James shouted up the stairs as she began to descend with her dress sweeping behind her.

'Coming, coming!' As she made it to the bottom of the stairs she was greeted by the kids and Jodie. 'Please don't touch the dress,' she begged them as she bent down to kiss them both. 'And please be good for Jodie, and straight to bed when she tells you.' Sharing air kisses with Jodie, Jen headed out and James held her arm as they walked down the steps.

'Just try and forget about it all and have a good time, okay?' he whispered to her as they climbed into the taxi. 'We'll get it all sorted out tomorrow, I promise.'

They arrived at the hotel to a jam-packed reception area. James picked up two flutes of champagne from the tray thrust in front of him. They weaved their way towards James' work colleagues who had already made a corner their own.

'Jen, you look fabulous as always!' James' boss greeted her, with air kisses and a hug.

James joined in conversations with his colleagues, who he had seen hours earlier, while Jen made her way to the circle of wives and girlfriends, who were chatting about the latest fashions and all the stuff she had no interest in. The one thing she always made sure she did when she attended these events was to greet the newcomer. There was always one of James' work colleagues who had brought someone different, someone who wasn't there last year – often a younger, prettier model.

'Hi, I'm James' wife Jen.' Jen greeted one obvious newcomer who was nervously shifting her weight from one foot to another while her new boyfriend laughed and chatted with his colleagues. 'You look a bit out of your depth.'

'Hi. I'm Alice, Tom's girlfriend,' she replied timidly as she wriggled uncomfortably in the purple ballgown-style dress she was wearing. 'Tom dragged me along, saying I'd enjoy it. Right now, I'm finding myself surrounded by women who resemble Greek goddesses, who I have little or nothing in common with!'

Jen laughed. 'I know what you mean, James drags me along every year, and every year it's the same. The food is good as long as you don't mind being ignored for most of the evening.'

'It makes you wonder why they ask us to come.' Alice chuckled. Jen had done her job and made the newcomer feel welcome. This time next year Alice would either have been replaced or earned Greek goddess status.

'Jennifer!' She'd been spotted by one of the Greek goddesses and there was no way out. 'We were just talking about the body they've found. Have you seen anything on your runs?'

'No, the cordon was up before I made it that way,' she replied.

'Isn't it awful? I thought Long Eaton was such a nice place.' Jen wanted to reply 'it still is' but knew she was wasting her breath. She was among women with money who lived it up on their husbands' wages in West Bridgford. Jen's thoughts turned to the meal and the dreaded seating plan they always implemented. Which member of the team would she be sat next to this year?

Suddenly James grabbed Jen around the waist, asking if she was okay. She could see the alcohol was beginning to take effect on him as he became louder and more confident. This was the James she loved; he always made sure everyone was included in whatever conversation he was having. 'Jen has put in to do the Nottingham Half,' James told everyone who was listening. *Cue the questions*, Jen thought. She was pretty sure she had answered them all last year when the same conversation had occurred.

'Oh wow, Jen. How long have you been running for?' Alice asked.

'About three years now, since both the kids were in the school. I was looking for something to take up my time and it kind of gets addictive after a while.'

'I could never do it. I'm far to self-conscious,' Alice said. Jen was about to respond when a tray of sparkling wine was offered. She'd just turned round to grab a glass when she saw him. Though he was dressed in a suit, she would have recognised him anywhere. Feeling James' arm still round her, she turned to him. 'Who's that bloke over there, with the purple bow-tie?' James turned for a moment to take a look.

'Probably someone from a competing firm.'

'James.' Jen looked over at him again and their eyes met. 'James, that's the guy who was following me earlier.'

'We've had this conversation. No one can keep up with you, let alone follow you!' Jen removed James' arm from her waist. The mystery guy was still there looking at her; she felt his eyes burrowing into her skin. 'Where you off to?' James asked as Jen tried to break away.

'I'm going over to ask him who he is and why he was following me.'

'Jen, you're being silly,' James said, taking hold of her hand. 'Come on, it's time to go and sit down.' James tried to pull her in the opposite direction, but the mystery man was still there watching.

'James.' As her voice rose everyone suddenly looked at her like she was some kind of weirdo. Realising her error, she switched into perfect wife mode as she let James lead her to their table.

'Once everyone is sat down I'll see if I can see which company table he is on, okay?' James soothed.

'Yeah,' Jen responded, knowing that there was no point in having an argument. She was strangely sober all of a sudden and very alert to everything that was going on. *Why would he follow me here?* she wondered.

They reached their table and Jen soon realised who she had been sat next to. James' boss would be wasted by now and would no doubt talk non-stop to her for the next two hours. James held out the chair for her and she sat down on it, feeling almost like a naughty child. While James remained stood up like he always did until the table was full, she spotted Alice sitting the other side of her husband. As Jen continued to look round, trying to spot the mystery man again, Alice caught her eye and sent a warm smile her way. 'You okay?' she mouthed. Jen smiled back and nodded, deciding that as soon as she could make a break for freedom she'd be off to find him. For now, she had to play the dutiful wife.

Once the table was full James took his seat and started to offer the wine around, like he always did. Once he had completed that job he squeezed her knee under the table, trying to offer some form of reassurance that she was so desperately lacking. The waiters started to bring out the food, and Jen felt like she was the only sober person on their table. The laughter and chatter got louder.

'So, Jennifer ...' James' boss began.

'Patrick, how are things with you?' she asked.

'Pretty good, pretty good. Wife has decided to put the house on the market so who knows? We might be moving near you soon.'

Jen laughed nervously. 'Have you not heard? Long Eaton is turning into a dangerous place to live.'

'Oh yes, I read about that ...'

As every new course came to the table Jen arched her neck to try to see the man and every time she failed to spot him, she panicked that bit more. There was no way of getting James' attention now that he had Alice eating out of the palm of his hand. Any other time she'd be fine with it, but she was scared and would have appreciated being able to speak to her husband properly.

'And how are the kiddies?' Patrick continued.

'They're both good thank you, Patrick. And your grandchildren?'

'Oh, they're growing up so fast. I was just saying to Rosemary the other day we must have them over to stay again soon ...'

This was getting painful. 'Excuse me.' Jen got up which immediately drew James' attention for the first time since they'd sat down.

'You okay?' he called over.

'I'm going to see if I can see him,' she mouthed. James just looked at her the way he did the kids when they did something he didn't approve of.

Before she could say anything or pull a face back one of the other wives, Rhonia, grabbed her attention. 'Jennifer, darling. If you're heading to the little girls' room I'll come along with you.'

Where else could she be going? Home? *No chance of that any time soon* Jen thought, looking at her watch. Plus now she had to go via the ladies'. As Jen weaved her way through the room, she studied everyone as they sat at their tables chatting away. No sign so far. There was no way she'd imagined it. He'd looked directly at her. *What if he'd gone after the kids?* Jen was starting to let her imagination run away from her. Why would he go after the kids? But then why was he following her in the first place if not to find out where she lived? Had she been found out?

Toilet trip successfully completed, Jen was returning to her table with Rhonia when she saw him. He was at their table talking to someone. As she got back to her seat, he looked straight at Jen and smiled.

'James ... James!' She tried her hardest to get his attention, aware that she was being watched.

'What's up?' James asked, unable to mask the annoyance in his voice.

'I'm going to get a drink, come with me,' she said, looking at him directly and hoping he would get the message she needed to talk to him away from everyone else.

'Can we get anyone else a drink?' James asked, getting up from his seat and addressing the table.

'Take my card,' Patrick said, flashing his gold Amex card.

'I'll get these. It's okay, but thank you Patrick,' James replied as he dug his hand into his trouser pocket in search of his card.

Jen was getting more and more impatient by the moment. She needed to speak to her husband urgently and here they were discussing who was paying for the god damn drinks. She took his hand and gave it a gentle pull.

'Anyone, anything?' James asked again as Jen led him away. 'What's up? Where's the fire?'

'The guy talking to Patrick's wife, it's him, James. He's the one that followed me earlier today.'

'Oh, him? I figured it out. I forgot to tell you – he works for Lords. They're just another accounting firm.'

'Are you sure?' Jen asked, beginning to doubt herself.

'Yeah, he came over and shook my hand while you were away with Rhonia.'

Jen looked back at the table from the bar and saw him stood talking to Rosemary. 'Here, help me with the drinks,' James added, handing her a bottle of wine and several glasses while he balanced numerous pints. When they arrived back at the table the music had started and couples were making their way to the dance floor.

'Jennifer, care to dance?' Patrick suddenly asked, holding out his hand before she had the chance to sit down. It was the last thing Jen wanted to do, but what choice did she have? Plus James' attention had turned back to Alice. What was he trying to do, get into her pants? Jen was getting more and more anxious. She needed to get control of herself.

'I'd love to dance,' she said as she took Patrick's hand.

'I hope James doesn't mind but I always make sure I dance with the most beautiful girl in the room,' Patrick told her as he led her to the dance floor. She could do this, she knew she could. After all, the mystery guy was there stood talking at her table. He wasn't going anywhere. She'd give Patrick his dance and then go and confront him.

As the music continued Jen tried to keep in time with Patrick's steps, making sure she kept a check on mystery guy with every whirl and turn.

'Another?' Patrick asked as the music ended.

'Between you and me, I think James might get a bit jealous.'

'Ah yes, Rosemary tells me that I shouldn't keep you young ladies away from your husbands for too long.'

Jen laughed. 'I would love to dance with you all night Patrick, but we also have to think of Rosemary. I'm sure she'd want to dance with her husband?' Patrick nodded his agreement. 'Who is it she was talking to anyway?' Jen continued. 'I thought I recognised him from somewhere?' She knew she'd find out one way or another who he was.

'That man she was chatting to while we were dancing?'

'Yes, him.' Jen looked over towards the table. He'd gone.

'To be honest m'dear, she has so many friends I can't keep track.'

'No worries Patrick. Thank you for the dance,' she said, curtsying in front of him.

The mystery guy was gone. She studied everyone she walked past but nothing. Part of her wished she smoked so she could check he wasn't outside. This was getting ridiculous; she'd had her chance and she'd missed him.

Jen wasn't sure how she'd got through the rest of the night, but like James she ended up getting suitably drunk. Maybe it had been the bottle she had brought back from the bar or the subsequent shots she had knocked back when the drinking games had begun.

As they grabbed their coats from the cloak room, Jen felt something in her pocket. She took it out and studied it. It was a white tablet with some sort of logo on it. *What the hell was this?*

'Jen?' James questioned. 'You okay?'

'Yeah. I just found one of the kids' sweets in my pocket. Not sure how it got there.'

'Nice.' James nuzzled into her neck. 'You smell divine, Mrs Garner.'

Jen's mind was too flooded with alcohol to process anything. The pill, the mystery guy and where he'd disappeared to. She was drunk, on the verge of wasted, and as they climbed into the taxi, James turned her face to his and started to passionately kiss her. She returned the favour until everything floated away and was forgotten.

Chapter Seven

WEDNESDAY
DI *Chris Jackson*

The text message that woke Chris up had become plastered onto his brain.

Meet me at Attenborough Nature Reserve at 8 a.m., please don't go into work or tell anyone that you're meeting me. Make sure you come alone. Riley – Derby Mortuary.

Chris rubbed his temples; he could feel a headache coming on and it was only seven-thirty. If he was going to meet Riley, he'd better get a move on. Why the nature reserve? What was wrong with the hospital or even the station? Chris tried to call him, but it went straight to answerphone. *Arggh!*

As Chris drove closer to the reserve, his mind continued to work away in overdrive. What could Riley possibly want? Why was he wanting to meet in such secrecy? As the traffic started to slow and come to a standstill, he searched in his glove box for painkillers. His headache was either caffeine withdrawal or a tension headache. Either way, one of these issues would be solved as soon as he'd found some coffee.

The nature reserve was a popular location for dog walkers and families in search of wildlife and adventure. Chris drove into the main car park and looked around for Riley. He got out of his car and headed towards the visitor centre in search of the much-needed coffee, but the drawbridge was yet to be lowered to allow access. He was about to sit at one of the picnic benches when he saw Riley heading towards him. He stood to greet him, noticing that the man looked like he hadn't slept for weeks.

'Can we walk and talk?' Riley asked. They headed over the bridge towards one of the many public footpaths around the reserve. 'Sorry for asking you to meet me like this.'

Chris looked at him quizzically.

'We got an ID on the body.'

'Who is she?' Chris suddenly stopped.

'That's where the problem lies.'

'Meaning?'

'When I was at university, we learnt about this database, which stores all the DNA profiles of undercover officers.'

'And?'

'So, I jokingly suggested to Amanda we should contact the government and check she wasn't one of their own. And we got a hit.'

'That's brilliant, isn't it?' Chris couldn't understand why Riley wasn't full of enthusiasm. Never mind why they were discussing this in the middle of a nature reserve.

'Well yes and no. So when we got a hit, they knew about it as well.' Riley fell silent, letting Chris take in all the information. 'I'm not 100% sure of the details but she was one of these undercover agents working for the force in central London. They're sending someone early this morning to collect the body and all information we have on the case.'

As the wind dropped, so did the conversation.

'Great, more politics.' Chris suddenly felt a sinking feeling. He stopped walking and leaned up against a fence post. He tried to collect his thoughts, not wanting to take his anger out on Riley. What was the point in the work they'd already done?

'You might want to go straight to your office and get as much backed up from the computer as possible before you lose everything.'

'Thanks for the heads up.'

'It's all good. Amanda is currently doing the same and will send any information over.'

'Is there anything you can give me? About who she was?' Chris asked.

'When we originally got the hit, it brought up Chloe Seaward, but there was minimal information about her on her file that we were able to access. Her file seems to have been locked and was for authorised personnel only.'

Chris' headache wasn't the only problem he needed to deal with now. His team morale would hit an all-time low. Everyone would be back to worrying about budget cuts again. 'Thanks, Riley. Tell Dr Walsh I owe her one.'

As Chris sped away from the nature reserve, he tried to decide how he was going to react to the information he'd received from Riley. He had to try to salvage as much as possible before they no longer had access to the case. He needed to act fast. As soon as he entered the station he would either be accosted by the Superintendent or his presence would be requested upstairs.

If he returned to Long Eaton, he would no doubt be spotted by someone and he needed to keep it all close to his chest and play the fool. He'd already taken the files home from Daisy's case so would be in trouble for that anyway. If the information on the police computers was about to be cleared, it wouldn't happen until they were backed up overnight. So he had a slight time advantage on those over removing any paper files.

Then his phone rang.

'Detective Inspector Jackson speaking.'

'Boss, it's Julie. Wanted to give you a heads up, something has happened and they're removing everything we have on our Jane Doe.'

Chris swore inwardly. 'Thanks, Julie. I'm on my way into the office now.' There was silence on the line for a second then she finally answered.

'Certainly, boss. I'll see you when you get in.'

It didn't take Chris long to arrive at the station. He was soon sat at his desk, saving everything they'd digitised about Chloe Seaward. With everything being logged, he was pretty sure there wouldn't be much of a gap from what was on paper and what was now sat on his USB. He was busy typing away when there was a knock on his door.

'Chris, I think you and I need to have a chat,' his boss said to him as he opened the door. So much for waiting to be invited in.

'How can I help you, Superintendent?' Chris was panicking that they'd discovered he'd removed files and taken them home, but he did his best not to show it.

'It's about the Jane Doe case. Dr Walsh managed to get a hit on the ID.'

'Oh great, do we know who she is?' Chris wasn't prepared to let on that he knew already, though he wouldn't be surprised if his facial expressions gave him away.

'As far as I understand it, she's an undercover officer from London.'

'Okay, and do we know what she was doing in Long Eaton?'

'In all honesty Chris, no. I received a call late last night from London telling me we were being taken off the case and that the body would be returned along with the files to the team the girl worked for.'

'What does that mean for myself and the team, sir?'

'You will all be reassigned work, most likely to do with the influx of drugs into Nottingham.'

'Isn't that DI Manson's remit?'

'He has asked for our assistance. There'll be a meeting request coming through.'

'The quickest stint as SIO ever,' Chris muttered.

'I'm not impressed about it either Chris, but my hands are tied.'

'Okay. Thank you, sir.'

'Take your team out for a drink. They deserve it for all the extra hours they've put in on this.'

'I'll make sure of it, sir.'

With that the Superintendent left Chris' office. Usually Chris would have been summoned upstairs – maybe his boss had fancied a walk to see what his other minions were up to. Chris fired up his computer and found the email trail he'd been included in from DI Manson and of course the meeting invite for the next day. *From one case to another*, he thought to himself as he clicked. At least he didn't have far to travel. Chris got off his chair and decided he would go and face the music. His team were probably already aware of the situation, but it was only fair that he told them to their faces.

'Can I have everyone's attention please?' Chris asked loudly as he walked into the team's office and was happy to see Julie typing away. 'As I'm sure you're all aware by now, we've been taken off the Jane Doe case, with her now being formally identified.' Chris stopped as the room broke out into chatter.

'Who was she, boss? Someone important?'

'From what I can understand Sally, she was an undercover officer, and her team have put in a request to investigate her death personally.'

'You'd have thought they would appreciate help from an outside source.'

'I totally agree with you Sally, but we pretty much don't have any say in the matter.'

There was silence in the room as Chris waited for someone to ask a question.

'So what now then, boss?' Greg finally asked.

'To the pub.' A voice that Chris didn't recognise shouted from the back of the room.

'Afraid not quite yet. You all need to return to your original workload.' Chris waited for a while and then spoke again. 'As for the pub, I'll be in Armstrongs at the end of shift if anyone wants to join me.' A promise of a drink seemed to cheer the room up no end. Chris returned to his office as Julie rushed to catch up with him.

'Chris, what's happened?' she questioned.

'Shit has hit the fan! The rug has been pulled from under our feet, and there is pretty much nothing I can do about it.'

'So we're supposed to just roll over and forget about the girl?' Julie asked as they arrived back at Chris' door.

'Come in, Julie. Take a seat …'

Chapter Eight

Jen Garner

At the sound of her alarm, Jen woke the children up who were strangely on their best behaviour. They'd dived out of bed, changed and had breakfast with a minimal amount of fuss while Jen had stared into space, wrapped in her winter PJs. Jodie had offered to take the kids to school the previous evening, no doubt after seeing how drunk she was. This had come as a huge relief when Jen woke up feeling the way she did. Human contact on a cold playground was the last thing she needed. She'd kissed the kids goodbye and decided to return to bed until she felt more human.

Jen woke again to the sound of post coming through the letterbox. Turning over, she noticed James still fast asleep, snoring away. This was her favourite kind of day; laying in bed relaxed and contented with her husband. She still had a huge headache from an all-consuming hangover and what felt like a mouth full of cotton wool.

She eased herself out of bed and walked carefully down the stairs, picking up the post before heading into the kitchen. Her first priority was to get a glass of cold water and some painkillers. With the amount they'd eaten and drank last night, Jen would need to run for miles to burn it all off.

She was about to return to bed when something caught her eye in amongst the post. There was a small brown package, addressed to her. *Another mystery package*, she thought as she opened it and emptied the contents onto the counter.

Her heart raced and her ears began to ring as her blood pressure plummeted. Everything went dark as she struggled to support herself. She grabbed the edge of the counter, and, as she lent over, the contents of her stomach came gushing out into the sink. When Jen was sure it was over, she slid down onto the cold marble floor and put her head in her hands, trying to ease the sickness and dizziness.

Pulling herself off the floor she returned to the sink to wash down the remains of last night, hoping that all the commotion hadn't woken James. She weakly grabbed a glass of water, as her stomach churned and her mind returned to the source of her queasiness. Jen tentatively picked up the necklace that had fallen out of the package and turned it over in her hands. She looked at the silver charm attached to it – St Christopher, the patron saint of travellers. Jen knew exactly whose it was. Unable to support herself, she slid back down onto the floor and examined the necklace further. She hadn't seen this since she left it in a box for her best friend, Chloe, on the day she'd left London to be with James. But what did it mean? How come it was suddenly in her possession again?

'You okay, Jen?' James asked as he walked into the kitchen, startling her.

'Yeah, just remembered why we shouldn't mix alcohol,' Jen said, laughing as she pulled herself off the floor, stuffing the necklace into her dressing-gown pocket.

James pulled her close. 'Fancy going back to bed and finishing where we left off last night?'

'James, I feel awful.'

'Shall I just carry you back to bed instead then?'

Jen chuckled as James attempted to sweep her off her feet while she was still holding the water, which in turn spilt everywhere. Then the phone rang, and it was game over as James became engrossed in some work-related emergency.

This was the perfect diversion she needed. James would likely be on the phone for hours. As Jen supported herself back up the stairs the necklace hit her thigh with each step, making sure she didn't forget it was there. Once safe in her room, she studied it again. None of this made sense. Other than the Facebook page she'd already checked, there'd been no other contact between her and Chloe for ages.

Jen started to have a sense of her old life coming back to haunt her. Everything she'd done to keep the past separated from the life she lived with James and the kids, the new role she had fallen into as a loving mother and wife, was about to come crashing down and she'd no idea how she was going to stop it.

Did the necklace mean something had happened? Had something happened to Chloe? Was she in trouble and this was her way of sending a distress call? There were procedures in place for those sorts of events that didn't need to involve her. Was this something only a best friend could solve? But they weren't even best friends. They hadn't been for the past ten years.

Jen suddenly found herself thinking about the flowers and the card. Were those other signs that something had happened to Chloe? Still wrapped in her dressing-gown, she logged into Facebook and began reading every single post and draft message between them since they'd set the silly thing up all those years ago. She'd finish doing this and then she'd have a shower and get changed. She thought about James and the kids. She needed to act normally until she had it all figured out. There was no point worrying them until she was sure they were in danger. Best to at least try to keep the past back in its box where it had been safely stored up until now.

'Do you want a coffee?' Jen asked James once she'd had her shower. She wrapped her arms around his neck and clung onto him. 'Come back to bed,' she purred. *This was acting normal, wasn't it?* She began to question herself and her actions.

'I can't. Something went wrong at the office overnight and I need to fix it.' This was what she'd been hoping to hear, and she nibbled his ear.

'Just a coffee then,' she said as she slinked away from James and his work. She wasn't sure how much time she had, but she was pretty sure she'd have until it was time to pick the kids up.

Jen sat herself down with her tablet opposite James who had now turned the kitchen table into his office.

'Thanks for the coffee, love,' James looked up, acknowledging her. 'This shouldn't take too long.'

'It's fine,' Jen said, smiling back at him, not knowing how else to respond because she needed to look for something too. Then she remembered the tattoo and what she'd heard on that first day. The body had a tattoo of an infinity symbol, and she had the same symbol on her wrist. She and Chloe had had them done at exactly the same time because their friendship was never going to end.

Jen's mind was all over the place. Was she in danger? Did she need to start thinking about getting her family the hell out of Long Eaton? Where would she take them? How could she just say to them, 'oh, by the way James, I need you and the kids to come with me we're in danger'? That would go down almost as well as her freaking out about the guy at the meal. Hang on, the guy at the meal … was he involved? Was that why he'd been following her? Where had James said he worked? She would Google it now. Maybe that would tell her either way if this guy was a threat to her and her family.

'Ahhh.' The company website didn't show photos of their staff members. How would she be able to find out who he was and whether he was a threat? She threw the tablet onto the table with some force, making James jump.

'Jen? You okay? Jen? *Jennifer*!' James spoke louder, trying to get his wife's attention.

'Sorry.' Jen snapped back to reality, unsure what James wanted or how long he'd been trying to speak to her. She quickly turned the tablet off.

'I wondered if you wanted to go out for a walk before we pick the kids up?'

'Yeah. Can do, give me a minute.'

James came over to where Jen was sat. 'You okay?'

'I was just looking at something and the bloody thing crashed,' she lied.

'Come here, let me look at it,' James said, reaching over for the tablet.

'No, it's fine,' she replied, standing up and brushing herself down. *Wife of the year,* she reminded herself. 'So where do you fancy walking?'

As Jen held James' hand and they headed towards the school, she knew that this was going to be the make or break moment of this whole mess. She could tell him everything and he would have the answers like he always did; he would sweep her off her feet and take her anywhere she wanted to go. They could pick up the kids from school, get in the car and disappear. James would protect her, wouldn't he? He would understand, he would know what to do. All she needed to do was tell him the truth. They said that the truth hurts, well this was about to sting like a bitch. 'The truth will set you free' was another one but, no, this truth certainly wasn't going to set anyone free.

'Are you sure you're okay? You're awfully quiet,' said James.

'Yeah, just thinking.'

'Are you sure? You've been up and down like a rollercoaster. One minute you're running around and then the next you're quiet.'

'I've just been trying to trace that guy from last night.' Well there was a part truth in it, wasn't there?

'The one you thought had followed you?'

'Yeah, the guy that was really friendly with Rosemary. You said he worked for Lords?'

'Yeah I remember now, seemed to be a nice guy when I briefly chatted with him.'

Great, just what she needed. This guy was now firmly planting himself into their family life. 'Did you get his name or anything?'

'No, I didn't have any reason to. What's going on, Jen?'

'He just scared me. Like you said, no one can keep up with me and he was there at the meal.' She was on a roll. She was going to tell him everything; there was no more hiding from her past. 'James you know when we met in London?'

'Yeah, at that nightclub.'

'Well—'

'—James, Jennifer! Fancy seeing you here.' The moment was lost as she turned towards the voice, realising who it was.

'Jess!' James greeted her. 'Harry said you'd gone back to London?'

'Yeah, it was a whistle-stop visit. I just had to pick some stuff up from my parents' house and then I came back again,' Jess said lightly.

Jen felt like an idiot just stood there, listening to the conversation going on in front of her. This had been her time with James to tell him everything and look who'd managed to turn up and ruin it? As Jess began to flirt with James and sneak in the odd touch of his arm, Jen felt like a spare part. 'We were just on the way to pick the kids up actually, Jess.' That was when the obligatory eye roll and visual inspection happened as Jess looked her up and down.

'We all need to go out together again. It was such fun last time,' Jess gushed.

It might have been fun for her, but watching Jess all over her husband wasn't her favourite thing to do on a night out. Jen looked pointedly at her watch.

'James, we need to get going …' James completely ignored her and was now in full-flow flirting mode.

'Well, I'm looking forward to it already,' Jess said as she placed herself between them, blocking Jen out of her and James' conversation.

'Let me know when you're back for longer, Jess,' Jen said, manoeuvring herself back to where she'd been stood. She took hold of her husband's hand and gently pulled him away.

'Yeah, okay, Jess,' James said as Jen led him away. The moment was lost; there was no way she could tell him anything now he had a head full of Jess.

'What on earth was that all about?' James asked, letting go of Jen's hand.

'Oh, sorry. Did you forget that I was your wife and maybe don't appreciate you stood there in front of me flirting with another woman?'

'Now you're really being silly.'

'Oh James, you're so nice. Oh James, you look like you've been working out. I'm bloody well surprised you didn't end up checking her tonsils.'

'Jen, it wasn't like that at all.'

'Whatever.' Jen stomped off in the direction of school, leaving her husband to choose who he was going to follow: his wife or that whore. Jen knew she needed to calm down before she made it to the school gates. The nice walk with her husband had now been forgotten because of that bloody woman. Jen had thought that she might finally have the chance to get her head straight, but perfect Jess had successfully put an end to that.

Jen looked up at the clear night's sky as she sneaked out of the house, having waited for everyone to fall asleep before she could get out unnoticed. She'd been lying there, pretending to be asleep whilst she thought about everything that had happened in the past three days. She was scared. Was she being followed? Had something happened to Chloe? Had Chloe had something to do with the flowers and the card? In her mind she knew what the answer was, but she was too scared to admit the truth to herself.

Her carefully crafted facade was beginning to fall away. Every time Jen played the perfect wife and the perfect mother, she knew the cracks were appearing as she lost her patience with the kids or James.

James hadn't been the same since they'd bumped into Jess; he couldn't believe the way Jen had spoken to Jess. He should have been on his wife's side, not sticking up for that stupid woman. Had James and her been secretly meeting up behind Jen's back? Had Jess caught him in her trap of perfectness? Jen stroked her wrist and her faded tattoo as she looked up at the sky. 'Where the hell are you Chloe?' she whispered.

A misty rain began to fall from the sky. As much as she wanted to continue sitting alone in the garden she wasn't suitably dressed for the downpour. Maybe she'd go and get her running stuff on. She hadn't had time for one the previous day and, though it was almost 1 a.m., hopefully the run would clear her mind.

She returned to the house and snuck around, trying to find her sports bra and trainers. She would be out the door and off to find freedom and clarification. Tying her laces she opened the door and noticed a brown envelope stuck to the front. *Strange*. Why hadn't the person who'd left it put it through the letter box? She pulled the envelope from the door and looked at it under the porch light. As she opened it, she was confronted with all her worst fears.

She immediately began to dry heave. Escaping towards the back of the house, she was disorientated and dizzy as her blood pressure plummeted. She needed to sit down and staggered towards where she'd been sat earlier. She began to shake as she rechecked the picture which had been so elegantly delivered to her as the final blow. Her stomach did flips and churned while everything spun as she tried to focus on the final confirmation that the body in the photo was indeed Chloe's.

The more she looked at the photo, the more she felt like she was about to vomit. For a moment she was at peace; at least she knew that the body they had found was Chloe. There was no more wondering and questioning. But then the panic started; everything was adding up far too fast in her head.

Was she in danger? Were they coming for her next? Were her family in danger? They hadn't made the choice to be part of the world she used to live in. She'd unwillingly dragged them in, and now it was her job to protect them from what might be coming. She'd ignored the warning signs, but maybe, just maybe, it wouldn't be too late to get them out of harm's way.

But first she needed to talk to someone, someone who wouldn't judge her and wouldn't question her motives. Melanie was so innocent, and the world to her was full of candy floss and playing games in the sun. Jen made her way back into the house, holding the envelope tightly. Where was she going to put it to stop anyone else seeing the horror of Chloe's dead body?

Grabbing a bottle of wine she headed up to Melanie's bedroom where she would spend the rest of the night. As she sat on the floor, she continued to stroke the faded tattoo on her wrist, wondering if it would send up a distress beacon or give her back that link she used to share with Chloe. But right now she needed to talk and share her secrets and, though asleep, Melanie would understand and when she woke up, she'd still get out of bed and cuddle her whilst telling her she was the best mum in the whole world.

Chapter Nine

THURSDAY
Jen Garner

With light beginning to shine through the curtains in Melanie's room, Jen knew it was time to do the right thing by her family. She'd told Melanie everything while she slept and silently cried away all the pain as she mourned the loss of her best friend. Jen knew she needed to ask for help.

She heard James in the bathroom and heaved herself off the floor. She ruffled her daughter's hair and stretched, leaving the half-drunk bottle of wine hidden in Melanie's room so she could go and greet James on the landing. *One more time with feeling*, she thought to herself.

'Morning sleepy,' she said.

'I wondered where you'd disappeared to.'

'Melanie had a bad night, so I spent most of it on her floor,' she lied, though it was partly true.

'Why didn't you wake me?' James asked, running his hands over his face.

'Because you've got work and once the kids have gone to school, I can always go back to bed, so there's no issue.'

'I love you,' James said, pulling her close and kissing her forehead. 'You smell like you've had a drink too.'

Feeling the lump in her throat, Jen fought back the tears. 'Well yeah, I had to have something to get me through Melanie's nightmares and that hard floor.'

Both the kids appeared in the doorway of their rooms and the madness of the next hour began. As the kids were both washed, dressed and fed, ready to get into the car for school, Jen watched James pull off the driveway, crying silently for what she was possibly about to lose.

'Mum, you okay?' Alex asked.

'Yeah, just got something in my eye,' she lied.

Jen dropped the kids off at the gate with extra hugs and kisses. She got back into the car and let her tears run more freely, blurring her vision as she drove home.

Entering the bedroom she shared with her husband, she moved the bed and pulled up the floorboard. In the exact place she'd left it, in the metal sealed box, she found her gun, one hundred pounds in cash, a phone number and a photo of Chloe and her out somewhere. Both had drinks in their hands and smiles on their faces. This was the only photo of Chloe she had taken with her when she'd moved to Nottingham to be with James. It was a picture of happier times when she had the world at her feet. Hoping that she'd be back before bedtime, Jen slipped her wedding ring off and placed it in the box for safe keeping. It was better to go back with no strings attaching her to home.

She replaced the floorboard and bed, grabbed a can of Coke out of the fridge and left the house, turning her back on everything she'd known for the past ten years.

She walked through the streets of Long Eaton until she found what she was looking for. She picked up the receiver in the phone box and dialled the number. 'This is Officer Lisa Carter, I need a safe house. I'm in immediate danger, please advise.' Starting to shake, she replaced the receiver and waited. Even though everyone had mobile phones these days and, a lot of phone boxes now housed defibrillators, the government had insisted that some should remain for the exact reason she was using it.

After a couple of minutes, the phone rang again. Picking up the receiver, she received her instructions and walked away.

James Garner

James was sat at his desk, looking longingly at his office door. It had been a busy day and he was ready to go home. He was about to get his last cup of tea when his phone rang. Sitting back down, he answered it.

'James Garner speaking.'

'James, I have your children's school on the phone.'

'Not a problem, June. Put them through.' His heart raced. Why would the school be ringing him and not Jen?

'James Garner.'

'Mr Garner, it's Kevin from Ashgrove School. I'm phoning about Alex and Melanie.' James began to twirl the phone cable in frustration. *Would they get to the bloody point?*

'Is there a problem?'

'I'm afraid no one has arrived to collect your children this afternoon.'

'Okay? Has something happened to my wife? She normally picks them up.'

'Mr Garner, they're with one of their teachers. Melanie is quite upset.'

'Okay, tell them I'm just leaving work and will be there as soon as I can.'

'Thank you, Mr Garner. We will see you shortly.'

James turned his phone onto loudspeaker, ringing Jen's number, as he rushed around his office trying to sort everything. Each time, it went straight through to answerphone. 'For fuck's sake!' Silence fell across the office as everyone stopped working and looked over at him. Grabbing his coat, he rushed out.

As he drove through the streets of Nottingham, he continued to dial his wife's number. Where on earth was she? Leaning on his car horn, he drove through the traffic at speed. He shouldn't be thinking this way. What if something had happened to her? She could be lying in a hospital, but her phone wasn't on. The kids needing to be his first priority. He sped into the school car park, took a deep breath, walked into reception and asked for the Head.

'I'm really sorry, I've no idea what's happened to Jen. I've been trying to phone her, but her phone seems to be switched off.' James rubbed his face as he explained.

'It's okay, Mr Garner, we totally understand. I'm sure Mrs Garner just lost track of time.'

Melanie and Alex came running down the corridor when they saw him. After hugs and kisses, James scooped them both up and took them to his car. 'I am so sorry that I was late picking you up,' he told them. 'My boss has been very mean all day, making me do all these things before I was allowed to leave.'

'It's okay, Daddy,' Alex said as buckled himself into the car. 'I looked after Melanie when she started to get upset.'

'Good on you, little man. You okay, Melanie?' he asked. Melanie remained silent as Alex stretched his hand across the car to hold his sister's.

'See Melanie, everything is okay. Daddy is here now,' he told her.

James took the kids home via the McDonald's drive-thru and, with Happy Meals purchased and plasticky toys compared, he headed home. As he drove he started to put on his boss's voice and in no time had both the kids in stitches and the late pick-up was soon forgotten.

It was bedtime before the kids asked where their mum was and why she wasn't home yet. James lied as best as he could. He told them she'd gone out with some friends and would be home soon to kiss them goodnight. After trips to the toilet and asking for drinks, they were finally settled and asleep.

James sat down and looked out towards the drive, willing Jen to run up to the door and apologise for everything. Every couple of minutes he'd get up and check outside. He sent text messages to all their friends asking if Jen was with them and begging them to get her to ring him if she was.

As he watched the clock, he started to get fidgety. What if she was lying in a ditch somewhere? Picking up his phone, he dialled Jodie's number.

'Hi, is everything okay?'

'I am really *really* sorry for ringing you this late, but I'm worried about Jen. She hasn't returned home yet. Would you be able to sit with the kids while I go and look for her?'

'Of course. Let me get changed and I'll be right over.'

'Thanks Jodie, I owe you one.'

Once apologies were exchanged James jumped into his car and decided to drive as much of Jen's running route as he could before searching the rest on foot.

Jen Garner

Jen had sat alone in a bland living room for the past three hours, watching the traffic pass from behind the plain net curtain and listening to the ticking of a carriage clock. She would get up and think about making conversation with Isabelle, only to change her mind.

She'd managed to make it to Mansfield. She wished she could have driven her car, which would have been so much quicker than the hour-plus she'd spent on public transport, trying to be inconspicuous and not memorable to anyone who happened to look her way. She was just a normal commuter who had taken the longest route possible to the safe house as per her training all those years ago.

But it had given her time to think, time to reflect on the past. She'd found herself wondering what they should get the kids for Christmas; the kids that she'd dropped off at school only hours earlier and abandoned.

Isabelle, who lived alone at the safe house, tried to be friendly and welcoming, offering her tea and biscuits at every spare moment while she pottered around. Isabelle wasn't stupid. She'd run the place long enough to know when to worry and act concerned about an officer.

Safe houses hadn't gotten any nicer since she'd last been in one. Maybe that was why they were safe houses. They weren't anything special: a normal house in a normal neighbourhood that was owned by a little old lady who usually had a cat and was visited by her 'family and friends' regularly.

As Jen watched the clock ticking on the wooden mantelpiece, she thought about what the kids would be doing and how James would be sitting in his office having his second cup of tea or, if it was a bad day, an extra strong coffee. When she closed her eyes, she could feel his warm body against hers, the smell of his aftershave and the ruffle of his hair. Was she really doing the right thing sitting in a safe house when at home she had two children and an amazing husband who provided everything for her and more?

There was no turning back now. Her past had pretty much landed on her doorstep, with Chloe being murdered. Was it a coincidence or was it a sign that she couldn't afford to ignore? She had done the right thing by phoning and sitting in this non-descript house for the past three hours. She was protecting her family, wasn't she? Or was she just running away from the problem, creating more lies that would come back and bite her? Then the doorbell rang, and she heard the voice that she'd tried so hard not to forget.

'She's in the living room. She got here at about eleven and has been sat staring into space ever since.'

'Thank you, Isabelle. I left as soon as I heard that she'd phoned in.'

Jen sat listening to their conversation, waiting for the moment when he would walk into the living room and back into her life. She felt the butterflies in her stomach and the ringing in her ears.

He entered the room and for a minute she had that excited feeling; like a little girl when Daddy came home from work. She stood up to greet him and then immediately sat back down, changing her mind. Max had changed so much over the years. He was older and the weight of the world showed on his face. His hair was still on the verge of non-existence.

All she wanted to do was to run to him and let him wrap his arms around her, telling her everything was okay. She wanted to tell him all about her kids and of course, James, and the new life she'd created. There were so many conversations she wanted to have. So many memories she wanted to share with him. As they both looked at each other, there was a deadly silence. Even the traffic seemed to have stopped. That moment between them seemed to last a lifetime.

'Lisa.'

She couldn't hold herself back any longer, as she stood up, rushed towards him and hugged him as the tears began to fall.

'Shhh, it's okay.'

As she sobbed, she became aware of a wet patch forming where she had rested her head on his strong shoulders. When she was growing up, she was always reminded of how much her parents disliked her. They'd always told her that she was an accident. They'd never wanted kids and she was a constant reminder of the mistake that they'd made. They never abused her as such, but she was always shut in her room while they partied and had their friends over and, as she grew older, she used to sleep up against her door at night, scared that someone would accidentally come in. As she got older and started to drink and experiment, she found herself going from one drug and sex-filled party to another. Until one day she woke up on someone's floor on one hell of a comedown and realised that if she didn't change her ways she'd end up dead. She'd decided then and there she would join the police force. Doing so had given her the stability she needed and she'd gained the father she'd never had.

'I'm sorry,' she whispered as she pulled away and the silence returned. 'Chloe?'

'I'm afraid so.'

'When did you find out?'

'Only yesterday. She was undercover, some historical case.'

'A ten-year-old case?'

'I'm not sure. We've pulled everything she's ever worked on. I've contacted her handlers and as far as they were aware, she was fine. She'd attended all the debriefs and check-ins.'

'So how did she end up dead where I now live in Long Eaton?

'I don't know, I'm sorry.'

Jen was trying so hard to not burst into tears again. Here was the man that she looked up to, the closest thing she'd ever had to a father, telling her he'd no idea how her former best friend had died other than the fact she was working some historical case. She wanted to scream and shout at him and hit him. He was Chloe's boss. How could he have let this happen?

'So where is she now?' Jen asked.

'One of the team picked her body up and transported her back to London yesterday.'

'Do you know how she died?' Jen really didn't want to know the answer. She wanted to stay detached from the situation. If he told her the cause of death, everything would become so real. It would no longer be just a body they found on a local footpath near the supermarket.

'The team at the hospital did a really good job on the autopsy. In fact, we only became aware that there was an issue when they managed to ID her.'

'So?'

'I've read the report and let's just say it wasn't nice.'

So many questions raced through Jen's head as silence fell again. She sat back down and grabbed a handful of her hair. She pulled it until she could feel the physical pain. Anything to try to block out the mental pain she was feeling for her best friend.

Why hadn't she kept in touch better than over Facebook? Why had she been so desperate for this new life, cutting everyone out? She was selfish. That was it. She was a selfish cow. The only person she had thought of was herself.

'For fuck's sake,' she shouted, rocking back and forth, shaking with anger. Max moved towards her to comfort her. 'Don't, just don't,' she growled at him.

'I'll ask Isabelle if she can make us both a drink,' he said, excusing himself from the room.

Jen didn't bother to respond, putting her head in her hands. Everything was a mess and if she'd stayed at home this morning, surfing the internet and drinking tea, none of this would have happened. Jen wanted to walk out the door, leave her gun on the table and get a taxi home. Though given what the time was, there would be some explaining to do and excuses to make. Jen could hear Max and Isabelle talking in the kitchen about the weather and the cricket scores as she sat and waited for the next blow to come.

'Isabelle asked if you wanted something to eat.'

'I'm good,' Jen replied as Max laid down the tea tray. She hadn't eaten since breakfast, but her mind was too preoccupied to even think about food. Max sat down and poured the tea, taking the mug and cradling it in his hands before sinking back into the sofa.

'Ah, I need to get one of these sofas in my office. Those office chairs aren't doing my back or neck any good.' Max's remarks went by unacknowledged as Jen stared into space.

'So, where do I fit into all of this?' Jen finally asked after another long silence 'Are my family in danger? Am I in danger?

'I really don't know. I'm not even sure that you are, as far as I'm concerned. I think it might just be one great big coincidence.'

'Coincidence? Chloe was working a historical case. She was dumped where I live. I've been receiving this strange mail and, unless he was one of your guys, I'm being followed. How can you call that a coincidence?'

'Hang on. You were being followed?'

She told him everything that had happened from the day

the body had been discovered. About the guy on the canal to the same guy being at her husband's client meal. She told him how James had told her that he was probably someone who worked at a rival firm when she'd pointed him out. Then Max said something that broke her heart all over again.

'You looked amazing on your wedding day. I wish I could have walked you down the aisle.'

'You were there?'

'Of course I was. I couldn't let my best asset disappear without a trace.'

'So, I guess you know about my kids?'

A smile appeared on Max's face. 'Kind of.'

Jen laughed, breaking the tense atmosphere that had formed between them. Max went on to tell her how he accidentally managed to track her down, and how he probably should stop calling her Lisa and use her new name instead. He told her that Fletch, his dog, had died some years back. He'd invested in a cat instead as that wouldn't need half as much looking after as Fletch did when he was away. He missed Fletch's boundless energy. His cat just sat on his knee of an evening. He knew it was for the best with the long hours he still worked. Jen joked that maybe he should take a leaf out of her book, but then the awkwardness fell again.

'So, what next?'

'I hate to ask this Lisa, I mean Jen, but will you come back and have a look at the case files? I just can't help thinking we're missing something.'

'What about my family? I can't just up and leave them. I came here to ask for help not to be recruited again.'

'I've already got my best people on it. You've come all this way. What harm would it do just to have a look at the files? I'll get you back home before tea time tomorrow.'

'Isn't there anyone else? Someone Chloe was working with?'

'You remember what she was like, and after you left she was more convinced she'd cope on her own.'

'Great. So this is more my fault than I already thought.'

The conversation paused and Jen began to absentmindedly run her finger over her tattoo again, trying to weigh up her options. Maybe after her trip to London, she'd go home and tell James everything.

'I see you never got that tattoo reinked,' Max commented as he watched her sitting there.

'I'm coming back to London with you.' Jen didn't acknowledge Max's question. 'But I need to be home in time to pick the kids up tomorrow. Okay?'

'Yeah, come and take a look, then you can go back to your life.'

Jen had been trained to protect the country. The kids and James had been her world for the last ten years. If returning to London was the only way she could protect them then she had to go.

'So how are we getting back to London?' she asked.

'Your chauffeur awaits madam,' Max said, standing up and pointing towards the door.

As they both headed out Isabelle reappeared to see them off, like any doting old lady would. Making sure the neighbours heard and saw as she kissed and hugged them both, she bade them goodbye and said she hoped she'd see them again soon.

Chapter Ten

James had returned home after checking everywhere he could think of. There was still no sign of her.

Thanking Jodie and promising to keep her informed, he started to phone around the hospitals. At 2 a.m. he searched for his hidden emergency pack of cigarettes and lit his first in eight years. Where the hell was she?

As day broke, James tried all the hospitals again, just to make sure. He checked everything on social media and news websites for any accidents or traffic hold-ups but there was nothing about Jen. Then he clicked on a story from Tuesday about the body being discovered. He found himself watching the press conference with the local Detective. James stood up, checked outside again and reached for his phone.

'Derbyshire Police, how can I help you?'

'My wife has gone missing. I think something has happened to her.' James' breathing started to accelerate, as he struggled to get the words out quickly enough. Whoever he was speaking to kept asking the same questions. He could feel himself beginning to lose his patience as his chest began to tighten.

An hour later, PC Curtis and Sergeant Gillroy sat in James' front room, taking down the basic information about Jen.

'When was the last time you saw your wife, Mr Garner?' Sergeant Gillroy asked.

'Yesterday morning, as I left for work.'

'Did she seem okay?' Sergeant Gillroy continued.

'Yes, of course she did. Why are you asking these stupid questions?' James said, rising to his feet and beginning to pace the floor.

'Can you think of anywhere else she might be?'

James became louder and more agitated as they continued their questioning. His wife was missing. Why weren't they out there looking for her? Why were they treating this as though she had stayed out too long with a friend?

'Why do you keep asking the same questions?'

'We're just trying to get a clear picture of what has happened.' Sergeant Gillroy spoke in a calming voice. 'Are there any friends or family that she could be with?'

'Jen's family all died before we met. And as for friends, she only really talks to the other school mums or our neighbours. Why aren't you out looking for her?' James shouted as he marched across the room.

'I'm sorry sir, but we just need to get some details of her movements yesterday before she failed to arrive at school.'

Just then Melanie appeared in the doorway, clinging to her teddy.

'Daddy?' she whispered, looking in awe at the two police officers sitting there in their bright yellow coats with buzzing radios clipped to them.

'Go back to bed, sweetie. Daddy is just talking to these nice police officers about something that happened at work.' PC Curtis and Sergeant Gillroy smiled at Melanie.

'Who's that? Why are you shouting? You woke me up. Is it time for school yet?' she asked, staring around the room.

'No sweetie,' James checked his watch. Almost 7 a.m.

'Where's Mummy?' she asked, wrinkling her nose.

James suddenly felt like the wind had been knocked out of him. Trying to catch his breath he said 'Why don't you see if you can go back to sleep for a bit longer, while Daddy talks to these police officers?'

'Where's Mummy?' Melanie repeated as tears began to glisten in her eyes.

'I'm sorry, I need to sort out my children.' James grimaced.

'Before we go, do you have a recent photo of your wife we can borrow?'

'Listen, I want to speak to that Chris guy. The Detective on the telly who's investigating that body they found.'

'I don't think it's going to be that easy, sir. DI Jackson is rather busy at the moment.'

He rubbed his hand over his face and led the two police officers into the hallway while he searched for a recent photo of Jen. Making sure Melanie was out of earshot he spoke: 'Someone needs to take action or Jen will be the next body, I know it.'

'Mr Garner, we'll be in touch later again today to check if you've heard anything from your wife.'

With that, James watched the officers walk up his drive towards their car.

DI Chris Jackson

Chris had been awake most of the night searching for answers in the case files. He had copied everything from the USB stick onto his personal laptop. He printed photos of both Chloe and Daisy, which were now plastered to his front room wall. He was silently grateful to his parents for the photo printer they had brought him last Christmas. It meant instant photos with no questions asked by nosey photo shop staff. He realised he had now well and truly broken the rules; not only had he removed files from work, he had made copies and reproduced photos. The Chloe case had been handed back to her old team and it had been made clear to him last year that the Daisy case was closed as there wasn't any new evidence to investigate. There *was* a connection between the two cases and if this is how he'd find it then so be it. His phone rang, startling him out of his thoughts.

'DI Jackson.'

'Morning sir, it's PC Curtis. We've had an interesting turn of events overnight that I wanted to speak to you about before I clocked off.'

'I'm just about to head into work now, Wes. Do you want to meet in the canteen in, what, thirty minutes, depending on traffic?'

'Sounds good to me. A nice hot cuppa before I clock off.'

With that, Chris' time at home was up. He tried to move everything into neat piles so when he returned home it would all be in the same place. The Maid Madness girls weren't due for another week so there was nothing to hide. He took one last look at the photos of Chloe and Daisy and headed to work.

Chris entered the station, swiped in and headed up towards his office to drop his things off before going to find PC Curtis. Arriving at the canteen he spotted Wes sitting at an empty table, drinking from a disposable cup.

'Sorry, Wes. You been here long?' Chris asked as he walked up to him.

'No, about five minutes or so. Can I get you a drink, sir?' he asked.

'No, let me get them. Plus if I ask the ladies nicely, they'll put mine in a proper mug with a couple of chocolate biscuits on the side.'

'I knew I was going wrong somewhere.' Wes laughed.

'Another tea is it?' Chris asked.

'Please sir, in one of those mugs if you can.'

Chris returned moments later with two steaming mugs and, as promised, a couple of chocolate biscuits on the side.

'So, how do I go about getting myself one of those next time I'm in the queue for a cuppa?' Wes asked.

'Secrets of the trade, I'm afraid. Plus, if I told you my secret, there'd never be any mugs or biscuits left for me. You'd make sure everyone knew about the secret code.' Both officers laughed out loud as people turned around, wondering what was so funny.

'Sorry for calling you at home, sir. We had an interesting

call in the early hours of this morning from a gentleman in the area.'

'It's not a problem. I should have been thinking about coming in anyway instead of being transfixed by daytime telly.' Chris chuckled.

'His wife had failed to pick up their children from school yesterday and hasn't been seen since.'

'Okay?'

'I went out to visit with Sergeant Gillroy early this morning. We've phoned round the hospitals and nowhere has any admissions matching her identity.'

'She hasn't stayed over with friends or family?'

'Not from the looks of things. He started to get a bit restless and then his daughter appeared, so we ended the interview. He was adamant he wanted to speak to you. I explained that you were busy which didn't deter him.'

'What did you make of it? Is it just another domestic?'

'I don't know, sir. Sergeant Gillroy seems to think so, but the gentleman had been surfing the internet, reading about the recent incident and your name came up. So he wants to see the man in charge.'

'You'd better give his number to those guys from London who came in yesterday.' Chris laughed, trying to make light of the situation.

'We've told him someone will contact him later today.'

'What do we know about him?'

'James Garner. Married to Jennifer Garner who hasn't been seen since yesterday morning. Two children, Melanie and Alex. He works as a Technical Manager and she is a stay-at-home mum.'

'Sounds a happy family unit.'

'Until she failed to pick the kids up yesterday.' Wes pushed a brown envelope towards Chris. 'We asked for a recent photo of his wife and he gave us this.'

'Give me his number and I'll get hold of him. You need to

clock off and get some sleep,' Chris spoke as he looked at the photo he'd just been given.

'Thanks, boss. Will you let me know if anything happens?'

'Will do.'

Chris studied the photo of Jennifer Garner, trying to decide what to do next. He had a dead woman and now a young mum missing; he needed to look into it. If she was being held captive or was about to appear in a ditch somewhere he needed to get ahead of whatever was going on in Long Eaton. He'd send Julie a message and see if she was in yet and fancied a trip out.

Chapter Eleven

James Garner

James sat at the breakfast table staring at the morning paper while the kids ate some high sugar content cereal. His phone rang.

'Jen?' he answered without even looking at the caller, hoping it would be her on the other end with some explanation.

'James, it's Mum. Is everything okay?' James signalled to the children to continue to eat their breakfast, got up and headed into the conservatory.

'It's Jen, Mum.' James tried desperately hard not to break down completely.

'What do you mean? Is she okay?'

'She didn't pick the kids up from school yesterday and hasn't returned home.'

'Did you have an argument or something?'

'No, Mum, everything is great between us. Well at least I thought it was.'

'What about the kids? What have you told them?'

'Nothing yet, I've told them she's out running.'

'You need to tell them the truth, son.'

'I know. I'm working up to it. It's finding the right time.'

'Make sure you do, James. You know I'd come straight over but your dad and I have got so much on at the moment with the local community group.'

'I know, Mum. I wouldn't expect you to. I'll give you a call back later. It's likely to be late, once I get the kids in bed.'

James headed back to check on the progress the kids had made with breakfast. 'Why don't you guys stay in your onesies and we'll have a movie day?'

'Instead of school?' Alex asked excitedly.

'I won't tell anyone if you don't,' James replied with a wink.

As the kids excitedly headed towards the front room ready for their movie day, James cleared the table and wondered how best to tell them the news.

They were all sat watching the first film when Alex asked the question. 'Daddy, when is Mummy coming home?' James stopped the film and prepared to have one of the most awkward and difficult conversations with his two children he would ever have.

'You both know Mummy loves you both lots?' James cuddled Melanie and Alex as he spoke.

'Yeah,' they both echoed.

'Mummy has gone away for a while.'

'Why?'

'I don't know, Alex.'

'Is that why she didn't pick us up from school yesterday?'

'Yes, and that's why the police officers were here this morning.'

The look of hurt and shock that appeared on both the children's faces almost broke his heart. Then the tears started. 'Do they know where Mummy is?' Melanie began to sob.

'They're looking for her and promise that she'll be home soon.'

'Will Mummy end up dead like that body they found?'

'No. Of course not, Melanie.'

'They've been talking about the body at school.'

'Melanie, I promise. Mummy has just gone away for a while. Maybe it's so she can train for her race?'

'But why, Daddy?' Melanie sobbed.

'Are you going to disappear too, Daddy?' Alex asked, wiping his tears on his sleeve.

'No, I'm staying right here with you two. We'll watch movies all day and eat pizza or hotdogs, together with popcorn and sweets. What do you think?'

'That will make Mummy come home. She's always telling us off for eating sweets,' Alex said, still fighting the tears.

'I'm sure Mummy will be home when she finds that out!' James hated lying to his kids. Right now, he was going to have to take one day at a time until he had at least some idea when his wife was coming home.

James continued to sit with the kids as they asked questions about where their mummy was and about the body that had been found. They asked him questions he couldn't answer but tried his best to help ease their young minds. He told them that he was going to ring the Police Detective and ask him if he had found their mum yet. They laughed together, and they cried together as they sat talking. In the end, it turned into a bit of a game, as they suggested places their mum could be and James pretended to phone to check. In between the bursts of suggestions, James was frantically messaging all his friends hoping someone somewhere had heard or seen something.

The second film of the day had just ended, and they were mid discussion of what they should watch next when the doorbell rang. The kids both dived up and ran to the door, fighting to open it in the hope it would be their mum. James reached over them and was greeted by the Chris guy he had spent the previous night watching online and a female colleague. James could feel his face redden as he stood at the door dressed in his Chewbacca onesie. After showing the detectives into the living room he made his excuses and disappeared upstairs to change. They would never take him seriously dressed as a Chewbacca, especially when the kids would no doubt encourage him to do his impression.

DI Chris Jackson

'Thank you for seeing us at short notice,' Chris said as James showed them both into the conservatory, leaving the kids watching some cartoon thing on TV.

'Have you heard anything about where my wife is?' James asked as he took a seat opposite the officers.

'I spoke with one of my colleagues who was here earlier. I wanted to come and meet you and hopefully take some more details if that's okay?'

'Yeah, yeah, of course.'

'Great. Thank you, James. Could you tell us about Jennifer?' Chris asked as Julie brought out her notebook and began to take notes.

'Jen ... well, I'm not sure where to start really.'

'Why don't you start at the beginning, when you first met your wife?' Chris suggested. If they started at the beginning then there would be less time-frame jumping and something from their early lives together might hold a clue as to where this woman was now.

'We met when I was out for a mate's stag do in London.'

'How long ago was that?'

'Ten years this year, I think.'

'Did she live in London at the time?'

'Think so, I never really went back to her place. We always met in a hotel or she'd come up here. She'd always tell me that things were complicated with her housemates so it was easier to meet elsewhere. Not that I minded.'

'So, was it a whirlwind romance?'

'I'm not sure what you're implying? We dated for a while, things were great, so I asked her if she'd move in with me.'

'And she did.'

'Well yeah, she was a bit unsure at first, didn't want to leave her job at some insolvency company, was worried about making new friends. I told her that I'd move down to London if she wanted. I just wanted to be with her. She was like this enigma. I just couldn't get enough of her.'

'So, once she'd moved here, did she change at all?'

'She became calmer, less of a mystery. When Melanie came along not long after we were married, she just fell into the mothering role. She was a natural, plus my parents adore her. Everything was great.'

'What about her family, brothers or sisters, her parents? Did you ever meet them?'

'She said pretty early on in our relationship she was an only child, which is one of the reasons we had Alex; she wanted Melanie to grow up with a brother or sister, someone to look after she'd tell me. As for her parents they'd died before we met, though she never talked about them, so I just assumed things were strained.'

'Okay. When do you think things started to change?'

'They didn't. Well, I guess she has been a bit manic and panicky these last couple of days. She randomly received some flowers on Monday and then a weird card the next day. She was convinced she was being followed as well. I told her it was nonsense. In fact, the guy she said was following her works at a rival firm and is friendly with my boss's wife, so I told her she was being silly.'

'Tell me about the flowers. Do you still have the card?'

'They're on display in the front room, well the lilies are. The rose she threw away, I think.'

'What spooked her about them?'

'I believe it was more the card if I think about it; the picture on the card was of the same lilies. I don't know what happened to it or I'd show you.'

'The flowers, did they come with a card or anything?'

'No, they were just left on the doorstep. We thought they had been delivered to the wrong house at first.'

'And it was after this she thought she was being followed?'

'No, it was the same day as the card arrived. Jen runs a lot, almost every day, and it was during her run she said this guy was following her. He then apparently appeared again at my client meal in the evening.'

'You said he was from a rival company. Do you know his name? Which company?'

'I told Jen it was Lords, but I can speak to my boss and find out.'

'That would be great, thank you James. We might need to speak to him.' Just then a young girl appeared in the doorway.

'You okay, sweetheart?' James asked.

'Daddy, Alex said I need to come and tell you something.'

'Okay?' James questioned.

'You know not last night but the night before, I woke up in the night and Mummy was sat on my floor crying.'

'Did you ask her if she was okay, Melanie?' James asked.

'No, I just closed my eyes really tightly as I didn't know what to do and didn't want to upset her more.'

'Melanie, is it?' Julie asked. 'Shall I come and sit with you and Alex and you can tell me all about it while Daddy finishes talking to my friend?'

'Okay. Alex told me I needed to come and tell you as it might help find Mummy.'

'You've done the right thing,' Julie said, ushering Melanie out of the door.

'James, do you have any ideas what your wife might have been crying about?' continued Chris.

'No, it's all news to me. The next day was when she disappeared. Do you think it might have something to do with why she left?'

'It could be. I'm sure my colleague will find out if Melanie knows anything else.' Chris tried to reassure James but at the same time he wanted to be careful about making any assumptions.

'I should be in there,' James said, standing up.

'It might be best if you give them some time.' Chris tried to reassure James, not wanting him to go and disrupt Julie if she was about to find something important out. He continued with his questions. 'James, tell me more about Jen. Did she have any tattoos, any scars or other distinguishing features?'

'She had a scar on her forehead, oh and a faded tattoo on her left wrist.'

'What was the tattoo of?'

'It's an infinity symbol. She said it was something she drunkenly got done when she was younger. In fact, she said it hurt so much that when it started to fade she never got it re-inked.'

There it was again, Chris thought to himself. Chloe, the dead girl, had one of those on her ankle. Could it be a coincidence that Jen had one too? Chris picked up his phone and started searching through his photos.

'In fact,' James started talking again, 'I used to joke and tell that if she'd managed childbirth, surely getting it re-inked would be nothing in comparison. But she'd just shrug me off or change the subject.'

Chris had found the photo he'd wanted. 'James, I want to show you a picture. Tell me if you recognise the girl in the photo.' He turned the phone screen towards James so he could see the photo of Chloe in the mortuary.

'Jesus, is that the girl they found earlier in the week?'

'Do you know her?'

'I don't recognise her.'

'So, you wouldn't say she was one of your wife's friends?'

'No, I've not seen that face before. What happened to her?'

'It's an ongoing investigation that I'm afraid I'm unable to comment on, but I'm sure you've seen the news reports. One final question James, before I let you get back to the kids, what was Jen's maiden name?'

'Sheridan. As in Sheridan Smith.'

'Thank you, James. I'll run the name through the system when I get back to the office.'

'You'll find my wife?' James asked eagerly.

'I will do everything in my power, but I can't promise anything,' Chris said, getting up from the chair he'd occupied. 'Thank you for your time today.' Chris held out his hand. 'I will get back to you as soon as I have some news.' Chris followed James to the front room, where Julie was busy playing Connect 4 with Alex.

'I think I've got to go now, Alex,' Julie said. 'Thank you for telling me all about your mum.'

'You will find her though?' Melanie asked.

'We will do our best. Try not to worry. You've done the right thing telling us about your mum crying, okay Melanie?'

Melanie nodded as Julie got off the floor.

'Thank you, James,' she said, walking over to shake his hand. Then she and Chris left the house. As they walked up the drive, Chris looked back through the window to notice the family were now all sat holding each other.

'What did you make of that?' Julie asked as she climbed into the car with Chris.

'I can see why PC Curtis was concerned. Did you get anything from the kids?'

'Not really, had a chat with Melanie about her mum sitting on her floor crying, but other than that nothing to report. Seems to have been a happy family unit.'

'It does all seem a bit strange that she disappeared after receiving the random gifts.' Chris started the car, and they pulled away from the house, heading back to Nottingham. 'What's bothering me though is the fact Jen shared the same tattoo as Chloe.'

'Do you think they knew each other?' Julie questioned.

'All the reports we've had back on the tattoo seem to say the same thing. That they are a common design and tend to have a unique meaning to the owner. James did say his wife's was faded, and he had told her to get it re-done. I showed him a picture of Chloe, but he didn't seem to recognise her. There was no hint of any recognition on his face.'

'So we've got a missing female who has a similar tattoo to the girl they found,' Julie summed up. 'Did James say much more about Jen's past while I was with the kids?'

'Not really.'

'I'm not sure what to think, Chris.'

'I think it warrants being looked into more if nothing else. Where are you with the drugs?'

'About the same as everyone else, boss. I think we've hit the same wall as DI Manson's team. So why on earth he wanted us to look at it, I don't know.'

'Probably as a distraction, no doubt. Leave it with me. If we have a team meeting first thing we can discuss a way forward for the case.'

'I'll do some digging boss and see what I can find out.'

'Thank you, Julie. I think I have some departmental meeting or something this afternoon so if you find out, drop me an email or something and we can look at it tomorrow.'

'Okay, you'll want dropping back at the station then?' Julie asked as they joined the A52 heading back towards Nottingham and the office.

Chapter Twelve

Jen Garner

For the split second when Jen opened her eyes, she thought she was at home. Any second the kids would come running into the room to wake her up, full of excitement for the day ahead ... but they never came. As she lay there coming round, she remembered where she was and what she'd done.

She'd spent the night in an old T-shirt Max had discreetly left on the bed for her; she began to wonder what she was going to do about clothes and underwear. She'd left home with nothing but her gun and some money.

She noticed how quiet the house seemed, as she changed back into yesterday's clothes and peered through the net curtains at life below. Sighing, she opened the bedroom door and headed down the stairs.

'Morning,' she said as she entered the kitchen to find Max sat in a rocking chair, reading some spy novel. 'Do you not get enough of that at work?' she asked as Max looked up to acknowledge her.

'They amuse me, how wrong authors get it sometimes ... or how frighteningly close to the truth they are.'

'Did you sleep okay? I didn't hear you come up.'

'I don't really sleep much anymore. I think I probably dozed for an hour or so in the chair. Can I get you a drink or anything?' Max added, getting out of his chair.

'I'll do it.'

'Don't be silly, you're my guest and I don't get much chance to entertain.'

Jen laughed, knowing exactly what he meant. Who could he entertain, living in such secrecy?

'How do you take your tea nowadays?' he asked.

'Milk, no sugar, please.'

'Toast? Afraid there's no sugar and E-number filled kiddie cereal here.'

Jen sat in silence while Max prepared her a drink and put some bread in the toaster.

'I'm sorry. It's only usually me and the cat for breakfast in the morning and we both tend to skip it.'

'Toast will be fine. Do you want a hand?'

'No, I'm good. You just make yourself comfortable and I'll sort the rest.'

As she sat eating, Max scooted his tablet over towards her. 'Here, order yourself some clothes and I'll get someone to go out and pick them up later.' Not wanting to argue, Jen began tapping away. 'Just don't bankrupt the service,' he joked.

'Here,' Jen said, sliding the tablet back to Max as he got out a card to pay.

'I'm going to grab a shower and call for a car. Do you need to do anything before we head in?'

'No, I'm good thanks, just looking forward to some clean clothes.' Jen sat and thought about her family; she should really check in on them. She wondered how James was coping and what he'd told the kids. She hated herself. It had almost been twenty-four hours since she had up and left. What the fuck was she doing sitting there ordering herself a new wardrobe? She was going into the office with Max, checking the files and then she'd get home as quickly as possible. She needed to see if she had anything left to salvage from her lies. She turned around as she heard Max come back into the room.

'Jen, before we head in, we need to talk about the day you left.'

Jen had known this conversation was coming. She hadn't been sure when it was going to happen or whether she could avoid it all together.

'I'm sorry I just left after the court case. I knew if I came back to the office, you'd have tried to talk me out of going.'

'I never had a problem with you leaving, Jen. You were starting to be like a caged animal, so I knew the time was coming when you'd want to break free.' Max sat down opposite her and helped himself to another slice of toast.

'I owe so much to the service. It saved my life when I first joined. It continued to save my life until the day I left.'

'Jen, you could've told me you'd met someone. I'd have still let you go.'

'I was scared Max, that you'd want to run background checks on him. I wanted to fall in love and make mistakes without knowing whether he had a criminal record or not.'

'He doesn't,' Max responded.

'See, I knew you'd want to check! So I didn't tell you. Chloe knew; she was with me when I met him and we went back to the hotel together. She'd already tried to talk me out of going. I just couldn't bear to have the same conversation with you.'

'Jen, you know I loved you like a daughter and I only ever wanted what was best for you.'

'And it all worked out okay in the end?' Jen let the silence lie for a moment. 'Well until my best friend ended up getting herself killed.'

As the car splashed through the rainy streets of London, she could feel the butterflies in her stomach. It was like the first day at school again but worse! Would there be anyone still working there she knew? What would they all think of her? How would she feel seeing Chloe's desk? Who would be sat at her old desk? Would the office layout still be the same? Would there be any new pictures on Max's wall? As they sat in traffic Jen felt like her head was already waiting to explode. Would it have not been quicker to get the tube? Although, then there was a great big safety issue to consider. At least they were dry and didn't have to deal with the hurly burly of commuter life. She tried to calm herself by concentrating on her breathing.

'You okay?' Max asked, noticing her agitated state.

'Yeah, just nervous.'

'Lisa Carter, nervous? I never thought I'd hear such a thing. You've definitely changed.'

As they passed the security barrier and pulled into the underground car park, Max directed her in the general direction she needed to go in and told her to just sit and wait when she got inside. He would need to get through security his side and then would come and meet her. So, there she was stood in this expansive hall, with people all rushing in different directions. She almost felt dizzy as she watched them. Did she really used to be this single-minded and focused on the task at hand to not just stop and take a minute to look at everything that was going on around her?

Max appeared from nowhere, handed her a visitor's lanyard and directed her towards the X-ray machines. Security had been significantly ramped up since she'd last been here, but she wasn't surprised if she was honest.

'Ready to meet the team?' Max asked, joining her on the opposite side of the machines.

'As I'll ever be,' she said, checking her watch as she found herself thinking about home once again.

She wasn't sure what or who she had expected to see as she followed Max towards his office. She noticed people whispering and looking at her. The new girl being paraded through the office, so everyone could check her out and form opinions before knowing who she was.

Their first opinions would probably be visual ones and weren't likely to be positive since she was wearing the same clothes as she'd left the house in yesterday. She hoped her Click and Collect would be ready to pick up soon, so she could at least have a clean set of underwear.

Opening his office door, Max invited her in. His office was just how she'd remembered it. Somehow the potted plant had survived; perhaps someone had started watering it more regularly, or it'd just been replaced with the exact same plant.

As she sat down, she looked at the pictures on the wall of various dignitaries and awards. Pride of place on Max's desk was a photo of Fletch.

'I bet it feels like you've never been away,' he commented.

Jen laughed nervously just as someone knocked on Max's door. *Perfect timing*, she thought to herself.

A young girl who Jen didn't recognise walked in with a notepad. She had short, pixie-like brown hair and big hooped earrings. She was wearing a brightly coloured dress that didn't at all match the dark dismal day that was forming outside or the decor of the office.

'Ah, Samantha,' Max greeted her.

'Good to see you back, sir. Did you have a successful trip?'

'Yes, I did thank you, Sam. I'd like you to meet Lisa, sorry I mean Jen Garner. She's come in to look at those files.'

Sam shook Jen's hand and smiled, displaying sparkly white teeth. Jen already felt really irritated by her persona. She was far too happy and pretty to be working for the service. The system would soon screw her up and spit her back out again.

'Sam is my PA.' Max introduced them. 'She's our little ray of sunshine and positivity.'

Jen attempted a smile in response. She had most definitely not taken a liking to Little Miss Sunshine.

'I've picked up the Click and Collect you ordered, boss. It's just on my desk. Do you want me to bring it in?'

'Thank you, Sam. I'll probably need you to point Jen in the right direction shortly, so keep hold of it for now.'

'Anything else I can help you with?'

'Not at the moment, thank you. I'll give you a call later if we need anything.' With that, the breeze of positivity left Max's office. Jen watched as she floated across the main office, stopping every so often to talk to someone, before returning to what looked like her desk. Jen couldn't help feeling paranoid watching Sam type away. No doubt she was telling her colleagues all about the new girl.

'Whoa, what was that?' Jen asked.

'Sam is really nice once you get to know her and get used to her. She's been a really positive asset, lifted the spirits in the office more than once.'

'I can't wait to work with her when the shit hits the fan.' Max gave Jen a disapproving look. Perhaps she'd warm to her in time, though right now Jen was tired and overwhelmed with being back.

'I need you to surrender your gun,' said Max.

'What, why?'

'When was the last time you fired a gun, Jen?'

Jen tried to think back. She certainly hadn't fired it in the last ten years. She hadn't fired it since she had hidden it under the floorboards in the house.

'I can't afford to let you out on the streets with a gun. Especially as you've not had recent training.'

Jen sighed as she passed it over.

'Now go and get yourself sorted, and I'll organise the stuff to show you.'

Jen exited Max's office and looked for Sam and her clothes order.

Being a parent had changed her. Carrying a little baby out of the hospital for the first time had been nothing short of scary and strange. Lisa would have never had that experience. She was too much of a career woman. But how different could Lisa and Jen be? She wasn't working a case when she met James. She was Lisa, but she used a different name like she always did, just in case it didn't work out. She hadn't planned on marriage and two kids when she met him on the dancefloor. Once she'd changed and put on the clothes that she'd chosen off a website earlier, would Jen suddenly be forgotten? Should she march back into the office and be the bitch she used to be? Who was she trying to pretend to be, Lisa or Jen? How could she forget the experiences that had changed her and shaped her into the woman she was today?

Jen felt more herself once she had managed to shower and change. The showers at the office weren't luxurious, but it was nice to feel the warmish water washing over her. Sam had been full of questions as she'd showed Jen the way.

'Are you who they say you are?' she'd asked. 'How long are you here for?'

Jen had tried to brush her off, telling her that it would depend on who they thought she was. All being well she'd be back home in time for tea, but it only led to more questions.

As Max saw her return to the office, he directed her to the meeting room. 'Find your way okay?' he asked her as she entered the meeting room. She noticed there was a man and a woman also sat at the large oak table. She vaguely recognised the man but, as for the other person, she had no clue.

'Yes, thanks.'

'Okay. Tim, Hannah, this is the former Detective Lisa Carter.' Jen nodded in their direction. Maybe it was time to go back to being Lisa again? 'Lisa left the service several years back, but has agreed to come and look at these files for us and tell us what we're not seeing.'

'Please call me Jen,' she responded, as she ran her fingers over her faded tattoo and decided to leave Lisa firmly in the past.

Detective Tim Brown. She knew she'd recognised him from the time she had spent at the service. As she poured herself a glass of water, she studied the computer tablets, which formed part of the table. She resisted the urge to check out the wiring under the table. James would have been under there as soon as he had entered the room. A large screen occupied the front of the room where Max was currently stood, looking through his notes.

'As we are all aware, Chloe's body turned up in Long Eaton on Monday morning. The Special Ops unit in Nottingham had made a start investigating and performed the autopsy. All the information is on your tablets in front of you.' Everyone started to swipe on their screens, looking at the information.

'The cause of death is listed as drowning. How sure is the pathologist? As I read earlier, she'd been badly beaten,' Tim questioned.

'The water in Chloe's lungs matches the water she was found in. The pathologist did confirm that, though she had taken a beating, it was likely she wouldn't have been conscious when her head was held down,' Max responded. 'As far as I have been able to establish Chloe was looking into this new batch of drugs that were coming in from somewhere.' Max loaded the picture of the drugs onto the screen and Jen took a deep breath in.

'Well, I remember that logo for sure. That's George Crawford's signature, but I thought he was still locked up in prison?'

'I suspected as much,' Max responded.

Jen was starting to get the feeling she'd been brought here under false pretences. If Max knew these drugs where connected to George, she was the only other person who knew the case as well as Chloe.

'If all this leads back to the Crawford empire, why was Chloe being left to her own devices?' Jen questioned.

'She was as stubborn and as independent as a certain former detective I once knew,' Max said, looking meaningfully at her.

'Chloe had told us that she was just going out partying, to get close to someone. I offered to go with her so many times, but she told me she'd be okay,' Hannah responded, clearly trying hard to disguise that she felt partly responsible for what had happened to Chloe.

'I'm guessing you've pulled all the Crawford files?' Jen asked.

'Yeah, the paper files are in the boxes,' Max said as Jen's eyes fell on the stacks of boxes around the room. She hadn't remembered there being this much. 'The electronic stuff is all on the system.'

'We managed to get some CCTV footage from the clubs

Chloe visited, but we couldn't see anyone that was of interest,' Hannah chipped in.

'That is what we wanted you to look at, if that's still okay?' Max said.

Jen sighed. She was being led into a trap, a trap that she had hidden from for the past ten years. But she needed to get home to her family. She looked at her watch. 'Let's see this footage then,' Jen replied finally, as she fought the internal battle between the buzz of being back working a case and the wish to go home.

As the footage began to play on the screens in front of her she immediately spotted Chloe, so full of life and happy. 'I'm not sure what I'm looking for,' Jen told the room.

'Well, can you see anyone you recognise?' Max asked.

'Other than Chloe? No, not really.' Then she saw something – someone – but she instantly dismissed it. 'I doubt it is, but that ginger lad on the left?' she said as she zoomed in on her screen. 'Could it possibly be Harry Greenidge …?'

'Who's Harry Greenidge?'

'My husband's best friend. They go out together all the time when Harry's girlfriend goes back home. But it can't be Harry. He seems totally out of place.'

'So, other than Chloe, there's no one else you recognise?'

'Nope, sorry guys, I've not really been much help after all that.'

'Thanks for taking a look. Hannah, will you show Jen Chloe's desk? And I'll get access to Chloe's computer system, if you're happy to whizz through her emails before you go, Jen?'

'Yeah. Max, can I use the phone though? I left my mobile back at home and I need to make a call.'

'Go into my office and use my phone,' Max directed her as Jen got up from her seat and walked through the door that connected the two rooms.

She really didn't have any choice, did she? Max had

brought her here and had known that this was going to happen. He knew she wouldn't be able to resist it, plus other than them knowing it was connected to the Crawford empire, they had nothing else to go on. Without Chloe for backup she was the only one that knew the history and everything else that went with it.

She picked up the phone and dialled her landline number. No answer. It was the only number she remembered, but he'd pick up the message as soon as he was home.

'James, it's Jen. I'm really sorry to have dumped all this on you. A friend from London contacted me and needed my help. I should be back in the next couple of days. Love to you and the children.'

After leaving the message, Jen walked back out of the office and over to where Hannah was now sat.

'Hi,' Jen said to her nervously. 'Max said you'd show me Chloe's desk?'

'The messy one.' Hannah laughed.

'You should have seen the state of the flat we both shared,' Jen reminisced, stroking her left wrist as she broke the tension between the two girls.

Arriving at Chloe's desk, Jen noticed that it was covered in files, scribbled notes and a single photo frame. She sat down at the desk and almost hit the floor

'Whoa, this is lower than I was expecting.' Laughing at herself, Jen tried to readjust the seat to a decent height. Why did people like sitting so close to the floor?

'I'm just over there if you need anything,' Hannah said, trying not to laugh as she pointed towards her desk, which looked much tidier than Chloe's.

Jen sat at Chloe's computer and looked around the office; here she was again. She used to sit just over where Hannah was now. Chloe and her were the A-team, having not realised they were training at the same time before Max had head-hunted them for his team and the career that had become their lives. As she studied Chloe's desk, she looked out for those little trinkets and mementos she remembered, but they weren't there anymore. She wondered where they had gone, and sat and got lost in memories about her lost friend. She hadn't realised that time had passed until Max had strode over to the desk.

'You okay?'

'Yeah, I think so. I'm just trying to get everything into some form of organisation,' she said, moving the files around. 'Have we managed to get access details for Chloe's computer, Max?'

'I've just been speaking to the Tech guys, and we think we've sorted access.'

'Super.'

'Log in as Cseaward with the password capital Whiskey Papa Zulu capital Alpha sixty-four Yankee Quebec.'

'I'm in,' Jen shouted, feeling like she had accomplished something.

'I'll leave you to do some digging.'

'I'm not sure if I should be worried about what I might find.'

Jen stared at the same pale blue desktop, complete with the service's logo. Not knowing where to start, she grabbed hold of the mouse, took a deep breath and started to explore. The system looked exactly the same as when she'd left, though everything seemed to be in different places. Chloe's computer wasn't giving much away; there were reports and letters she had typed, her internet history was pretty boring too. Opening the calendar application, she quickly flicked through the past year's worth of appointments but nothing sparked any interest. Once Outlook was opened, Jen was faced with dozens of unread emails; then something caught her eye.

'Hannah, do you know anything about an Adam Coulthard?'

'No, why? What have you got?' Hannah asked, getting up from her desk and wandering over.

'He emailed Chloe last week asking if she was okay. Said

that he was worried because it wasn't like her to go this long without making contact.'

'No idea. Are we able to run a trace on the email address at all?'

'Drop the Tech team an email. They'll probably be able to trace it.'

'Great, is it worth running his name as well?'

'Might be worth waiting to hear from Tech, just in case there are thousands of Adam Coulthards.'

'Good point.'

Jen typed an email and sent it through to the Tech guys, waiting eagerly for a response.

Chloe's desk was beginning to resemble organised chaos. Jen's mind kept replaying the last time she and Chloe were together, the silent goodbyes between them, each knowing what was coming. Having worked so many cases together they had become inseparable and, just like a blood sister, Chloe hadn't approved of her relationship with James – but it had been too late, because Jen was in love.

'Here I've got something for you, seeing as you're staying with us for an extra couple of days?' Max's voice brought her crashing back to reality. He always could read her better than anyone else. He clearly knew that once she was back in the office she would get that buzz again and want to see the case through to the end.

'Oh?' she questioned.

'I've got you a standard issue mobile phone,' Max said, handing her a black mobile phone box. 'I'm afraid it isn't touchscreen and you can't download apps onto it. But wherever you use it, you'll have a secure connection.'

'Okay, thanks … I think,' Jen said, studying the phone as she took it from the box and turned it over in her hands. She hadn't seen this make of phone before. Probably made specially for the government. All being well, it would be robust as well.

'All the numbers you'll need are programmed onto it and the speed dials are set up too.'

'Thanks, Max. I think I might have found something on Chloe's computer. There's an email from an Adam Coulthard asking if Chloe is okay.'

'Have you run him through the system?'

'Nope, just waiting on a response from the Tech team with an address before I attempt that one.'

'Great. Keep me updated. I'm in my office if you need anything.'

'Will do.'

Moments later an email arrived back with an address.

'Do you mind running Adam through the system, Hannah? I've got an address for him in Reading.'

'Give me a minute and I'll be on it.'

Jen continued to explore Chloe's computer when she heard Hannah walk over to her desk. 'I think we've got something here.'

'You found something on Adam Coulthard?'

'Yes. He has a series of drug-related charges on his criminal record.'

'We'd better bring him in.' Jen suddenly felt hopeful that this was it; she had found who had killed her best friend. Now she just needed to find out how and why she was connected to this mess.

James Garner

After the detectives left the kids had plenty of questions about their mum and hers and their dad's lives together before they were both born. James loved telling them stories about what he and Jen used to get up to and how they had first met in a club in London.

As evening fell, James had ordered takeaway from the local pizza place and they pic-nicked on the front room floor. The kids seemed happy and James couldn't remember the last time he had spent quality time with them. It was a shame that they were being forced to because of the circumstances. He had told them both that they could stay up late, but he knew that he would end up having to carry them to bed when they finally dropped. When everything was back to normal, he promised himself he would make sure they spent time together like this more regularly.

His phone had spent the day buzzing as text messages were sent and received. James had sent everyone he could think of a message asking if they had seen Jen or knew where she was.

After more pizza than he'd have thought two kids could ever eat, they finally fell asleep. As he carried each one up to bed, he kissed their foreheads and told them he loved them more than anything in the world.

Remembering he had promised to update his mum, he picked up the phone and dialled her number.

'Hey Mum, sorry it's late.'

'Has there been any news? Did you get a chance to speak to Melanie and Alex?'

'No news. The police were round today asking questions about Jen and our lives together.'

'Did they give you any idea as to what they're doing about her disappearance?'

'Not really, but I will chase them up tomorrow.'

'Do you need me and your dad to come down to yours, so we can give you a break? It's been ages since I've seen those two monsters.'

'No, Mum. We're good, I promise.'

'How about we take the kids away from it all, bring them back here? You know, some fresh country air?'

'But what about school?'

'Oh, I'm sure they'll understand. The kids aren't going to learn much while their mum is missing, are they?'

'Maybe.'

'That settles it. Your father and I will be down tomorrow morning. We'll wait for the morning traffic to settle and then we'll head over. It'll take us about an hour depending on which way your dad decides to drive.'

'Okay, Mum. You guys drive carefully, okay?'

'We'll be fine, don't you worry. See you tomorrow.'

'Bye.'

James was about to head up to bed himself when the doorbell rang. *Who on earth would be coming over at this time of the night?* he thought as he checked his watch.

'Jess!' James answered the door, surprised to see her. 'Is everything okay? Is Harry okay?'

'I've just heard and wanted to come round and check you and the kids are alright.' She didn't need to say any more. James knew exactly what she was talking about.

'Come in. Do you want a coffee or anything? I was about to pour myself a whisky if I can tempt you?'

'Might as well,' Jess said, following James into the living room.

'Take a seat. I'll go and pour us a drink.'

'Just bring the bottle, James, as I am guessing you'll be needing more than one.' Jess laughed.

Doing as instructed, James grabbed the bottle of whisky and two glasses and returned to the living room.

'Thanks for coming over. You didn't need to.'

'What's gone on with Jen?'

'In all honesty, I don't know …'

Chapter Thirteen

SATURDAY
DI Chris Jackson

'Morning all. I trust we all had a good night?' Chris said as he entered his team's office to murmurs of agreement. 'As some of you are aware, a local lady, Jennifer Garner, was reported missing by her husband yesterday morning. Julie and I visited and have decided we are going to do a bit of digging into this missing person.' There was the sound of movement in the office as everyone stopped what they were doing and turned their attention to their DI.

'So ...' Julie began as she stuck a picture up on the incident board. 'This is Jennifer Garner last seen on Thursday, taking both her kids to school. We know from talking to the neighbours she returned at ten past nine, left again at about nine-thirty and hasn't been seen since.'

'When did the husband first realise she was missing?' Colin asked.

'James received a phone call at twenty to five from his children's school as no one had arrived to pick them up. So that is approximately eight hours from when she left the house until the first alarm bells sounded,' Julie responded.

'What time did the husband call in her disappearance?'

'Control received the call at 4 a.m. on the Friday and PC Curtis and Sergeant Gillroy attended.'

'Did the husband give any explanation as to why he left it so long to report her missing?' Colin continued to question.

'In all honesty, I think he just waited and hoped that she would arrive home full of apologies.'

'Could we be looking at a domestic case, given the timelines?'

'In my honest opinion no, Colin. There have been no calls to this household prior to today.'

'Thank you, Julie,' Chris said as he stood up. 'I have the team in Long Eaton sending me copies of all the CCTV files for the area. All being well, we should be able to locate her.' A groan echoed around the room as they all realised they were in for a day of watching CCTV footage. 'Julie, I have a couple of things I want to look into as well regarding this case. Are you happy to sort the footage as soon as it arrives?'

'Not a problem.'

Chris wandered back to his office via the kitchen for his second cuppa of the day. There was something really bugging him about this case. It was like there were too many coincidences and the fact that Jen shared the same tattoo as Chloe Seaward concerned him the most.

Cradling his cup of coffee, he logged onto the system to see if there was anything left on there on Chloe. As he expected, he was greeted with a lot of restricted access warnings. He decided to check Jen's Facebook to see if there were any photos where her tattoo was visible, but there was nothing. Her Facebook was pretty secure, and he would need to speak to the Tech team to be able to check any deeper. For now, he was busy looking at lots of happy smiley photos of Jen and James, or the kids; everything that was needed to portray the perfect life – though it clearly wasn't because why would she have just upped and vanished if things were so great? He was about to bring up the electoral roll when there was a knock on the door.

'The CCTV is here, boss. Are you wanting to join us?' Julie asked.

'No it's fine, Julie. You go ahead. Give me a shout if you spot her,' Chris responded. He was getting one of his headaches again and staring at a video on a computer screen probably wasn't a good idea right now. He typed Jen's name into the electoral roll and soon after she came up as living with James Garner. She had also completed the census in 2011 where she had listed herself as a housewife with no past career history or qualifications. It looked to him that she had filled out the bare minimum about herself. Some people were like that and kept their accounts and data secure. If so, why did she have a Facebook and work so hard at portraying the perfect life though?

He moved on to James' Facebook page which had even less information, other than the photos he had been tagged in by others. Chris wondered if he could find anything about the apparent stag do James and Jen had met at. Chris scrolled through James' Facebook page in search of photos. He did find photos of a wedding James had been tagged in and with a bit of cross referencing came across the stag do photos. Sadly nothing of Jen, though it had been worth a try.

'Boss we've got something.' Sally suddenly appeared at his door. 'It's not much but, we've picked her up on the leisure centre cameras heading south, so we're focusing all our efforts on that general direction.'

'Great. Thank you, Sally.' Chris pulled up the area on his computer to see where she could have possibly been heading. 'What do you think the likeliness is that she's going to catch a train, Sally? As that's the direction of the town's train station.'

'It could be that, boss. Do you want me to ring the train station and get copies of their CCTV in case she was heading that way?'

'Let's try to get ahead of her. Hopefully we'll locate her quicker that way.'

'On it, boss.'

Things were moving in the right direction and hopefully they'd have found Jen by teatime and have her home shortly afterwards.

'What we got Sally?' Chris asked as he walked into his team's office.

'Let me put it on the main screen,' Sally replied, typing away. 'If you watch the screen, Jen walks past this camera at 9.45 a.m.'

Chris stood and watched the figure pass the screen as Sally had said. 'She doesn't look like she's in much of a rush.'

'Though she doesn't look like she's on a morning walk either, boss.'

'Good point. So have you followed up with the train station?'

'Greg and Julie are watching the footage as we speak and I've been on the phone to the train station. They're going to send over what they can but have asked for a more precise time-frame.'

'All being well we should be able to give them something once we pick her up again. Where is the next camera situated?'

'Surprisingly enough boss, it's a traffic camera and one for the train station itself.'

'Well, at least we'll be able to give them an exact time-frame.'

Chris wandered around his team's office, standing behind Julie as she watched footage of the train station car park. She was sat there with headphones on, glued to the screen. He turned and looked up at the main screen again where Jen was now stood in a freeze frame. There was no doubt about it being her, based on the descriptions the neighbours had given of when they saw her leave.

'I've got something,' Greg shouted as Sally and Chris moved over to where he was sat. 'There she is.' Greg pointed. 'I've watched it on a couple of minutes but she seems to go into the phone box, comes out of it and then re-enters again, before finally exiting and heading in the direction of the main road.' Sally and Chris stood silently as they watched Jen and her bizarre movements.

'Do we think she is trying to phone someone and then receives a call back again like she's awaiting instructions?' Sally asked.

'Put it up on the main screen Greg, so we can see it a bit clearer.' At this point everyone had stopped searching to watch the main event unfold on the big screen.

'Colin, will you get onto the telephone company? I want to know who she's phoning and who phones her back.'

'On it, boss. Do we have a time-frame?'

'Camera says nine fifty-five,' Greg responded.

'So where does she go from there?' Chris pondered.

'Judging by her direction, I'd say she crosses over and heads towards Tamworth Road,' Greg said, pointing to his screen with his pen.

'So definitely not the train station,' Sally suggested.

'So where could she go along Tamworth Road?' Chris asked. He let the video continue playing as Jen disappeared from the camera screen. Moments later the camera view changed as a bus could be seen passing the view.

'Boss, is it possible she got on the bus that has just passed the camera view?' Sally asked.

'Rewind it back a couple of seconds,' Chris said as they all stopped and watched the bus pass the screen. 'Sally can you get hold of the train station and ask if they have their own cameras on the car park? See if we can get a better picture of Jen and what she's doing. Trudie, will you contact the bus company —Trent Barton, I think – and make your way to their head office to check their CCTV for around the time Jen possibly got on the bus?'

'Yes, boss,' they both echoed.

'Anything from the telephone company, Colin?'

'On hold boss, while they try to work out who I need to talk to.'

'Great, keep me informed. We'll meet back here later.'

Everyone was happy and doing their jobs while Chris trudged back to his office, noticing his coffee was now cold. He decided he needed to write things out so he could understand them more clearly. Moments later there was a knock on his door and Julie arrived with a fresh coffee in hand.

'Things are looking good, boss.'

'She's definitely on the move somewhere, but where?'

'I didn't think she looked that panicked or scared either, from what I can see.'

'I agree. Things don't really add up. If I'm honest with you, Jen seems to be one great big mystery.' Just then Chris' email pinged. 'Hang on, I might have something here,' Chris said, returning his attention to his email. 'Damn it, thought I had something.'

'Bad news, boss?'

'No, before the meeting I was searching the electoral roll for Jen. When I searched Jennifer Sheridan, there wasn't one living in London at the time James said he met her.'

'Right okay,' Julie said, sitting down and leaning in to the see the email.

'So, I typed out a quick email to the electoral roll team in London. They've just come back saying that the search was right. There was no record for anyone called Jennifer Sheridan.' Chris wrapped his hands round his newly acquired coffee. 'There is no trace of a Jen Sheridan until she pops up in Long Eaton once she had moved here with James.'

'So, where did she come from?'

'According to this, she didn't even exist.'

'It doesn't make sense, boss.'

'All this is making me more and more convinced she is linked to this Chloe Seaward.' As Chris started to type away, his phone rang. It was Trudie.

'Boss, Jen gets on the eleven o'clock bus to Nottingham.'

'Great. Thanks Trudie. Can you get copies of the bus's CCTV and run them back?'

'Not a problem, boss. I can tell you now she paid cash and remained on the bus until Nottingham, getting off at Friar Lane at eleven-forty.'

'Thank you, Trudie.'

'The picture is pretty clear of her, so it is definitely her without a question.'

'See you when you get back in,' Chris ended the call. 'Guessing you heard most of that?' Chris asked, turning his attention back to Julie.

'So, we've traced her to Nottingham.'

'Could you phone the council and arrange for us to go over tomorrow and view their CCTV footage and hopefully we can track her to her final destination?'

'Okay, boss.'

Things were moving again. They had managed to track her that far but her apparent non-existence prior to moving in with James was puzzling. Chris wondered if it was worth contacting the team that had taken Chloe and asking them if Jennifer Sheridan had been one of theirs? Maybe it would be better to track Jen to her final location before he gave anything away to the other side. He didn't want this case being taken off him as well. A local girl missing from the same town where a body had recently been dumped would go down a storm if the press ever got hold of the information. Never mind his suspicions that all this was linked to Daisy somehow.

Colin appeared at Chris' door. 'Sorry, boss. Just got off the phone with the phone company. They're being difficult due to GD bloody PR or something. They said they'd give me a call back in five.'

'Okay, thank you. Keep us informed.' Colin ducked back out of Chris' office. 'I don't like this,' Chris said, turning to Julie 'There is too much in this case that doesn't add up.'

'Jen seems to go out of her way to get on a bus, when she is right next to a train station that would get her into Nottingham quicker,' Julie replied.

'And why is Colin having so much trouble getting hold of the number that she rang?' Chris added.

'You checked into her social media?'

'Yeah, I was flicking through hers and James' earlier.'

'Find anything?'

'Not really, but she doesn't appear in any of the stag do photos where they were meant to have met.'

'Did you find those on James' page?'

'No, I had to do a bit of searching around, but I found the account of the groom and managed to find the photos that way.'

'Guessing she was camera shy around then?'

'Or not there at all?'

'You reckon James is making all of this up?'

'I don't know. There are too many loose threads for my liking.'

'Another thing – I phoned around the local florists, and no one remembers making up the combination of flowers Jen received on Monday.

'So there's another thing we can't explain …'

James Garner

James had spent most of the previous evening downing his sorrows with Jess and trawling missing persons' websites, reading up on police procedure and the first forty-eight hours of a missing person case. Sighing, he looked at his watch, counting the hours.

The children had slept through the night, which had surprised him. He'd half expected them to get in bed with him during the night. His mind was working overtime, trying to work out where Jen was. He was struggling to remember if he had told her he loved her when he last saw her. He thought back over the past couple of weeks, trying to recall if there had been any noticeable changes in her behaviour. Every time he kept coming back to the flowers and card and her reaction.

He could hear the bed above his head beginning to creak, then footsteps heading into his bedroom.

'Dad?' a voice came from above.

'I'm down here, little man.'

'Has Mummy come home yet?'

'Afraid not, little man' James said as Alex bounced down the stairs.

'Oh, I thought she might have come back in the night.'

James went over to Alex and picked him up, taking him into the kitchen.

'What do you fancy for breakfast?'

'Anything?'

'Anything, but quickly decide before your sister comes down.'

'Can we have eggy bread? We haven't had that in ages.'

James checked in the fridge and asked Alex to help by finding the frying pan and the bread. James tried to remember the last time he'd cooked the kids' breakfast. Usually there was a rush to get them out the door, so cereal was all he had time to offer.

The smell and sound of the frying pan must have woken Melanie up as she was soon downstairs too, excited about the promise of eggy bread for the first time in forever. James found himself unable to keep up with the kids' demands for more and more.

When breakfast was done and the kitchen resembled a decent state, the doorbell rang.

'I bet that's Grandma and Grandad,' James said as he walked to the front door, followed by two excitable children.

James unlocked the door, trying to contain Melanie and Alex's excitement that Grandma and Grandad had arrived. After the hugs and kisses were over, James led his parents into the conservatory as the children continued to bounce off the walls. But, all of a sudden, Melanie stopped and broke down in tears.

'What's the matter, Melanie?' James asked, scooping her up from where she was sat.

'I … I miss Mummy, Daddy. I wish she was here,' Melanie sobbed.

'Oh sweetheart. We all do. Come and help me make Grandma and Grandad a drink and we can talk about it.' Melanie clung to her dad as he carried her into the kitchen.

'I bet Mummy misses you too,' James told Melanie as he placed her down on a stool.

'I can't be happy Daddy because you and Mummy aren't happy. Every time I laugh I keep thinking of Mum.' She broke down as snot and tears flooded out. James could feel his heart breaking as he looked at his daughter and pulled her closer to him. How could Jen be so selfish? Look what it was doing to the children!

'Daddy! Daddy! Grandma says that she's brought us some special cakes. Can we have them now?' Alex bounced into the kitchen, suddenly stopping as he saw his sister in tears. 'Melanie?'

'It's okay, Alex. Melanie is a bit upset. Are Grandma and Grandad okay?'

'Yeah.' Alex tried to manoeuvre himself next to Melanie, joining the snot-filled embrace.

'I hear someone has cake?' James spoke as he carried mugs of steaming tea into the conservatory. The kids followed seconds later carrying plates.

'She okay?' his mum asked as she took the mug.

'Think so,' he whispered. All of a sudden, the excitement of Grandma and Grandad returned as the cakes were given out and consumed. James kept his eye on Melanie, occasionally winking at her which she attempted to replicate much to James' amusement. James hoped the kids didn't notice the tense atmosphere that filled the room as he attempted to have silent conversations with his parents. No one wanted to mention Jen but at the same time, his parents were keen to find out what had happened.

'Grandad, do you want to come and see the Lego models that I've made in my room?' Alex suddenly piped up.

'Yes please, Alex! Melanie why don't you show me your bedroom as I don't think I've seen it since you decorated it?' The kids raced out of the door, dragging their grandad along with them. Diversion tactic implemented.

'Tell me, James. Are you really okay?' His mum asked, making sure the kids were safely upstairs.

'I have to be, Mum. For the kids' sake.'

'You've still got no idea where she is?'

'I keep trying to think of places we haven't checked. I've phoned the school mums over and over and they haven't seen her or heard from her. I just don't know where else to start looking.'

'Did you two get into a fight or something?'

'No, other than a few cross words the other day over something trivial, things have been brilliant recently, better than they have been in ages. Which is why I can't understand why she's just disappeared.'

'She didn't leave a letter or anything? No clue she was planning something?'

'No, Mum.'

'I can't understand why she would get up and disappear. What do the police think has happened?'

'I spoke to the DI earlier. He said that they were looking at CCTV footage tracking her movements.'

'So, a waiting game then?'

'I guess so. I don't really know what else I can do.'

'What about all these TV appeals you see these days?'

'The police aren't too keen on the idea. You heard about the body they found here recently?'

'Do they think it's connected?'

'I don't know. No one is telling me anything.'

'Maybe it's for the best that we take the kids back with us for a couple of days. Get them away from all this.'

'I don't see how taking them to a different county will do any good, Mum. Their mother will still be missing.' James felt guilty, suddenly regretting his response. 'Sorry, it's just my head is a mess, and I don't know what's best anymore.'

'Have you spoken to work?'

'Not had a chance. All they know is that I had to leave early on Thursday. I guess that will be another call I need to make on Monday.' James sighed. 'Mum, why don't you and dad stay here? There's plenty of room, the kids' school routine won't be disrupted, and you're both here if anything happens.'

'I'll speak to your father, James. You know how much we've both got on at the moment with the community group.' His mum sighed. 'Oh, stuff the bloody community group. You need my help. I'm sure they can manage without us for a couple of days.'

James felt guilty for asking his parents to stay. Truth be told, he didn't want to be alone in an empty house without the kids or Jen. Did he need to start planning for life without her? Right on cue the kids suddenly came bouncing back into the room.

'Grandad says he'll take us both to the park on our bikes.'

'You better get your stuff ready then,' James said as he stood up and his mum pulled him into an embrace.

'We'll take them if you want to stay here, son,' his dad said, appearing in the doorway already looking worn out.

'No, I could do with some fresh air.'

Bikes safely out of the garage, James was about to return to the house when he noticed a black car with tinted windows parked on the opposite side of the street. He noticed it because this was usually a quiet neighbourhood where everyone knew everyone else. He was about to walk over to the car, when it started its engine and pulled away before he could make it over the road. He'd send a message to everyone on the street and check that no one had had anything stolen or vandalised. He pulled out his phone but was soon distracted by the excited noise coming from the children and his parents ready for their bike ride to the park.

Chapter Fourteen

Jen Garner

'Adam Coulthard, this is the police ...'

It was 5 a.m. on a Saturday and Jen found herself stood on Adam Coulthard's doorstep. Surrounded by armed police officers, Hannah and one of the area's top DIs, Tony Fox, they were giving Adam an early morning wake-up call. With Adam's association with drugs and his previous arrests, they weren't taking any chances when it came to bringing him in.

Just as the commander had finished saying Adam's name, a blurry-eyed male answered the door. 'What the fuck?' were the first words that came out of his mouth before he bolted through the house.

'Ah, I love it when they run,' DI Fox said as he gave chase, closely followed by a whole raft of armed officers. Though Jen wasn't going anywhere, as she felt herself frozen to the spot as armed officers filed into the house. Moments ago, in front of her, had been stood the guy from the message Chloe had left on Facebook. She had been kidding herself that it would be someone different. The guy who had just bolted through his home while others were giving chase was the person Chloe had fallen in love with. Had he been Chloe's knight in shining armour like James had been to her, or had she just been faced with Chloe's killer?

'We've got him, bringing him back through,' came the message through a radio near where Jen was standing.

Jen glanced at her tattoo and entered the house as Adam was hauled back into his living room.

'Adam Coulthard, I am arresting you on the suspicion of murder.'

'Hang on, what?' Adam interrupted the officer who was reading him his rights.

'It's okay, Officer. We'll handle it,' Hannah said, walking into the room.

'And who the fuck are you?'

'I am Detective Littlefair, and this is my colleague Jen Garner.' It was at that point Jen noticed a facial change in Adam; a hint of recognition? 'We've come here to speak to you about a colleague of ours, who you emailed recently. We have questions in regard to your relationship with Ms Chloe Seaward.' Adam fidgeted in his seat.

'We are in a relationship, we were about to move away and get married.'

Jen took a moment to steady herself as she began to survey the room, which was full of pictures of Chloe and Adam together. This wasn't the living room of a drug dealer. She went and picked up one of the photos. She studied it, trying to place it and work out whether that was her with her back turned towards the camera.

'When was this taken?' Jen asked, out of the blue.

'I'm not sure. It was one of Chloe's that she liked. Is someone going to tell me what's going on and why I'm sat in my own living room cuffed while you two circle me like vultures?' Adam asked.

'Adam, we have reason to believe that you may have been involved in the murder of Chloe Seaward.'

'You *what*? I only saw her last week, she said everything was fine, she had one more thing to do and her case would be over and we could leave here, start again …' Adam paused as he tried to stand. 'I loved her. We were going to run away and get married,' he shouted as he continued to struggle.

'Adam, if you promise to remain seated, we'll get someone to remove those cuffs, but if there's any trouble from you, they'll be back on.' DI Fox spoke up from the doorway. 'Plus, I wouldn't put it past one of these girls to floor you if you try anything.' He laughed as he started to remove the cuffs.

As Adam sat there rubbing his wrists, Jen could see the dozens of tattoos that were inked onto his arms. She wasn't completely sure, but she thought she recognised at least one gang tattoo.

'Adam, Chloe's body was found in Long Eaton a couple of days ago. Someone had brutally murdered her.' Jen noticed tears form in Adam's eyes.

'No … she said she was going to leave the service, and we were going to go somewhere, where no one knew us and our pasts and we could start afresh.'

'So you knew she was a detective?'

'Yeah, it's how we met. She was undercover, and I tried to sell her drugs, though as I am sure you're aware it didn't work out too well for me.' Jen couldn't believe what she was hearing; Chloe had been dating someone who had sold her drugs! Wasn't there a rule about that or something?

'So, let's talk about these drugs you were selling. Who were you selling them for?' Hannah continued to question.

'This is the stupid thing. I don't know, I never knew who I was working for.'

'How can you sell drugs and not know who the boss is?'

'None of us did.'

'When you say none, how many sellers were there?'

'Look, everyone I knew that was selling had one contact number. It was never the same person, each time someone different would show up. It was almost impossible to know who was at the top. But I'm clean now and have been for the past five years, thanks to Chloe.'

'So, you're expecting us to believe that you didn't know where the drugs were coming from?'

'Some of us wondered if it was George Crawford, because all the drugs had that branding on, but whenever you asked questions you were told not to.'

Jen zoned out momentarily. There was that name again: George Crawford. But Max had checked and he was still safely locked up in prison somewhere.

'So, tell us about Lisa Carter,' Jen found herself saying.

'What Chloe's so-called best friend? Who fell in love and left her and the service?' Adam responded as Jen took a step closer to Adam, ready to slap him if he stood up.

'Now say that to my face,' she boomed at him as DI Fox quickly manoeuvred himself to be between Adam and Jen.

'Ha, so you've turned up again, have you? I guessed you would once I sent you that stupid necklace that Chloe loved so much.' Jen took a step back as Adam shouted at her over the DI's shoulder. 'Chloe always told me if she got into trouble to find you. She even told me if she was missing to send that stupid necklace to you and you'd have an answer. Pity it involved me being woken up at silly o'clock.'

Jen didn't know how to respond to what was going on in front of her. Chloe had fallen for one of the people they had spent so much time chasing down and trying to put away. She watched as the DI forced Adam to sit back down. None of this was making sense. How could Chloe have been so stupid? Is this how she had gotten herself killed?

'Look,' Jen heard Hannah say. 'Tony, if you would ask your officers to stand down, I think Jen and I have a handle on this, thank you.'

'Do you want me to leave someone here just in case?' he asked.

'No, like you said. I'm pretty sure one of us could floor him if there was an issue.' Hannah reassured, laughing to herself. 'Thank you for letting us use your resources.'

'It was my pleasure,' DI Fox said as he left the room and gathered his colleagues.

'Right, Adam. You've got tea and coffee in this place, right?' Hannah asked.

'Yeah.'

'Go and get yourself dressed, I'll put the kettle on and we'll start again.'

'You sure you can trust him?' Jen asked Hannah as Adam left the room.

'You two have got someone in common and you are both going to want answers. So, let's see where it leads us. He clearly didn't kill Chloe. It's obvious from his reaction to the news.'

James Garner

James had been sat in the local pub, looking at his pint of beer. His mum had been insistent that he went out with one of his friends so he could escape from the kids for a while and relax. He had to admit that it was nice not to be stuck between the same four walls thinking and worrying about Jen's whereabouts.

'Hey mate.' James stood up and greeted Harry.

'You don't look so great?' Harry said. His friend was, as always, full of life, bouncy and enthusiastic. Harry was a totally different person since he'd started dating Jess. He was always on top of the world, no matter what was going on around him.

'I've had a rough couple of days. I think Jen might have left me.'

'What! Don't be silly.' Harry responded as his eyes widened. 'I thought you said in the message she'd disappeared?'

'She has, and the only logical explanation I can think of is that she has left me'

'What about the kids?'

'They're at home with Mum and Dad.'

'You can't think like that. You two are solid. I'm sure she has a reasonable explanation for all this.'

'Yeah, I thought that too,' James said as he took a sip of his pint.

'What about the kids, are they okay? You know if you ever need someone to look after them, Jess and I are more than happy to come and watch them.'

'A night with my two, I think that might seal your fate. How are things going with you two anyway?'

'Yeah everything is great. She's amazing, everything about her is amazing. Look I'll go and get us a round,' Harry said as he stood up and headed to the bar, leaving James to sit and think. He looked around the busy bar; everywhere he looked all he could see were loved-up couples.

'You should go and check out the barmaid James, she's pretty hot,' Harry said, returning with two pints and a couple of shots.

'I think after this I'm going to be staying single, mate,' James said as he picked up the shot and knocked it back. The sharp liquid burned the back of his throat as it slipped down. James immediately reached for his pint to cool his throat.

'What have the police said about it all?'

'They say they're investigating. I don't know. The longer I have to wait for news the more I'm convinced that she has either left me or she is lying in a ditch somewhere.'

'There's no way she'd leave you guys, especially the kids.'

James downed the rest of his pint. He didn't know anymore. The more he replayed that morning in his head, trying to pick holes in Jen's behaviour and the fact she was crying on Melanie's floor, the less it made sense.

'What's Jess doing tonight anyway? You two are usually joined at the hip.'

'She's out with some friends or something, and I am only getting one word answers from her when I message her, so she is clearly off having fun somewhere.'

'Another one?' James asked as he stood up and reached for his wallet.

James returned from the bar with drinks in hand, noticing that Harry was chatting away to someone he didn't recognise so he placed the drinks down and continued to look out at the sea of faces, almost hoping to see Jen somewhere in the crowd.

'Bottoms up, mate,' Harry shouted as the music was suddenly turned up and lights dimmed. James watched his friend knock back another shot shortly followed by a swig of his pint.

'Harry,' James shouted over the music.

'What's up mate? You're not crying off are you?'

'No, I wanted to ask you about Jess.'

'You want me to ask her if she's up for a threesome when she's back?' Harry shouted back, laughing.

'No, no … what?'

'Then spit it out. mate.'

'When did Jess get back from London? It's just I saw her Wednesday and then she came over to mine last night to check if I was okay…'

'She couldn't have. She only got back this morning.'

'No really, Harry. She turned up on my doorstep at about eleven, said she'd heard about Jen and wanted to know if I was okay?'

Harry took a step back, looking at James like he was crazy. 'You're telling me my missus came round to yours last night for a cup of cocoa before bed? Or did you offer her something more?'

'What, no? I'm happily married to Jen.'

'Ha, and that's working out well for you, isn't it?' James looked at Harry. *What was wrong with him?*

'Look I'm gonna get us another drink, double yeah?' Harry didn't wait for an answer and left James stood at their table. He was beginning to feel the alcohol haze falling in front of him and time seemed to speed up as Harry returned with another pint and another shot that burned his throat. James wasn't enjoying himself but he needed to speak to Harry about Jess. Maybe Jen hadn't overreacted when they saw Jess on Wednesday. Had she really been all over him and he hadn't noticed?

'Harry,' James tried to shout at him over the music. 'Harry!'

'Look, I know you're jealous about Jess and I and how great things are between us now your wife's gone running off 'cos she's bored of you.'

'*What?*' James roared.

'Come on, James. What girl appears from nowhere, no family, no friends, and just happens to be the girl of your dreams?'

'You don't get to speak like that about my wife when you don't even know where your missus is or who she's seeing.'

'At least she isn't a slut. I warned you in the beginning she was only after your money and now look—' Before Harry could finish James took a swing at him, knocking him in to several tables.

'Don't talk about my wife like that,' he roared, going for Harry again, who took a moment to react, trying to defend himself. 'No one calls my wife a slut.' James continued to roar as they began to take chunks out of each other. The bouncers appeared and attempted to pull them apart, but James was having none of it as he turned on the bouncer.

Harry tried to calm the situation down as a crowd started to gather around the commotion whilst the bouncers had James pinned to the ground. They pulled James to his feet and practically carried him out of the pub and threw him onto the street. But James still wanted more, trying to take on the world as he attempted to get back into the pub. The blue lights began to flash and there was nothing more anyone could do as James began fighting with the police officers.

Chapter Fifteen

Chris was fast asleep when he became aware of buzzing. Forcing his eyes to stay open, he began to search round in the dark for whatever was making the sound, finally resting on his mobile phone.

'DI Jackson.'

'I'm sorry for waking you, sir.' Chris tried to stretch as he held the phone to his ear. 'We have a drunk and disorderly in the holding cells who's demanding to speak to you.'

'Okay.' Chris tried to remain calm as an irritation began to creep over him. He had been woken up for a D&D? Most drunks in the area knew his name. Why was this person any different to the others? The nervous officer continued.

'We checked his driving licence and bank cards, and they both confirm that we have a James Garner in the holding cells.' As soon as Chris heard the name, he was awake. Rubbing his eyes, he manoeuvred himself so he was sat on the edge of his bed, squinting at the time on his alarm clock.

'Can you inform Mr Garner I will speak to him first thing, but he needs to sober up first?'

'Will do. I really am sorry for waking you, sir. We checked his ID on the system and the Desk Sergeant instructed me to contact you.'

'Not to worry. Can you confirm where he is being held?'

'The Nottingham holding cells. He was arrested in Stapleford.'

'Thank you, I'll be there as soon as I can.' Chris was now awake and moved into the kitchen to make himself a coffee. What the actual fuck was James playing at getting himself arrested? He should be at home looking after his children.

The officer hadn't mentioned anything about the children. Had they been caught up in James' arrest? The last thing the family needed was social services knocking on their door. As he looked out of the window towards the football stadium, his concern got the better of him. He dialled the station's number in the hope there would be someone available to check on the family.

Wandering back into his room, he noticed the commotion had also woken up Fluff. 'I'm sorry,' Chris said as he stroked his cat, receiving a loud purr in response. 'Better sort you some food.' It was 3 a.m. and Chris knew there was no point even attempting to get back to sleep. His mind was in overdrive and he needed to check that those kids were safe.

Chris found himself powering up his laptop in order to try to distract himself from worrying about the Garners. He went back to studying Daisy and Chloe's files, looking for similarities. Other than the beatings they had both received which were similar, and the manner they were both found, Chris was unable to find anything else to connect the two girls. He'd look into Chloe's policing background once he was back on the system at work. No matter how many times he stared at the photos and reports, nothing was standing out.

Chris received the call he had been waiting for an hour later. The kids were safe. James' parents were with them and they had been none the wiser. The officer who had woken Mrs Garner said she was under the impression that her son was asleep. He had told her that someone would be in touch as soon as they had more information about her son's arrest. Chris wondered if it was too early to phone the house himself but decided it was best not to wake them again.

A couple of hours later Chris headed down towards his car as his thoughts returned to James. What on earth was he playing at? Though, at the same time, he felt sorry for the guy. His wife had disappeared, leaving him with two young children. He deserved some form of outlet but getting himself arrested probably wasn't the best way. Chris wished he could speak to the arresting officers in hopes of a heads up about what had happened. Though it was early, so they were most likely sat writing up reports and looking forward to clocking off.

Chris parked his car easier than expected at the Nottingham holding cells. Greeting several of his former colleagues, he swiped into the station. 'Morning,' Chris greeted the Desk Sergeant. 'I'm here to see James Garner. I believe he was brought in for D&D last night.'

'Ah, Inspector Jackson. Mr Garner has been asking for you.'

'Are you able to give me any further information regarding the events that led to his arrest?'

'James Garner …' The Desk Sergeant began as he typed away on his computer. 'Arrested at Wetherspoons in Stapleford at around 2 a.m. Having got into a fight with a fellow drinker, when asked to leave he then moved on to the doormen and later my officers.'

'Did your officers sustain any injuries?'

'Luckily for Mr Garner, he was easily detained at that point and thrown in the back of one of the vans.'

'Any witnesses to the altercation?'

'I'd say a whole pub full. The arresting officers got everyone's contact details.'

'Do we also have James' sparring partner?'

'No, a Mr Harry Greenidge said he didn't want to press charges. It was just a misunderstanding.'

'One great big misunderstanding! Did James himself sustain any injuries?'

'On his arrival, he was placed straight into a cell due to his violent nature. He is yet to see a doctor as we've been waiting for him to sober up. The officer who brought him in hadn't noted any substantial injuries that needed immediate attention.'

'Am I okay to see him?'

'PC Pinkington,' the Desk Sergeant shouted across the crowded room. 'Can you check on last night's D&D and see if he's suitable for an interview please?'

'Sir, interview room one?'

Chris watched the officer disappear down a maze of corridors. Absorbing the early morning chaos, Chris reminisced about his days as a PC. A busy night shift also led to a busy booking-in session, followed by the paperwork.

'Do you need any assistance with the interview?' PC Pinkington enquired as he returned to escort Chris.

'No, I'm good thanks. It's an informal chat for now.' Chris placed his hand on the door handle and opened it slowly, unsure what lay behind it.

As Chris entered the interview room, he saw James slumped in the chair, his face swollen with dried blood streaks down it. Chris wondered whether he should have brought a large coffee or something but it was too late now. He hoped he wasn't in for the long game as he walked around the other side of the table and took a seat. He waited for James to break the silence.

'Do my parents know where I am?' James eventually asked in a voice barely audible to the human ear.

'Yes, we had an officer call and speak to your mum earlier this morning.'

'The kids?' James asked as he rubbed his hands over his face.

'Yes, they're fine. I doubt they've even noticed you were missing.

'My wife?'

Chris moved closer towards James as he struggled to hear him. 'We've begun to track her movements. I was planning on visiting you later today with an update on the progress we've made.'

'Do you know when I can go home to my family? Are Wetherspoons pressing charges?' James asked, seeming to remember where he was.

'I expect you'll be let off with a caution and a fine.'

James nodded, taking it all in, as Chris stood up and cleared his throat. There wasn't really much point staying any longer. James clearly knew he had done wrong and was full of remorse.

'Listen, James. I don't know what last night was about, but you need to take a long look at yourself. You need to be there for your kids. Their mum has gone missing and they are probably scared. The last thing they need is for their dad to disappear too.' Chris headed towards the door. 'Go home, get yourself cleaned up and be there for your family.'

Returning to his car, Chris sank down in his seat and hoped he wouldn't be spotted. He wasn't in the mood for friendly chit-chat. The case was beginning to get to him. It didn't seem to be progressing. How could a woman disappear into thin air? Why was he so sure that Jen was connected to the body? Had he read James all wrong? He was a detective so he should be following the evidence. Right now, the evidence was showing that James was someone who lost his temper and resorted to violence. He wondered if Jen had escaped a violent marriage. Wouldn't she have taken the kids too, though?

He needed to contact the Garner household and speak to Mrs Garner, at least to reassure her that her son was okay and would be home later that morning. He had asked the Desk Sergeant to make sure someone took James home; though this was against protocol, it was the least he could do. Hopefully it would give James time to think about what he had done and how he was going to explain it to his family.

Jen Garner

Jen was glad that she had listened to Hannah when she suggested that they go for a couple of drinks when they had finally left Reading. Jen had been starting to see why

Chloe had fallen for Adam. Behind his tattoos and hard man persona, he was a nice guy who had made the wrong choices in life. He'd finally made the right one when he met Chloe. She hoped that now that Chloe was gone he would be able to move on and stay away from drugs and the violence that came with them.

After she had made a comment about her hair and how unpractical it was for detective work, Hannah had also taken Jen to her hairdresser who was a strange sort of guy; very friendly, open at nine at night. He'd cut Jen's hair with no questions asked. As Jen looked in the car mirror, she saw her old self staring back at her … it was scary. With a few snips here and there and make-up to match, she was back. But what about those she had left behind so easily?

Right now, she had bigger things to worry about as she sat outside HMP Reedmoor about to face her nemesis: the man and his network that Chloe and herself had brought down all those years ago. She wasn't even sure how she had found herself sat there in the quest to find Chloe's killer.

'You ready?' Hannah asked. They hadn't spoken much on the journey to the prison; for one, Jen was nursing a killer hangover and was sure Hannah must have been as well. Though she was clearly better at hiding it than she was.

'I'm good when you are, Chloe.' It was out of Jen's mouth before she could stop it and it floored her. In that moment she could have sworn it was Chloe with her, like back in the good old days. Hannah had either not heard Jen or chose to ignore her as she climbed out of the car and headed towards the prison, notebook in hand. Jen had just brought emotional baggage along with her. With the slip of the tongue and the knowledge she was about to face her past head on, it was all she really had room to carry.

'Detectives, take a seat.' Jen and Hannah sat directly across from Governor Paul Brady. Reedmoor was like any other prison with rigorous searches and items taken from you to be returned once you left.

'Thank you for seeing us on such short notice,' Jen said, reaching out to shake the Governor's hand.

'Not a problem. What can I help you both with?'

'We're looking for some information on George Crawford.'

'Ah yes, inmate two-seven-five-one. He's one of our more popular residents.'

'Does he have many visitors?'

'He has contact from one of those prison pen-pal schemes and the odd visitor. He used to have a wife or girlfriend who visited once a month but stopped coming about three years ago. I'll run you off a list while you're speaking to George. I'm afraid it won't be a long list. Like I said, he hasn't had many visitors over the years, but still remains popular with the other inmates.'

'That would be good, thanks. Has there been any reason to suspect he has any other contact with the outside world?' Hannah asked.

'All personal mail in and out of the prison is checked and we also have mobile phone jammers installed. If someone really wants to get something in or out of the prison …' Governor Brady tailed off.

'What is his relationship like with other inmates?' Hannah asked.

'There were some issues at the beginning of his sentence, though things seem to have settled down.'

'Any issues with radicalisation?'

'George is a funny one. Despite his notoriety, he'll keep himself to himself, unless something is kicking off, or he feels that someone is being bullied or radicalised.'

'I guess he never was one to get his hands dirty,' Jen commented as the Governor stopped to take a breath.

'I wouldn't say he was a model prisoner, but he has respect

for my staff, which is the most basic thing we ask from our inmates.'

'Is George aware of our visit today?' Jen asked.

'He has been informed he has members of law enforcement visiting. I decided it was best to not reveal your identities for your safety during the visit.'

'Thank you, Governor Brady. We much appreciate that.'

'Please call me Paul. I've set up a private room for your use. My staff member will be stationed in the room in case of any incidents.'

'Thank you, Paul.'

Paul picked up his office phone, and within minutes an officer was knocking on the door to escort Jen and Hannah to their interview. Jen wasn't sure what to expect but whatever happened, she was going to deal with it as a detective and not a mother and wife.

'Officers, George Crawford is currently in the waiting area. Once you are both settled, I'll bring him down. If I can ask you to keep your hands on the table at all times. If at any time you wish to end the interview, please signal to the officer who will be in the room with you and remain seated until the prisoner has left the room.'

Jen pulled out both of the chairs, tugged her sleeves down to hide her faded tattoo and took a seat. She had to wriggle into a more comfortable position as the chairs were still as uncomfortable as the last time she had been there.

'You okay?' Hannah asked.

'All good,' Jen replied, turning towards her colleague and hoping she couldn't tell that inside she was freaking out like hell.

'Do you want me to lead?'

'No, I can.'

'I'll sit and watch Mr Crawford and see if he gives off any facial and body language signals.'

They hadn't been sat waiting long when the door opened.

Jen heard the heavy footsteps and jangling of keys and moments later George Crawford was sat facing Jen for the first time in what felt like a lifetime.

'Mr Crawford …' Jen began, studying the person sat in front of her, waiting for some form of recognition on his face, but instead he continued to look straight at them.

'Officers, how can I help you? It's been a long time since you guys have asked to see me.'

'We're here to speak to you about an officer by the name of Chloe Seaward.'

'Nope, I'm afraid the name doesn't ring a bell.'

'Are you sure Mr Crawford? She was instrumental in putting you in here.'

George looked long and hard at Jen and then to his fingernails. 'Nope, no recognition. I'm sorry, Officers. I think you may have had a wasted journey.'

'Mr Crawford, can I call you George and get past these formalities?'

'Of course, and how shall I address you?'

'Michelle, and this is my colleague, Emma.' They were the first names that came into Jen's head and she needed to think quickly.

'Ah, now that's better. Do you think we could possibly get a cup of tea as well? I usually see my visitors in another room, and I get brought a cuppa.'

'Do you get many visitors, George?'

'I used to, but well, the old gang as I'm sure you're aware, were put in prisons across the country. I guess they've all moved on from our heyday.'

'I wouldn't call drugs and people trafficking a heyday.'

'Each to their own.'

'So, George, Chloe Seaward. Did she come and visit you?'

'Not that I'm aware of, Michelle. But I'm getting old and my memory … Maybe you should ask her yourself?'

'I'm afraid that isn't going to be a very easy job, as we recently found her body.'

Jen watched, waiting for a reaction but all she got was 'Oh dear.'

'I'm afraid she met her end in, let's say, not the most pleasant of ways. I won't bore you with the details.'

'So, you've come to visit me to find out what I know. I hate to tell you I don't know anything. I'm unable to commit murder in another city let alone from my prison cell and be back in time for roll call.'

'You must realise investigating Chloe's murder is one of our top priorities. Can you think of anyone from your past who wished to cause Ms Seaward harm?'

'Afraid not, Officers. Like I said, we've been scattered across the country. I can't say for certain we're all still alive. Prison can be a tough place.'

'Do you have many friends in here, George?'

'I wouldn't call them friends. We're all doing our time for our crimes.'

'How are you getting on with the more, let's say, radicalised inmates?'

'Now, they're a nasty kettle of fish. I keep myself to myself. No point trying to force their views on me. I'm a man of God.'

'Have you always been a man of God?'

'Yes, I was brought up as a proper Christian, church on a Sunday then home for a roast.'

'You surprise me, George, given the path you went on to take.'

'Those weren't my finest moments. I've made my peace with God. It's all between me and the Big Guy.' George's eyes looked up to the ceiling as he made the sign of a cross.

'A regular visitor to the prison pastor on a Sunday then?'

'Oh no. I believe that I don't need to be involved in a formal worship to praise the Lord, officers.'

'How did you get involved with the prison pen-pal programme? I hear you're in regular contact with your pal?'

'Oh yes, I look forward to the letters arriving each week. We aren't allowed to share our real names. Apparently, it's protecting our identities, but we talk about our lives and gardening. You should give it a go.'

'I'm good, thanks. I deal with enough of you guys on a daily basis not to want to go home and write to you,' Jen replied.

George looked around the room, clearly trying to buy time while he thought about his next move.

'Pretty dull colours in here, Officers, wouldn't you say? They could do with livening it up, like the main visitor area.'

'Well George, seeing as you have no knowledge of our victim, I guess we've wasted your time.'

'Not a problem. It was nice to get away from the same four walls for ten minutes.'

'Can you escort Mr Crawford back to his cell, Officer?' Hannah spoke up.

George waited for the officer to refasten his hands before he stood up and began the walk across the small space

'I'm glad to see that marriage and childbirth have been kind to you, Lisa. I hope you're keeping a close eye on them,' George said as he left the room. Jen immediately felt sick as her stomach dropped with worry, but she knew she had to hold it together and get out of the prison and away from everyone before she freaked out.

'I think we might have just been played. He knew exactly who I was,' Jen said as soon as he was out of the room.

'He knows something. There's certainly something he isn't letting on. Shall I ask the Governor to do a cell search? Shake him up a bit,' Hannah asked.

'It's not worth the manpower, Hannah. It won't gain us anything. I'd like to have copies of his mail. See if that yields any information.'

'Officers, can I escort you back towards the Governor's office?'

As Jen and Hannah broke free of the stagnant air of HMP Reedmoor, the rain began to pour. Jen felt like her heart was about to explode out of her chest and she felt sick. They had most certainly been played. Someone must have tipped George off and that was what worried her the most. She pulled out her phone and wandered across the car park to get some distance between Hannah and herself.

'Max, it's Jen, we need to get my family into a safe house now,' she almost shouted as soon as Max picked up and took a breath to speak.

'What, slow down Jen. What's happened?'

'He knows who I really am Max, and about my family. I need them pulled out and put into a safe house.'

'Jen, calm down. They're fine. I've got my best people watching them.'

'But what if they're not good enough Max? And he gets to them?'

'George is safely tucked up in prison. How's he going to get to them?'

'I don't know, I really don't. I can't afford anything to happen to them because of me.'

'Why don't you take Hannah to Croydon and I'll give you a shout when your old flat is clear?'

'Should we not be looking through all this stuff from George?'

'There's plenty of time for that. Let's get your flat cleared in case there's stuff there that needs to be brought in.'

'Okay.'

'Promise me you won't do anything rash.'

'Like what?' Jen asked as the rain started to soak her through to the skin.

'Jen, I know you probably better than anyone else. Just

get to Croydon in one piece. No diverting from the plan, okay?'

'Yes, sir.' Jen ended the call. It hadn't even crossed her mind to do anything else. It would take them at least two hours to get back to Long Eaton. Which was more or less the same amount of time it would take to get to Croydon. Could she even provide better protection from George Crawford?

'You okay?' Hannah asked as she put her umbrella over Jen, offering her shelter.

'Depends which answer you want?' *She could trust Hannah, right?*

'The you answer.'

'I'm in a panicking mess.'

'Come on, let's get back to London. I'm sure Max will have everything under control. He usually does.' Hannah directed Jen back towards the car, opening the door and making sure she was safe inside before going round to the driver's seat.

Chapter Sixteen

DI Chris Jackson

'Any news on Jen overnight?' Chris asked his team as he entered their office.

'None that we're aware of boss, though I'm sure one of the officers mentioned an issue with Mr Garner or something?' a voice replied somewhere in the room.

'Yeah, guess who got the call?' he said, raising his eyebrows. 'Anyone else?' Chris asked a silent room. He noticed that the timeline had been updated with all of Jen's movements and key CCTV images pinned to the incident board.

'The telephone company have at last supplied us with the number Jen phoned. We've run it through the system with no hits. It's a 0976 number which has no geographical location,' Colin explained.

'Thank you. Any luck when you've called the number?'

'It rings several times and then goes dead. I've even tried talking to the silence but nothing.'

'Anybody got anything else?' Chris surveyed the room. No one seemed interested in sharing, so he went on. 'This morning, I received a call from the Nottingham holding cells. James managed to get himself arrested for drunk and disorderly behaviour. I'm awaiting the reports to be filed by the arresting officers.' Chris let his team digest the information before continuing. 'Do we think that there is an underlying issue of domestic violence we need to investigate?'

'We've both visited the family and haven't noticed any of the indicators,' Julie spoke out. 'Plus neither Sergeant Gillroy nor PC Curtis flagged anything from their visit.

'But he was arrested for violence this morning,' Sally argued.

'Do we need to bring him in for questioning?' Chris asked. Suddenly the room came to life with his whole team talking at once. 'We haven't got any evidence that anything has happened to Jen now or in the past. I myself, don't believe James is the violent type,' Chris stated to everyone who was now voicing their opinion.

'Is it worth asking him to come in voluntarily? Or bring the kids in for a chat?' Sally asked.

'Guys, we need to look at this from the human angle,' Colin shouted over everyone. 'How many of us have had a bad break-up and gone out for a drink? We all go to the pub after a bad day at work. I am not defending his actions, but he has obviously gone out for a drink with a friend and somewhere, something has gone wrong and he has ended up in a fight.'

'When I spoke to James in the holding cells this morning, he was very remorseful. Almost a broken man,' mused Chris.

'We can't ignore that James could have done something to Jen,' Sally argued back.

'But we've no evidence from the CCTV that she was in trouble,' Trudie responded.

Chris looked around the room for inspiration. He was glad that Colin had stuck up for the guy; he made one mistake and was immediately accused of murder? It didn't seem fair. Chris stood at the front of the room and looked towards his team. This case was at a dead end. What should he do? How best to direct them all now? There wasn't anything to investigate other than more hours of CCTV.

'I want to go and do some research in my office. Can we make some enquiries with women's shelters and see if she is hiding out there? Also, can someone chase up going to view further CCTV at the council?'

'Yes, sir,' the response came back as Chris headed back to his office to search Chloe's policing career.

Chris wasn't sure what he was looking for when he pulled up the policing database on his computer. He wanted to see what he could find out about Chloe and the possible connection to Jen, as flimsy as a matching tattoo was.

'Chloe … Seaward …' Chris typed into the search box and hey-presto the name appeared on the screen. Chloe graduated from Hendon Police College in 2004 with glowing honours and commendations but that was when his luck ran out. There was nothing else on the database to view. So she graduated, then what? She vanished until she ended up dead in Long Eaton and a mystery force swooped in, took her body and all the files that went with it?

This was so frustrating! He typed out an email to the people who maintained the database, asking where the information was. People didn't train to be a police officer and then decide, actually, I don't want to do it any more. And, if they did, the end of their service was dated.

Okay, so maybe he needed to try to search for Chloe another way. Would she be on the electoral roll if she was proving to be this hard to track through her police record? He knew he was wasting his time even looking on there but he gave it a go. As suspected, there was no record.

Then an idea hit him; it would be a risky one, especially if he was asked why he was accessing such files. His policing rank gave him access and he was putting it to good use. He could check the approved police housing list for new officers who had qualified and moved to a new area. The housing was a bit like student accommodation but full of police officers, usually on probation. As this mysterious team was based in London, Chris was all too aware of the impossible house prices. So, it was worth a shot searching all approved housing and who was living in it at the time.

He soon struck gold. Detective Officer C Seaward was listed as an occupier of a flat in Shirley, in the London borough of Croydon. He had found an address for her but that wasn't going to get him very far or prove any connection to either Daisy or Jen. Then something else caught his eye – listed as living with C Seaward was a Detective L Carter. *Liam?* he thought to himself, *Leon? Lesley?* Was this Chloe's husband or boyfriend? If it wasn't, wouldn't he have been there when they cleared the files out?

Returning to the policing database, he entered L Carter and soon discovered that 'L' was a Lisa Carter. Her police record had her graduating from Hendon at the exact same time as Chloe. Could Lisa have been working with Chloe for this mystery team? But who the hell was Lisa Carter?

Jen, Daisy, Chloe and now Lisa Carter: all women. Was this Lisa dead or in danger from the same person who'd killed Chloe and quite possibly Daisy?

'Boss.' Julie stood at his doorway.

'Can you give me five minutes and I'll be with you guys?' Chris responded, not looking up.

'Okay, it's about the CCTV.'

'I'll be with you in five, I've just found something.'

'Okay.' Julie left the doorway. Chris wondered vaguely if they'd found something important but he was too wrapped up in his discovery.

Was Daisy the key to all of this? Chris partly wished he was at home surrounded by all the files. He remembered her being a hooker, and then the investigation that followed her death. She had a nasty drug habit and the arrest prior to her death was when she was caught in a compromising position with a well-known football star. The hotel room had traces of drug use, but Chris could never get anything concrete enough together to get the footballer in for questioning. Every time he tried, the footballer's lawyer was in Chris' office giving him the third degree. So the footballer had got away with it and, as for Daisy, she'd turned up dead a week later.

He knew it was a stretch, but Chloe and Daisy's bodies were left in the same position with similar injuries. Was Chloe investigating the drugs Daisy had been using and maybe even used that night with the footballer? Did this mysterious team that had whisked Chloe's body away also know about Daisy? Had they made it harder for Chris to close the investigation into her death, leaving it to go unsolved because they were onto something already?

Now he just felt more anger at the secret team for keeping him in the dark, even with one of their own turning up on his doorstep. But where did this leave Jen or even Lisa Carter? What was this team investigating and, more importantly, who were they?

'Boss.' There was the knock at the door again

'WHAT!' Chris said as his head snapped up to see Julie stood at his door again, less than thirty seconds since she had last been stood there.

'Boss, I really need to talk to you. I'm sorry, but there's a problem with the CCTV.'

Chris stood up. 'What do you mean there's a problem with the CCTV?'

'They've lost it.'

'Lost it, how can they have lost it when it was on the system, what ...?' Chris looked at his watch and realised he had been searching longer than he realised.

'Sorry,' Julie said meekly 'I mean the council. I phoned them to chase up about us going over to view the footage, and they say they've lost the footage.'

'How can a council lose CCTV? Come in, sit down. I'm sorry I snapped. I lost track of time and was trying to find stuff on Chloe,' Chris apologised, inviting Julie into his office.

'I'm sorry to distract you boss, but I couldn't wait any longer without telling you. I phoned the council as you returned to your office and they said they hadn't been in touch because the footage has vanished.'

'How does footage just vanish?'

'They're looking into it now, but they said that it was there last night and something seems to have happened when the system backed up overnight. The footage is gone.'

'So, have they lost everything? All footage from all cameras?'

'No, just certain cameras, boss. They've said we're welcome to come over and have a look but all footage from Friar Lane, Maid Marian Way and St James' Street for Thursday is gone.'

'Their chances of finding it?' Chris asked as he rubbed his face.

'They've got a team on it as we speak, boss.'

Chris got up and picked up his coat. 'I'm going down there now to see them. You coming?'

Chris was fuming as he marched over towards the train station and city council. How on earth had they lost hours of CCTV footage that they'd had the day before? Julie had clearly phoned and warned them that he was on his way over as he was greeted at the reception desk by the Head of Security who immediately took him to the control room. There the gravity of the situation was explained to him. It wasn't just his missing person's case that had been put in jeopardy. They had bigger problems to deal with because this data had to have gone somewhere.

After a long walk back to the office via the canal and the park area of Nottingham, Chris was back at his desk trying to decide which direction to take when Superintendent Gray and the Press Officer appeared at his door. Chris didn't need to ask them if there was anything he could help with. He already knew why they were there.

'Chris, I've brought Felicity down with me to talk about this missing female your team have been investigating.'

'Take a seat, sir. How can I be of help?'

Julie appeared at the door with a tray of drinks, offering Chris a weak smile and mouthing the word 'sorry' as she put the tray down.

'You know exactly why we're here, so let's cut to the chase. Tell me what you've got on this Garner woman?'

'Well, I guess you've seen from the team's office, sir?'

144

'So you've got nothing, other than CCTV footage of her looking happy and healthy. She gets on the bus and off again in Nottingham. Am I correct?'

'Yes sir, but I think there is a connection with the hooker from last year, Daisy Chambers, and also Chloe Seaward ...'

'See, here lies the problem, Chris. Chloe is no longer your case. It's being investigated by her own team. I'm less familiar with Daisy but I'm sure if I checked, her case is now classified as a cold case as no further evidence could be collated.'

'Yes, you're correct but—'

'—you and your team, Detective,' the Superintendent cut him off, 'have a high profile drugs case you're supposed to be working on with DI Manson. Am I correct?'

'Yes sir, but what about Jennifer Garner's family?'

'As harsh as it sounds you're going to have to tell them that you will keep the investigation open but, as far as you're able to tell at this point, it's looking like Jen left of her own accord.'

'What about reaching out to the media? The dead body won't have been completely forgotten about and it might help bring Jen home?'

'This is where I come in,' Felicity, the Press Officer, interrupted. 'The husband, James, hasn't done himself any favours getting arrested for drunk and disorderly conduct. If the media get hold of it, they would crucify him. Imagine the headline. "Wife runs away from violent husband ..."'

'Okay, I get your point,' Chris responded, not needing Felicity to give any further examples.

'I want this wrapping up Chris, and your team back to the drug investigation. I will get DI Manson to get in touch and give you an update,' the Superintendent ordered, turning on his heels and making his way out of the door.

Chris slumped down in his chair. There was no use arguing, it had been inevitable. He just needed to find a way of telling the family.

James had been let off with a fine and a caution. He felt rubbish. He had cocked up big time! He had seen the police doctor and got himself cleaned up; the cut above his eye had stung as the doctor attempted to clean it. Luckily, it didn't need any stitches as the blood seemed to have clotted nicely.

James asked the officer who had brought him back from Nottingham to drop him in Long Eaton. He needed the walk to clear his head before facing the family. He had no idea how he was going to explain it to his mum, never mind the kids. He didn't even know how he had ended up in the state he had. He remembered having a drink with Harry. What had happened to Harry? He vaguely remembered punching him. He would phone him as soon as he got home, though without his mobile phone, which was also missing, it would prove difficult as he didn't know Harry's number off by heart.

He gingerly opened the door, not knowing what to expect. The smell of toast hit him, followed by the familiar sound of his children coming from the kitchen. Feeling like a naughty schoolboy, he hung his head and walked in.

'Daddy!' the children shouted, running towards him.

'Hey guys. Having fun with Grandma?'

'Why are your eyes black, Daddy? Have you been fighting?' Alex asked as James met his mum's disapproving gaze.

'Daddy's been naughty,' he responded, which brought on a flood of questions as James crossed the kitchen towards his mum.

'I'm so sorry, Mum,' James whispered as he pulled her into an embrace.

'What the hell happened, James? We told you to go out and have a drink and relax. Not end up in a police cell,' she hissed, pushing him away.

'I know, I'm so sorry.'

'Go and get yourself cleaned up and we'll talk about it later when the kids aren't around.'

James headed upstairs towards the bathroom. He checked his room and noticed the bed had been made. Oh, how he longed to sleep, forgetting everything that had happened. He sat on the edge of the bed and thought about Jen. She hadn't been far from his thoughts while sat in the police cell. He tried to think of places where she could have gone that hadn't been checked. She had no reason to leave, did she? The police would only have more questions about their relationship, especially after the previous night.

After a long shower, James finally felt normal again. He could hear his parents talking in hushed tones below, no doubt about him. They would need to go back home at some point and, judging by his behaviour, was it even wise to leave the kids with him? James started back down the stairs to be greeted with a disapproving look from his father; the same one he'd used when James had done something wrong at school. James followed him into the living room, neither of them wanting to bring up the subject of the night before.

'The kids okay last night?' James asked. 'No nightmares or anything?'

'No. They were fine, son. Alex woke up this morning asking if his mum was home yet, but your mother spoke to him.' The two of them sat in silence, listening to the children's excited chatter radiating through the walls like they didn't have a care in the world.

'Daddy, Grandma is going to take us out on our bikes!' Alex squealed as they ran into the living room.

'Come on you two,' his mum shouted, appearing in the doorway with coats in hand.

'Come with us, Dad,' Melanie shouted as she bounced around the room.

'You two go out with Grandma. Maybe we will do something later,' James answered as his mum and dad exchanged knowing looks. At thirty-six years of age, James knew exactly what those looks meant. They'd had this planned from the moment he'd walked through the door. The excited noise of Alex and Melanie began to fade as they peddled off on an adventure with their grandma.

James sat face to face with his dad in awkward silence. James knew from experience this meant his dad was trying to figure out how to approach the conversation. Then almost on cue, his dad sighed heavily.

'Fancy a coffee, Dad?' James asked as started to stand up.

'Son.'

James turned to face his dad's stony expression. 'Dad.'

'What happened last night, James?'

James sat back down in his chair and started to tell his dad where he thought it had all gone wrong.

'You know this won't have done you any favours with the police?'

James didn't have an answer. He already knew that he would have increased his chances of being seen as responsible for his wife's disappearance.

'You need to pull yourself together, son. You're thirty-six. You have two adorable children and right now you're all they've got.'

'I don't know what to do. Jen always handled the emotional stuff,' James said as he rubbed his nose and soon regretted it as he was reminded of the soreness.

'What would have happened if they'd woken up and you weren't here? I know we encouraged you to go out but … you've got to think of the kids, James.'

'I know. I made a mistake Dad, and I'm sorry. I just …'

'Look James, your mum and I will help out as much as we can, but you've got to do your bit too. Your mother is concerned about the children and their wellbeing and who can blame her?'

'Why, what's happened? Have they said something?'

'No, she … we … just can't keep trying to avoid conversations with them, about where their mum is.'

'I just don't know where to start. I don't want to scare them or worry them unnecessarily. What if she returns tomorrow?'

'And what if she doesn't?'

James knew there wasn't an answer. He just wasn't prepared for all the upset it would cause.

'Why don't you ask that DI for some advice, son? I'm sure they're used to dealing with cases like this.'

'Hmmm.' Clearly this wasn't the response his dad wanted as he raised his voice.

'Come on James, take some responsibility.' Then he left James alone with his thoughts.

James sat alone in the living room. The kids were still out on their bike rides and the house was silent. James felt his eyes become heavier as he started to drift off.

'James, Harry is here to see you.' James woke up with a start, having not realised that he'd fallen asleep. He stood up, stretched and rearranged himself. 'Harry,' James greeted him as he walked into the living room.

'Listen you two, I have two children who are missing their mum. The last thing they need is to see their dad fighting, okay?' Mrs Garner warned as she followed Harry into the living room.

'Listen, mate. I'm sorry about last night, it was entirely my fault,' Harry said as he took a seat on one of the spare chairs.

'Don't be silly. I'm as much to blame for it all.'

James noticed his mum hovering in the doorway. 'It's okay, Mum,' James reassured her. 'Coffee, mate?'

'I'd kill for one.'

'I'll bring them through,' his mum said as she left them and headed towards the kitchen.

'So, what the hell happened last night?' James asked, turning to Harry who also sported a black eye.

'I don't know. You were knocking them back like there was no tomorrow.'

'Yeah, my head knows it too.'

'It was all a misunderstanding, mate. You said something,

I said something and it got a bit out of hand but we're cool.'

James ran his hands over his face as Harry recounted the evening. He hoped his mum wasn't still listening as the shame crept over him.

'Maybe I'd better go over to the pub later, apologise and offer to replace whatever I broke.'

'If I were you mate, I'd avoid it over there for a while. You know, let the dust settle.'

Right on cue, his mum re-entered the living room with two steaming hot coffees. She handed one to each of them.

'You two made up?' she asked.

'Yeah.'

'I'm just outside. Please don't start fighting in front of the kids.'

'We won't, Mrs Garner,' said Harry. 'That's all water under the bridge now.'

'Good,' she said finally, heading out of the room again.

'You in trouble with your mum?' Harry asked once she was out of earshot.

'Yeah. They didn't know I wasn't home until she was woken up by a police officer in the early hours of this morning.'

'Not good, mate. I'm sorry for causing so much grief.'

'It's really not your fault.'

Harry reached into his pocket and pulled out James' phone. 'I'm afraid it isn't in a very good state. I didn't want to try to turn it on, in case you had stuff you needed to try to back up.'

'I was wondering what happened to that,' James said, taking the phone in his hands and studying it.

'I'm guessing you've not had any news about Jen?' Harry asked, changing the subject.

'No, I'm waiting for news from the DI. Hopefully, now I've got my phone back I might hear something.'

'Do they still have no idea where she is?'

'When I spoke to the DI at the station, he said they'd traced her as far as Nottingham. He'll be coming to see us later.'

'I'm sorry, mate,' Harry said. 'You and Jen are solid. She can't have gone far.'

'I keep going over and over the conversations we had before she left, but I can't pinpoint anything in her behaviour.'

'Maybe she needs space, wherever she is.'

'Space for what? I just want her home. The kids need her home. I wish there was a way I could reach out to her.' James stared out of the window, searching for Jen somewhere in the distance, just out of view.

'You thought about reaching out through the media? Set up a press conference or something?'

'Yeah, I'll go on with my two black eyes and they'll be labelling me as a violent husband.'

An awkward silence fell between them again. James wanted to be left alone. He felt as if he'd been answering the same questions over and over, and he still wasn't any closer to knowing where Jen was or bringing her home.

'Look, mate, I'm going. I just came to drop your phone back.'

'Thanks. I'm sorry I'm not more chatty. I'm just tired and what with Jen and ...'

'It's okay. Look, try one of these before you go to bed. They'll help you sleep.' Harry placed a plastic packet on the table as he got up to leave.

'What is it?'

'Just give it a try. Think of it as a gift from me and Jess.'

James laughed as he wondered what on earth Harry had placed on the table. It looked like Paracetamol tablets, but he doubted very much that it was. He picked it up and placed it into his back pocket as he followed Harry towards the front door.

'Take care, mate. You know where we are if you need us.'

James watched Harry walk up the drive, and then returned into the house and studied the contents of the plastic packet. What the hell was this? It couldn't be legal, whatever it was. He was about to head upstairs when he heard the front doorbell ring again.

Chapter Seventeen

DI Chris Jackson

Chris pulled onto James' drive as a short, ginger-haired man was leaving the house. Chris studied him, convinced he knew him from somewhere. What with the thousands of criminals he must have dealt with in his time, never mind witnesses, victims and general passers-by, he was forever seeing faces that he recognised but couldn't quite place. As the person walked towards the car he turned and smiled at them before continuing off down the street.

'I recognise him from somewhere,' Chris said, climbing out of the car.

'No ideas. Sorry, sir,' Julie responded as she joined him in walking towards the house.

'Hmm, probably just a passer-by that I've encountered in the past.' They walked up the drive towards the door, assuming James would be in, given he had just had a visitor.

'You ready?' Julie asked as they approached the front door.

'Yeah, I just wish we were bringing them more positive news,' Chris said as he reached over, pressed the doorbell and waited.

'Mrs Garner? DI Chris Jackson and this is DS Ryan.' A look of worry crossed the woman's face as she studied their ID cards.

'Is this about Jen?'

'Can we come in Mrs Garner? Is James home?'

'Come in,' she said, directing them towards the conservatory and calling for James and her husband as she followed the officers in. 'Can I get either of you a drink?'

'Tea please,' Julie spoke in her calm, reassuring voice. 'Milk, no sugar.'

'DI Jackson?'

'Water, please.'

They sat down in the well-lit conservatory as the evening began to draw in. Chris could hear the chatter of children from the back garden as they chased each other around the swings. Chris wondered how they were coping without their mum. Right now it sounded like they didn't have a care in the world.

'James.' Chris stood up to meet him as he entered the conservatory, followed by his mum with the drinks carefully balanced on a tray.

'I've asked Derek to keep the kids occupied, so we can talk without distraction.'

'Thank you, Mrs Garner.'

'It's Rita,' she said, reaching over to pour the tea.

'How are the children taking their mum's disappearance?'

'To be honest, they're going through phases. One minute they're playing happily, then the next they're asking where their mum is,' Rita responded.

Chris turned to talk to James. 'James, when I saw you this morning, I promised I'd have some news.'

'You found her?'

'Not quite.'

'What do you mean?'

'We've managed to track your wife's movements, and she was last seen getting off the Indigo bus in Nottingham.'

'Okay. So, does that mean you've found her in Nottingham?'

'Your wife, as your neighbours suggested, left here around 9.30 a.m. She walked towards the train station, made a phone call and went on to answer a second call from the phone box.'

'James, do you have any idea who she would have been ringing that she couldn't phone from home?' Julie asked.

'No idea. I hadn't spoken to Jen since I left for work that morning, I've checked my phone and my answerphone dozens of times, but nothing.'

'Your wife doesn't look in any form of distress at any of the points we've managed to pick her up.'

James looked towards his mum for support.

'James, was Jen planning to meet anyone in Nottingham? I remember from reading the file that you work in Nottingham.'

'I do. I wasn't aware of any plans.'

'Could she have possibly be coming to meet you for lunch as a surprise?'

'Not that I know of. I was pretty busy most of Thursday. So if she'd called the office, I wouldn't have been free anyway.' James looked uncomfortable.

'James, we need to ask some difficult questions regarding your wife's disappearance, which are all routine questions. We would appreciate it if you could remain calm and answer them honestly.' Julie took control of the interrogation, seeing as Chris had clearly riled him.

James began to look even more anxious.

'James, do you have any reason to believe your wife was planning to leave you?'

'*Leave me?*' The words had clearly struck James like a stab wound. 'No, we were happy. Everything was great.'

'Have you noticed any money missing from anywhere? I know you told us that Jen left all her personal belongings, but we've reason to believe she paid for her bus ticket with cash.'

'No …' Chris could see the pain etched on James' face. The conversation had stalled as James sighed and ran his hands over his face. 'You're saying that you think my wife has left me and the children?' James asked.

'We're exploring every possibility, James. But as Chris explained, at no point have we witnessed her showing any signs of distress.'

'Then where in Nottingham do you think she is?'

'At this point, we don't know. We've only managed to track her as far as getting off the bus.'

'What are you doing about locating her?' Rita interrupted.

'The team and I are currently conducting a case review.

Hence our visit to you now.' Chris decided to respond to this one, stamping his authority on the answer.

'You're going to stop looking and just wait for her to return home?' James looked like his world was falling apart.

'No, James. I promised you we would find her and we will. It's just going to take more time than we originally expected.'

'Is there anything we can do to help? What about the newspapers?' Rita asked.

'I've spoken to our Press Officer, and she doesn't think it would be a good idea at this time.'

'So, we're really just going to have to wait for Jen to come home?' Rita responded sarcastically.

'What do I tell the kids?' James' voice broke and his mum moved over to comfort him.

'Detective, you must understand the position we're all in here. We need Jen home. We want her home,' Rita pleaded.

'I do, I feel for you all but without any signs of distress or cause for concern from what we've seen, there is little more we can do.'

'Do we need to prepare ourselves for the worst?' James asked.

'In most cases like this the missing person does make contact eventually, but this isn't something we can put a time-frame on.'

An uncomfortable silence fell across the room.

'Have you looked any more into my wife's background?' James asked.

'What makes you ask?'

'When I first met Jen, I was head over heels in love with her, like I said. But whenever I used to ask about her parents and her family she told me that they were all dead. Other than the girl she was supposedly living with at the time, all her other friends lived miles away. So, when we moved here I asked after the friend she was with in the nightclub and she'd go all quiet and change the subject. After a while I stopped asking, thinking that she'd tell me in her own time but she never did. I don't know, I'm just beginning to wonder whether you think she could have been on the run from something or someone?'

Julie pulled out her notebook and started to record what James had said about his wife.

'I wish I had the answers, I really do James,' Chris replied.

Rita stood up, collected the cups and returned to the kitchen.

'I'm afraid I also need to ask about your wife's mental health. Are you aware of anything that might lead you to be concerned for her wellbeing?' Chris continued.

'Not that I'm aware of. Why?'

'I'm afraid it's another avenue we need to explore. I'm sorry this isn't a more positive meeting, James, but as I originally promised, I wanted to keep you and your family informed every step of the way.'

'Is there anyone who could help us speak to the children?' Rita asked, returning to the conservatory.

'I will ask one of my family liaison officers to get in contact with you tomorrow. If you think of anything else James, please give me a call. You have my card and we'll be in touch as soon as we have more news,' Chris said, rising from his seat to leave. 'Please remember what I said this morning. Make sure you look after those two children of yours. They're going to need their dad more than ever.' They walked into the hallway, leaving James, once again, a broken man. Derek met them to see them out of the house.

'Thank you, Officers.'

James Garner

James sat in silence with his mum, neither of them wanting to say anything and break the silence, but then something in James snapped. He got up and stormed out of the room.

'James?' His mum's concern was met with silence as he

marched up the stairs and straight into their bedroom. He immediately started pulling out drawers.

'James! What are you doing?' his mum cried.

'I'm going to search through her stuff until I find something that tells me where she is,' James said through gritted teeth as he pulled another drawer out.

'Derek!' his mum shouted, running back down the stairs.

'What's the matter, love?'

'It's James. He's up there now pulling their bedroom apart.'

'Okay love. Grab the kids and take them out to the cinema or something. They don't need to see him like this.' She grabbed the kids' coats and ran into the garden, scooping them up with promises of ice cream and the movies. 'I'll text you later,' she shouted, as she bundled the kids into the car before they had a chance to see their dad back on a collision course.

James was so angry, he pulled out everything and let it crash to the ground. God only knew what Jodie would be thinking next door, but he didn't care. As he came to Jen's dresser he caught sight of his face. He picked up the vanity chair and threw it at the mirror.

'Seven years bad luck, I've had ten being married to that stupid bitch,' he seethed as the glass shattered, falling onto the tiny table which had been filled with make-up and perfume. James started throwing the bottles and tubes with force at the wall.

'James.' A voice he knew came from the doorway, but he didn't even turn to acknowledge his dad as he continued to throw Jen's perfume bottles. He was going to find something if it took him all night he decided, as he moved to his side of the bed, upending furniture and anything that was in the way.

Satisfied he had checked the whole bedroom, he moved into the en-suite, choosing to smash the mirror in there with his fist. Given the fight he had been in the previous night, it caused more pain to him than damage to the mirror. Then he remembered somewhere in the bedroom he hadn't checked. Walking back in, he pulled all the sheets and quilt off the bed and with a thud he upended it. He wouldn't be needing the bed in future anyway. Why would he want to sleep in the same bed as she had, for all those years? He'd go back to his glory days of university; an eligible bachelor of the city. Out every weekend with his mates, a different woman every night, living the high life. He began to feel his way around the carpet which once held the king-sized bed when he noticed something that wasn't quite right. Pulling the carpet back, he saw that one of the floorboards was loose. Somehow, managing to squeeze his fingers into the gaps, he leveraged the board up and there it was. A small wooden box with a lock on it. *Bollocks to that*, he thought to himself as he lifted it above his head and brought it smashing down onto the floorboards, but it didn't budge. Getting up, he made his way over the upturned bed and brought the box crashing down onto the metal frame. After several more attempts, it sprung open.

In all his anger and rage he hadn't been prepared for what fell out of the box. A single white-gold wedding band, a photo of what looked like Jen with some other woman and a scribbled down address for somewhere in Mansfield.

'Gotcha!' James shouted in triumph, until a different photo caught his eye that had become part of the carnage. Melanie and Alex looked up at him from the broken frame. His rage lifted, as finally the tears fell and he gulped for air.

Chapter Eighteen

Jen Garner

'Well, here we are,' Jen said as they pulled up outside a house down a dead-end street in Croydon. It had metal shutters over all the windows and front door.

'Doesn't look like there is much happening here now,' Hannah commented, looking around at their surroundings.

'Well, I guess it has changed a lot over the years. Believe it or not, this is where the Crawford Empire began.'

'You wouldn't think it to look at it.'

'I don't think the local force realised what they had stumbled upon when they started to investigate.'

'How did we come to be involved?' Hannah asked.

'It all started with a little old lady who lived in that house there.' Jen pointed. 'At the time, the yard which was situated where those houses are in front of us was a wasteland with a couple of derelict buildings.' Jen needed to talk through the events surrounding the case. She had never gotten closure. She had left the service before the mandatory counselling and final debrief had taken place.

'There was a lot of concern for the resident's safety as she was living alone next to this derelict yard, so the local officers installed a camera. There had been a break-in at the builder's yard over the road, so the team decided to review the footage from the camera. To their surprise, they spotted people coming and going from the yard at all times of day and night. So further surveillance was set up in this lady's front bedroom.'

'I bet she loved that.'

'All of a sudden she had a house full of people again and despite her age, she couldn't do more to help. She fed the officers; I think some of them ate better than they did at home.

There was endless supplies of tea and conversation about last night's telly.'

'That's always good. I've been on many a stakeout and lived off takeaway meals here and there.'

'The local team noticed that the people coming and going were local dealers. To cut a long story short, not only were they dealing drugs from these abandoned offices they were manufacturing and cutting various drugs. The local detectives basically fell upon a drugs network that was being run out of these buildings that stretched beyond the boundary lines of Croydon.'

'So how did Chloe and you end up being involved?'

'The local team had managed to set up undercover operations, but the more they investigated the further the network expanded and started to involve trafficking and prostitution. Drugs were showing up across the country, with the distinctive logo that could be linked back to those buildings down the dead-end of a quiet road in Croydon.'

'Whoa.'

'So that's how Chloe and I got involved. It became very big and widespread very quickly and there were some concerns regarding national security.'

'What happened to the old lady?'

'I guess she moved, maybe into a home. Though she was eighty at the time so …' Sitting in silence, they watched people come and go from the newly built homes.

'When were new houses built?'

'I'm not completely sure, but once the drug manufacturing was cleared out, the site was sold pretty quickly to a housing developer.'

'So, where do we go from here?'

'I'm not sure, to be honest. I don't think there's any point chasing around London because when George went to prison so did his whole network.'

Hannah's phone began to ring, making them both jump.

'Sir? Okay, we're heading there now.'

'Max?' Jen asked as Hannah ended the call and started the engine.

'Your old flat has been cleared. We can go straight over.'

Hannah and Jen gained entry to the complex with little issue and now stood at flat number twenty-one while a uniformed officer checked their IDs.

'I hope you're not expecting to find much in there, the place has been ransacked,' he told them as he studied their IDs and then his clipboard. 'You know what they say, if your name's not down you're not coming in.' He peered over the top of the clipboard, scrutinising them. Jen could feel herself getting more and more irritated as the seconds passed. She felt like snatching the damn clipboard off him. Her heart rate was increasing rapidly.

'I can ring my boss if it'll help?' Hannah said, in an attempt to play along as Jen got more and more frustrated.

'Ah, here we go,' he said, taking his pen out and ticking their names off. 'Enjoy your stay ladies, and please make sure you exit via the gift shop on your left.'

'Thank you,' Hannah said as she pushed Jen through the door before she could do any damage to the poor officer who was clearly just trying to bring a little fun into his day.

'You okay?' Hannah asked her once they were inside.

'Yeah, sorry. I was so close to losing it there with him.'

'I could tell. I'm sorry you had to go through that. He clearly has no idea what he has been asked to guard and was trying to make light of the situation.'

Jen looked around the room and her heart sank. Any chance of finding anything in the mess that was now in front of them was near impossible. Someone had done a proper job on the place, looking for something.

'I knew Chloe was messy but Jesus, Jen ...' Hannah said, trying to make light of the situation.

'Oh, you've not seen anything yet.' Jen laughed as the tension was broken. The amateur dramatics they had to go through to get into the flat were soon forgotten. Hannah passed a pair of disposable gloves over to Jen and they both gloved up, making sure they didn't transfer their prints onto anything. Jen began to look around the open-plan kitchen while Hannah headed into the side rooms.

'The bedrooms are pretty much the same,' Hannah said as she came out of one of the rooms. 'There doesn't seem to be any signs of a struggle. The place just looks like someone came in and ransacked it,' she added.

'Do you think whoever did this found what they were looking for?' Jen asked. 'Because I don't think there is any chance of us finding anything useful here at all.' Jen continued to poke around and picked up a table that had been turned over. 'Do you think there could be anything of use under all of this?' she asked out loud.

'I don't understand what you mean?'

'Look at my kids, for example ...' Jen tailed off. There they were in the back of her mind as they always were. How could she even consider trying to be a detective when she was holding onto something so precious? Undercover detectives weren't known for being able to do the job they did and then go home to their kids and husband. It was considered too dangerous. Could someone ever detach themselves fully from maternal instinct? Children were too innocent to be collateral damage. Jen wondered how best to explain what she meant.

'My two ...' she began again. 'When their rooms are a mess and they want to play with a certain toy, they change their minds when they realise the toy is underneath the rest of the mess. They get something else out and then the mess builds up. Until they tidy their rooms and suddenly discover something they haven't seen for ages.' Hannah still looked confused. 'Never mind, it's easier to hide something under all of this than in a drawer for example.' Hannah nodded again, and Jen gave up trying to explain, but she knew what she meant.

'So, what do you suggest? We start tidying?'

'Ha! Hell no! I get enough of that at home! Let me give Max a call and get a team sent down here.'

'An army of cleaners and when they're done, they can come over to mine.' Hannah laughed.

Jen found herself back in the office sat at the conference table with Hannah and Max talking noisily in the background. Jen still couldn't work out how George knew about her family; she had been so careful when she left the service. She had sourced everything herself: birth certificate, driving license, passports, all for Jennifer Sheridan. When she married James, she was able to do it all over again but legally this time. She knew the service would have probably provided her with all the documents, but she wanted a fresh start, to do it all on her own – and she had.

'Jen, I've loaded all the data from the prison onto the system and asked Sam if she will compile it into a spreadsheet,' Hannah said, pulling her out of her daydream.

'Okay,' Jen responded, not paying attention to what was going on in front of her.

'Jen, do you remember if George had any family?' Hannah asked her, but Jen's mind was still elsewhere. 'Jen,' she said, louder this time.

'Yeah, I'm with you. Sorry, my mind is somewhere else. Sam's got the visitors' list.'

'And?' Hannah prompted before Max stepped in.

'Jen, Hannah and I were discussing if George had any family. Prior to his incarceration?'

'Not that I remember,' Jen said, reaching over and typing on the tablet in front of her. 'When Chloe and I were undercover,' she began, 'there never seemed to be any one particular female with George at any one time.'

'So, the visit to Reedmoor Prison and Mr Crawford has achieved nothing? We still have the branded drugs, a dead detective and no suspects because our chief one is behind bars,' Hannah summed up.

'We've got his communications. Hopefully when Sam has finished compiling it, something might ping,' Max suggested.

'I'm at the same conclusion as Hannah. We're at a dead end and pretty much chasing ghosts,' Jen cut in.

The team sat in silence, trying to figure out a way through the mess when Sam knocked on the door. 'Sorry to disturb you,' she said in her annoying sing-song voice, 'I've done it, it's on the system.'

'Thank you, Sam. Care to join us while we check through it?' Max asked as he located it on the system. Jen had a horrible feeling that what she was about to witness would be a multi-coloured spreadsheet complete with swirly fonts, and was almost disappointed when the boring old spreadsheet loaded.

'So,' Sam began. 'This is just a list of names of people who visited George Crawford. I can go and work Excel magic when I know what we're looking for.'

'Sam, having typed all those names in, did you notice anything out of the ordinary?' Jen asked.

'Not really. He seemed to have a lot of visitors at first which then stopped and became just his solicitor.'

'Maybe his star began to fade,' Jen offered.

'It clearly didn't fade that well if these drugs are back on the streets,' Hannah responded as she started to search through the list of names on the spreadsheet for anyone with a matching surname. She came up with nothing.

'Sam, could you have a look at the list and see if you can compile something that tells us when everyone visited and how many times?' Jen asked.

'Of course, I'll get right on it. Unless anyone needs anything else?'

'No. We're good thank you, Sam,' Max said as Sam got up from the table and left the room. 'Jen, I know you've already looked at one set of footage, but I want to show you something.' He typed away on his screen, transferring it on to the main screen. 'I've been looking through the other footage. The ginger blob you thought was James' friend Harry seems to appear on most of the footage, regardless of its location.'

Jen stared at the footage, playing out in front of her. 'So, you think Harry might have something to do with this?' she asked.

'To appear in one nightclub is a coincidence but to appear on most of the footage ... something isn't right.'

'But he's a salesman and he travels a lot, I know that much. There's no way it's him,' Jen argued as she tried to think back to the last time she and James went out with Harry and Jess.

'I think we need to consider it, Jen. I've been in touch with someone from the drug squad and the main place these drugs have been turning up in is Nottingham.'

Jen didn't think she had heard right for a second. Had her former best friend been so close to her without her knowing? Could her husband even be involved in all of this? He was always out with Harry, but she was sure James wasn't on the footage. She'd looked for him herself. 'Pull Sam's spreadsheet up and search Harry Greenidge and James Garner.' Jen felt a sense of relief when the results came back with nothing.

'Can I make a suggestion, Max?' Hannah interrupted, breaking the awkwardness. 'Why don't I make my way down to Nottingham and insert myself into the drug task force and see if we can smoke Harry out? If he isn't dealing, there's nothing to worry about.'

'Good idea.' Max agreed. 'You can also see if you can steer Jen's missing person's case in the wrong direction.'

'Hang on, what?' Jen said, realising what Max had said.

'You're a missing person. Your husband reported you missing, the day after you left.'

'But why? I left him an answerphone message and explained everything.'

'I'm guessing he's not got it. I've done all I can to steer the Detective running the case in the wrong direction. It would be good to have someone on the ground just in case. Make your way to Nottingham, Hannah. Let's see if we can smoke Harry out.'

'I'll go and get my stuff together,' Hannah said as she left the room.

'You know you should be letting me go as well.' Max didn't have to answer. She was far better off out of it than walking into the middle of her own missing person's case. They were getting close; she could feel it. She just needed to find the damn connection and pray to God that it wouldn't be James.

'Hannah, I need you to do me a favour,' Jen said as she approached Hannah's desk whilst she was packing a bag with some stuff she might need.

'Anything.' Hannah paused. 'Within reason though, right?'

'Something has been bugging me about what Adam said about the necklace. If he didn't send the flowers or the card, why send the necklace?'

'So, you want me to break into your house and get it?'

'No ... well, kinda. I didn't bring my keys, or I'd give you them.'

'Don't worry, house breaking is one of my specialities.' Hannah laughed. 'They won't even know I've been there.'

Chapter Nineteen

MONDAY
James Garner

James woke up to find himself lying on his bedroom floor, alone and cold. He still had Jen's wedding ring on his little finger and the photo of her was lying nearby. As he sat up, he studied the photo more carefully. They looked incredibly close, whoever the other woman was. Had she been there the night he had met Jen? He was sure he hadn't seen her. Hang on a minute, wasn't this the girl that they'd found on the towpath?

James closed his eyes and his thoughts turned to Melanie and Alex, remembering Jen coming out of Melanie's room the day she disappeared. Should he go and check in there to see if she'd hidden anything? Melanie had mentioned about her mum being sat on the floor crying when she woke up. Was she crying because of the other woman in the photo?

What on earth had Jen got herself into? Did he even know his wife? What had suddenly made him doubt Jen's motives? Since when was it a crime for her to go into Nottingham and not give him a call to meet her? He remembered fondly what they used to get up to on his lunch breaks. All his life, things had been set out clearly in front of him. Now, sat on his bedroom floor, holding his head in his hands, he was lost. Jen was his everything. He needed to retain his focus and trust the woman he loved. The DI had said he wouldn't stop until he found her. For once he had to trust in someone else and know that he couldn't save the day.

As he sat there, the house seemed strangely quiet. No children running around getting excited about school, no nagging voices. Where was everyone? Brushing himself down, he got up, reminding himself who he was, what he was responsible for and who he loved. He made his way down the stairs and couldn't help notice the silence that engulfed him.

Walking into the kitchen, he realised that everything had been tidied away. Moving from room to room, everything seemed to be the same; no trace of anyone other than the light on the answerphone flashing. Hopefully it would be Jen or a message from someone telling him they'd seen her ...

'You have one answerphone message left on Sunday at 1500, beep.'

'Mr Garner, it's Dave from the garage about the service due on your car. If you could give me a call back on ...' James pressed the delete button.

'You have no saved messages.' James put the phone down in defeat. What was the time anyway? Where were the kids? James returned to his room in search of the broken mobile phone he had thrown somewhere. As he turned it on, he prayed that it would work, only to be greeted with a blank screen.

'Fuck!' he shouted in frustration. He had lost everything. Hopefully it could be rescued if he plugged it into his laptop, but where was his laptop? Most probably buried under everything else in the bedroom. Is this how the kids felt when their room was a mess? Taking everything apart had seemed like a good idea at the time, but now he couldn't find what he needed. His thoughts were broken when he heard the front door open and a voice called up the stairs. *Jen?*

'James?' His mum greeted him.

'Mum.' There was an air of disappointment surrounding them both, neither knowing what to say.

'I just need to grab my laptop, Mum.'

'Good luck on that one.'

James raced upstairs and began to search for his laptop, not noticing his mum following him up and standing in the doorway to his room.

'Did last night actually solve anything?' she asked.

'Mum ...'

'I'm not interested in your excuses, James. First you get

yourself into a fight and arrested, and then you totally flip out, scaring everyone. Did you even stop to think about the kids?'

James stood for a moment, taking in everything his mother had just said. 'Where are the kids, Mum?' he asked, suddenly realising they still weren't at home or with her.

'At school.'

'You took them both to school?'

'They need some normality, James. Seeing as you are failing to provide that, I took them to school.'

'Did you at least warn the school?'

'Yes, I spoke to both their class teachers and the Head, who were all very understanding. Look, I'm going back downstairs to make lunch. Do whatever you need to do. Then I suggest we all sit down and have a talk because if you continue on this road you are going to crash and burn.'

James searched out his laptop and stood alone in what was now a bomb site. How was he going to explain everything to his family? He was a thirty-six-year-old man having to explain his bad behaviour to his mum.

He hoped that the kids would be okay at school. Hopefully the distraction would do them some good. He plugged his phone into his laptop, praying that something could be saved, and then walked down the stairs to face his mum.

As James entered the kitchen, he noticed his parents sat around the dinner table. His mum had a notebook open in front of her while his dad was sat holding his drink. This was the last thing James needed.

'Shall I ring Deb? Let her know there's a family meeting?'

'Don't be flippant with me, James,' his mum responded.

'What's going on, son?'

'Isn't that a bit of a silly question, Dad?'

'We're concerned about you and the kids,' his mum interrupted.

'What do you want me to say? My wife is missing, the police seem to think she has just left us.'

'They didn't say that, James.'

'Okay, she went into Nottingham, and they don't seem to think she was in trouble.'

'So, you decide to take it upon yourself to trash your bedroom? What do you think the kids thought last night with you banging and crashing around?'

Silence fell between them all as James contemplated his answer.

'If you're going to continue on this path, we're going to take the kids back to Wetton with us for their own safety,' his mum said, breaking the silence.

'Did you even find anything last night?' his dad asked.

'No,' James lied, not wanting to have to explain everything to his parents. 'I stopped myself from searching any further.'

'I don't understand where this sudden doubt has come from?' his mum questioned. James looked at them both, in search of the answer. He didn't even know himself why he doubted her.

'It just doesn't make sense, Mum. She had no reason to get up and leave us.'

'People do crazy things all the time.'

James knew his mum was right. He needed to be positive and proactive; he had no reason to doubt his wife or their marriage. 'So, we just sit and wait for her to come home?'

'That's all we can do, James. The police are out searching for her. It's just a waiting game until they have more news or she comes home of her own accord.'

'I just don't know what to do, Mum.'

'Your dad and I are here to help you, but you need to start helping yourself.'

James stood up and walked around the table towards his mum. 'I'm sorry,' James said as he hugged her.

'Just think how scared Alex and Melanie are right now. You need to be there for them more than anything else.'

'What's the plan?' his dad asked, bringing everything back to the present.

'I'll stick the kettle on.' James felt more upbeat, more like himself again. He knew his parents were right. It was time to take control of the situation, be more assertive and look after the two most important people in his life. He didn't know the answers but he needed to accept that. If she had left them, then he would fight tooth and claw to get her back. He hoped that wherever she was, she was happy and safe.

Jen Garner

After another sleepless night, Jen found herself back in the same office, sat at the same conference table, rubbing her wrist while staring at the same spreadsheet of George's visitors over the past ten years.

'I've got something,' Sam said, finally giving Jen some hope.

'Go on, Sam.'

'I've just noticed that during the first year he was regularly visited by a female and a child. I guess I spotted it as I was wondering who in their right mind would take a small child to a prison visit.'

'Good spot, Sam. I don't remember him having any family when we were tracking him. Max?'

'No, me neither Jen.' Max typed into the screen in front of him. 'At the time of his incarceration, he was listed as having, I quote, no dependant that he was aware of! He also stated having no living family.'

'Who was this woman and what was her connection to him?' Jen pondered out loud.

'I've got a Gwen Adams and I'm guessing her daughter, Tilly Adams,' Sam read off the spreadsheet in front of her.

'When did they stop visiting, Sam?' Jen asked.

'According to the visits log they visited for about four years, then just stopped.'

'Have you seen any written communication from them?'

'I don't think so, let me check,' Sam said, standing up and reaching over towards the boxes where George's fan mail sat.

'Pass me a box, Sam, and I'll help you go through them,' Jen offered, feeling like she had nothing else to do until they heard back from Hannah.

DI Chris Jackson

'Good Morning, all.' Chris found himself sat round a conference table with his boss, DI Clive Manson from the drugs task force and an unknown female he had never seen before. 'If I can just begin with introducing you all to Detective Littlefair. She's a former colleague of Chloe Seaward and is part of the team investigating her death. Detective, do you want to start us off?' Superintendent Gray asked.

'Thank you. As you will no doubt be aware, the body you guys found last Monday belonged to one of our own detectives. We've been looking into the drugs we believe she was investigating and have found links to Nottingham.' Hannah passed several sheets of paper to those around the table.

'This possibly fits with an investigation my task force are currently looking at,' DI Manson commented.

'Have you had any progress with this case, DI Manson?' Detective Littlefair asked.

'Up until now it's been a painstaking investigation, with little progress. DI Jackson and his team have offered to assist us on this case.'

Chris nodded his acknowledgement, unsure if any of them had really started looking into the drugs.

'Are you happy to start with what you and your team know about the current drugs situation and we can take it from there?'

'Of course, Detective,' DI Manson replied.

'Please, it's Hannah.'

'We have become aware that there's a potential turf war brewing in Nottingham. Historically, there have been two main players in Nottingham. But there are signs of someone else muscling their way in. The task force has been trying to identify who this new player is and where the drugs are coming from.' DI Manson began to explain what he and the task force were working on.

'Can I ask how you became aware that there was a new player?' Hannah asked as she tucked a loose hair behind her ear.

'We started seeing a new batch of drugs which we hadn't seen before. When we spoke to our contacts, they were very unwilling to tell us where the drug had come from.'

'Am I right in assuming that this drug was distinctive from the others?' Hannah prompted

'Yes, all the pills seem to have the same engraving on them.'

'I think we may be looking for the same people, Inspector.'

DI Manson's face lit up with the realisation that he had stumbled onto something big. Chris sat wondering why on earth they needed to do this in his station and not wherever DI Manson and his amazing task force were based.

'DI Jackson, have your team had any success in tracing these pills?' Hannah asked, turning to Chris.

'As far as I'm aware, we've not yet been able to collate any information,' Chris lied. He didn't have a clue about these pills or what his team had managed to find out so far.

'Chloe had managed to collate some CCTV footage prior to her death. The team have been looking through. If you flick to page three in your pack you will see that we have identified a male we would like to speak to.' Chris screwed up his eyes as he looked at the picture in front of him.

'Do you have any idea of this person's identity?' Chris asked.

'I'm not familiar with this figure either,' DI Manson commented.

'He's another reason we've come up to Nottingham as we suspect that it could be a man called Harry Greenidge.'

'Harry Greenidge? He's currently part of an investigation I'm working on.' The name suddenly piqued Chris' attention.

'How so?' Hannah questioned.

'He's connected to a missing person's case.'

'Which is coming to a close,' the Superintendent interrupted.

'Has his name come up in any of your investigations, DI Manson?' Hannah asked, clearly trying to change the subject.

'Not that I'm aware of. I assume he's local?'

'I know this is very short notice but are we able to put a tail on Harry, DI Manson?' Hannah asked.

'It shouldn't be a problem. Chris, I'm guessing with Harry being part of your investigation you've got contact details for him?' DI Manson asked.

'He was part of a bar fight on Saturday night so he's on the system and should be pretty easy to trace.'

'If you could both excuse me, I'll get the team onto him,' DI Manson said as he got up and left the table.

'Detective Littlefair,' Chris started. 'I was wondering if you had any other names linked to what Chloe was looking into?'

'We're hoping that Harry is going to be the key to this, as we are pretty much at a dead end at the moment. Why do you ask?'

'It's a bit complicated, but Harry is best friends with a guy named James Garner, whose wife Jennifer Garner is currently missing.' As Chris spoke his boss shot him a look, clearly trying to communicate to him that he needed to drop this, but if he could get some information from this detective then he would.

'The name Garner hasn't come up my end, Detective. Do you think they could be involved?'

'I'm not sure. James and Harry got into a fight on Saturday night and I'm wondering if they were fighting over drugs?'

'Possibly, Detective Jackson. But I think we are best focus on Harry's location and, if this James is involved, we' pick him up through Harry.'

'Sorry to keep throwing names at you, but are you aware of a Lisa Carter linked to the investigation?'

'Not that I'm aware of. Sorry.'

Chris didn't have any more names to throw in, but he was now even more worried about Jen's welfare with the possibility of James being involved in these mystery drugs. Just then Clive re-entered the room.

'I've got someone sat outside Harry's house now, and we'll keep a tail on him.'

'Thank you, DI Manson.'

'I also double-checked and Harry's name isn't linked to either rival drug gangs. So it will be interesting to see which side he falls on, or whether he is our mystery new dealer.'

'I'm hoping that Harry is going to crack this thing wide open for us,' Hannah responded.

'I'm going to head back to my office,' the Superintendent said as he stood up. 'Chris can I just have a word, please. Outside?' Chris knew exactly what was coming. He was going to be told to concentrate on the drugs and to forget Jen and the Garners.

Chapter Twenty

Jen Garner

Jen had been sat at Chloe's old desk, wading her way through George's fan mail. Since Sam's discovery of his mysterious visitors earlier in his sentence, she'd busied herself with reading his letters. She looked at the time and wondered how Hannah was getting on back home with the Nottingham force and her apparent missing person's appeal. Max walked over towards the desk holding an earpiece; they'd certainly got smaller since she had last worn one.

'Hannah is at your house so will be with you shortly. You okay with this? Remember how it works and everything?' he asked.

'They can't have changed that much?' Jen questioned and then decided better of it. 'I'll put it in my ear and hope for the best, unless these things go somewhere else now?' Max handed her the piece, and she inserted it into her ear.

'I'm going to move into the meeting room Max, so everyone doesn't have to listen in,' Jen said, getting up from Chloe's old desk.

'Hello? Jen, can you hear me?' Hannah's voice came through the earpiece.

'Loud and clear,' Jen replied. 'Can you hear me okay?' Jen was conscious that she should really be talking into something.

'Loud and clear.'

'Great.'

'I'm just at the end of your road. It looks like James and two other older people are leaving the house now.'

It sounded like James' parents were in Long Eaton. James must be really worried about her if he'd called the cavalry. 'They'll be off to get the kids from school, so the coast should be clear.'

'I'll make sure before I go in. You know this would have been so much easier if you'd brought your keys with you.' Hannah chuckled as Jen heard a clicking sound in the background.

'I'll make sure I remember that next time.'

'Okay, I'm in.'

'How did you get in so quick?' Jen questioned.

'Conservatory. I need you to guide me to where I have to go, Jen.'

Jen closed her eyes and thought of home. 'Right go out of the conservatory and you should be in the kitchen?'

'Yeah.'

'Okay, this is the easy bit – the island in the middle of the kitchen,'

'Yeah, I'm stood looking at it now.'

'You're going to have to bend down. I posted the envelope under there.'

'There wasn't anywhere else you could have hidden it?'

'I was in a rush.'

Jen could hear Hannah's knee's clicking as she bent down. 'Got it.'

'Is it still in the envelope?'

'Yup.'

'Hannah, will you go up the stairs and head into the main bedroom and get something for me?'

'While I'm here …' Jen listened as Hannah started to make her way through the house and then climb the stairs. 'Holy shit, Jen. What happened here?'

'What?'

'I think someone got a bit angry. One of the rooms, which I assume is yours, has been totally trashed.'

'What?' Jen repeated as she stood up, almost wanting to drive back home so she could see what Hannah was seeing. 'Are you able to get to my wardrobe?'

'Here to serve,' Hannah responded as Jen listened to her muttering as she stepped over things.

'There's a shawl thing with pockets. I wore it to the meal the other night with James.'

'Red? Yeah got it.'

'Can you check the pockets?'

'Okay. I think I've got it.'

'I vaguely remember putting something in there. What is it?'

'It's a pill with the Crawford branding on ...'

'So that means—'

'—Jen, I've gotta go. Someone's coming. I'll speak to you when I'm clear of the house.'

'Over and out.'

So, the person who had been at the meal had been spying on her? Why else would she have one of George Crawford's pills in her pocket? Was this the confirmation she was waiting for that everything was linked to George Crawford and he was back running his empire?

'Okay Jen, I'm clear. They all arrived back with some other female I'd not seen before. Pretty, dark hair ...'

'You've just described half of the street.'

'Well she seems pretty cosy with James and the family'

'Jess?' *What the fuck was Jess doing in her house with James, the kids and the in-laws? Had they already started to replace her?*

'Jen, I'm just looking at the necklace now. Who's Chester Bennington?'

'He was the dude from that band who took his own life. Why?'

'Because on the back of the St Christopher, it has engraved "RIP Chester Bennington".'

'That's a bit strange. Why has that been put on there? Can you send a picture through?'

'Will do. I'm gonna sign off as I need to get back. Talk later.'

Chester Bennington, Jen thought to herself. *Was it some clue or something?*

'Oh my god, Chloe. You are a genius!' Jen shouted as she moved quickly over to Max's office. 'Max, I need to go out. I know where Chloe has left us something.'

'Woah, slow down.'

'We used to have a hamster called Chester, named after the singer from Linkin Park.' Max's face was blank

'He died, and we buried him under a tree in the park.'

'Right?' Max seemed completely puzzled as to why she was telling him this.

'On the back of the necklace Chloe got Adam to send me it has "RIP Chester Bennington" engraved on it.'

'And you think she might have hidden something where you buried your dead hamster?'

'Look, I know it sounds crazy, but I couldn't work out why Chloe got Adam to send me the damn necklace. Hannah just retrieved it when she went to my house.'

'Okay, did she find anything else of interest while she was there?'

'Max, I need to go to South Norwood Country Park ...'

Jen stretched her legs as the car pulled up outside the gates of the park. Max had let her escape out of the office but asked Sam to go along with her just in case. She wasn't really sure what the PA was going to do if she got into trouble, though. Give the attackers paper cuts? What difficulty would she get into in the middle of a park anyway? Well, she might get told off for digging up the park, though she had come armed with a hand shovel and she and Chloe had buried Chester in a secluded spot.

'So, run it past me again, why did you bury him here?' Sam asked.

'Because we wanted him to be free. Chloe and I used to run here, so we knew we could see him every day and know he was watching us like he did at home.'

'Except you moved away.'

'Yeah there is that ...' Jen went quiet for a moment. 'I bet Chloe used to still run here though.' Sam didn't say anything as they continued into the park. Jen wasn't warming to her in the slightest. She'd have preferred to have been let out the office with Detective Brown or just a driver.

'Okay, this is where we buried him. Under this tree.' Jen started to march off over to the secluded area with Sam dragging behind. 'Just here,' Jen said as she bent down and started digging.

'How far down did you bury him?' Sam asked as she watched.

'Far enough that no one would ever find him. We made him his own coffin.' Sam rolled her eyes as Jen kept digging. 'Bingo, found you,' Jen said, lifting a metal box from the ground and sitting back against the tree.

'Wait, a minute ...' Sam interrupted her. 'You're not going to open it, are you?'

'Of course I am. If Chloe left me something it would have been left in here,' Jen said, cracking open the lid

'I think I'm going to be sick.'

'Pull yourself together, Sam. We buried him in a cardboard box. There'll be nothing of him left other than some bones.' She was right. She opened the tin and saw that someone had taken the time to wrap Chester's remains in a cloth. Right next to him was a USB stick. 'Wanna see?'

'No.'

'Take this, then,' Jen said, handing Sam the stick which she immediately dropped like it was on fire.

'I'm not taking that. It might have dead rat on it.'

'Sam, first off Chester was a hamster. Secondly, this isn't the box we buried him in and thirdly I would think by the time Chloe had dug him up, he'd have been long decomposed. His bones have been wrapped up. Sure you don't wanna look?'

'No, no, I'm good,' Sam said, bending down to pick the USB up.

'Great.' Jen was about to put the lid on the tin when she saw the tiniest bit of paper with the tiniest handwriting. It said 'sorry'.

No more needed to be said. Chloe either knew she was in danger or this was her back-up plan. Chloe told Adam to send the necklace if she was ever not back. She'd have known that Jen would have realised who Chester Bennington referred to, leading to their old pet's burial ground. She could cry all the tears she needed to once this was all over and whoever had killed Chloe was safely behind bars.

'The Tech team have put a rush on the stick, Jen,' Max told her as she sat in his office, playing the waiting game. 'How did you and Sam get on?'

'She wasn't too impressed when she discovered we were digging up my hamster, but I'm sure she'll be over the trauma soon.'

'She has shown some promise. I was going to speak to her about training to join the team.'

If Jen had been drinking anything she would have spat it back out again. 'Judging by her performance out in the field it might be best to leave her doing her day job,' Jen warned. 'I'm gonna grab a cuppa while we wait. Want anything?' Jen added as she stood up, knowing that she needed to move or do something before it drove her crazy.

'I'm good.'

Jen left Max's office and offered a friendly smile to Sam. Had she been too hard on the girl if Max was considering recruiting her to the team?

Upon her return to the office, she noticed Max standing seriously at his desk.

'Is everything okay?' she asked.

'I've received the files back from Tech.'

'Great, what's on them?' Jen asked excitedly as she moved around to look at Max's computer.

'It's James.' Right on the front of Max's computer there was a photo of her husband and Harry at some nightclub.

'What the fuck?' Jen shouted. 'Is he on the other ones too?' She was beginning to panic now. Had this all been a set-up from the day she met James at the nightclub? Had he groomed her all those years in what she thought was wedded bliss?

'No, he's just in the one. Harry is in the second with someone I certainly don't recognise.'

Jen tried to wipe the picture of James from her mind. She had to forget about it and focus. 'Nope, no idea who he is. Sorry.'

'The third is just some pub,' Max said, flicking onto it.

'Don't recognise that either,' she said with some relief. 'Is that all that was on the stick?'

'No, I've got a list of dealers and a list of ports along the Thames.'

'Okay, any idea what that means?' Jen couldn't shake the image of James from her head. If Chloe had taken these photos she must have seen or even known her husband. This was something that Jen hadn't even considered; she couldn't even imagine being so close to her former best friend and not realising it. She wondered if James had even noticed he was having his photo taken, given the relaxed body language and the smile on his face.

'I'm going to contact Hannah, get the list of dealers sent over to the team in Nottingham. Who knows? They might be able to separate them into rival gangs.'

'Max, what about James?' she said, unable to keep the panic from her voice.

'I've got someone watching him. He isn't going anywhere without me knowing.'

'There's no way he's involved in this, I know my husband!'

'What, like he knows his wife?'

It had come as a hard blow as the words left Max's mouth. He was right, she had been hiding from James in plain sight for the past ten years. Had he done the same to her? There was no way he was a head of a drugs empire, was there?

'Max, I've got to fight for my husband. There is no way he'd be involved in this. How would he have known about the pills to start with? Let alone leave it for so long to start up again?'

'What if he was already involved?'

'I knew everyone who was involved in George's network and neither Harry nor James were part of it.'

'But how do you know Jen? You've been so blindsided by all of this. You need to have a really good think about how well you know James.'

Jen didn't answer. She didn't have the energy to stand there and argue with Max, but she knew, she just *knew*, that James was innocent. Didn't she? Or had the last ten years of Jen's life been a bigger lie than she ever imagined? Was that why George knew about her family? Maybe James was working for him …

DI Chris Jackson

'DI Jackson, I've just received something from the team in London. Are you able to show me how I can put it on the screen?' Hannah asked as she walked in on Chris and Clive talking in the team's office. Chris couldn't help but notice her flushed complexion, like she'd been rushing around.

'Yeah of course,' he said, getting up to help her as she did that thing where she pushed the loose strand of hair behind her ear. 'I'm guessing they've been sent to your phone?' Chris asked as he held out his hand for the phone.

'Am I able to Bluetooth them over or something?' Hannah replied, seemingly not wanting to give up her phone.

'I guess you could send them to me and I'll open them in my work email on the system?' She wasn't half making things more difficult.

'You'd better let me have your email address, Detective.' As they stood close to each other at the main computer Chris became more aware of her. He noticed the freckles on her face, though she had clearly tried to hide them behind her mask of make-up. He needed to move away from this woman. It was bound to be a trap. She was an undercover detective; she knew how to lure lesser men than him.

'Right, do you want to talk us through it?' Chris asked triumphantly as the information appeared on screen.

'This is a list of all the dealers we believe Chloe compiled before her death. We were hoping you'd both be able to check the list and separate them for us?'

'Well, I can see several names straight away,' Clive spoke up. 'To me they look like a list of the main players in Nottingham. With a couple I don't recognise.'

'Clive, you said there were two rival gangs in Nottingham?' Hannah asked. 'Would you and Chris be able to separate this list into who is who on each side, so we're left with the main players?'

'Shouldn't be a problem, Hannah. Will take us all of five minutes.'

'Good to hear, DI Manson. One more thing. If we wanted to see first-hand these drugs being distributed, when do you think would be the best time to head out to Nottingham?' Hannah asked.

'I'm afraid the weekends tend to be the best time, but with the influx of students arriving in Nottingham, there's always something happening.'

'I'm not sure which hotel I've been booked into, but would you mind giving us a tour of Nottingham's hot spots?'

'I was about to suggest the same myself,' Clive answered, looking over at Chris.

'How about ...' Chris began 'you go and get yourselves checked into wherever you're staying, and Clive and I will begin looking at the list. I'll grab one of my female officers and meet you in town later tonight and Clive can give us all the grand tour?' Chris couldn't believe he was volunteering himself for a night out on the tiles. He knew he wouldn't be short of volunteers, but he had surprised himself.

'Sounds good to me,' Clive responded in agreement, rising from his seat. 'I need a stretch. Meet you back in your office, Chris?'

There was nothing more Chris could do other than nod in agreement. Clive led Hannah towards the car park, hastily making arrangements. Chris wasn't sure what type of undercover stakeout Clive and Hannah where planning. He'd better hurry up and recruit one of the female officers for what would no doubt be a fun-packed night out.

Chris wasn't sure what to expect when he pulled up outside Detective Sally Croft's house. She wasn't hard to convince once she learnt the stakeout wouldn't involve sitting in the back of a van. He and Clive had sat there for over an hour going through the list they had been provided, splitting the names into three groups: the two known groups in Nottingham and those names which were unknown. Hopefully after the night on the town, things might become a bit clearer.

Chris watched as Sally kissed her boyfriend goodbye and wobbled her way towards his car. As always the scent of her perfume assaulted his nose seconds before Sally climbed in, and tonight she had laid it on thick.

'Sorry, boss. It took longer than I expected to get ready.'

'Not a problem.'

'What's the game plan? I was pretty surprised when you said it wouldn't involve sitting in the back of a van people-watching all night.'

'Basically, we're having a night out with Hannah and DI Manson.'

'Okay, I hope she's paying,' Sally muttered. Maybe Sally hadn't taken much of a shine to Hannah barging her way in.

Chris drove into Nottingham, filling Sally in on Harry's lack of movements since the car had been stationed outside his house.

'Do you think he knows we're watching him?'

'If he's the hardened drug lord Hannah and her team seem to think then possibly.'

Chris was in two minds whether to park up at the Nottingham holding cells and walk into town. After seeing what Sally was wearing on her feet, he didn't think she would appreciate the walk. Chris had offered Clive a lift to Nottingham, but he had declined and said he wanted to pop into the office prior to going into town. They all agreed that they would meet up in the Market Square at 9 p.m. and, just after Chris and Sally arrived, Clive appeared.

'Clive, this is Detective Sally Croft.'

'Detective Croft,' Clive said as he went to greet her with a kiss on the cheek.

'Have you seen Hannah?' Chris asked.

'Not yet, but I haven't been here for long.' Chris looked around the Market Square. Sally soon started flirting with Clive, giving Chris the sinking feeling that he was about to be paired up with Hannah if she ever appeared.

'Excuse me,' Clive said as he answered his phone and Sally peeled herself away from him. Chris tried his hardest to make small talk with Sally but after being in the office all day with her there wasn't much left to say.

'Well, well, this is a turn up for the books. Our Harry boy seems to be on the move.'

'I wonder where he's off to?' Chris asked.

'I've asked the team to keep a tail on him and not lose him.'

'Will be interesting to see if he turns up in Nottingham,' Sally commented.

'I wonder what's happened to Hannah?' Chris said. He was already beginning to feel like a gooseberry.

'There must be a bar we can go in? That'll be warmer than us standing outside in this,' Sally said, visibly shivering.

'Where do you suggest we head first?' Chris asked as he looked around again for Hannah. She made a living tracking people, so surely she'd find them in one of the many bars around here? 'Maybe if we head up into Hockley, we can make our way around from there.' Chris began walking ahead but started to slow down. He needed to look like he was with Sally and Clive. Although they were both too busy flirting with each other to notice he was up ahead, anyway. Should he have brought one of his other team members who would at least look like they were taking things seriously?

'Where is best to start?' Chris turned to ask Clive again, who was completely preoccupied with talking to Sally.

'The drugs have mainly come out of the nightclub on Plumtree Street. We can either head straight there or we could hit a couple of bars first.'

Chris really wasn't sure what he was doing. He couldn't stop seeing himself as a police officer, not a reveller. Maybe that was where he was going wrong? He was meant to be undercover. They wouldn't see anyone dealing or even be offered anything if he looked like a police officer. He needed to relax into it. Clive and Sally seemed to be acting like drunken fools and they hadn't touched a drop of alcohol. Did he just need to lighten up?

'Let's make a start in here.' Chris found himself declaring as he led the way into one of the bars they were about to pass. 'What can I get you guys?' He memorised their orders and then pushed through the crowds, finally making it to the bar.

'I know you ...' one of the revellers came barging into Chris as he stood waiting to be served. 'You're that DI Jackson bloke from that Unit thingy.' The guy was starting to sway and slur his words as Chris looked at him, unsure how he was going to get out of this one. It was only just after 9 p.m., and it was far too early for him to be calling for back-up and arresting someone if they got violent.

Just then, a girl came up and put her arm over Chris' shoulder.

'Sorry, the queue for the ladies' was crazy. You got them drinks yet?' Chris wasn't sure how to answer as he looked at the female and her jet-black hair. 'Oh, who's your friend?' she asked. Chris needed to think fast. He needed to get out of this situation and he'd decide what to do about the girl afterwards.

'Some guy who thinks I'm some detective from the ... what was it?' Chris responded.

The girl laughed. 'That's the funniest thing I've heard all week. We come to Nottingham for a quiet night out and now you're a detective. We should come here more often.'

'Sorry, think you're mistaken,' Chris clarified for the guy.

'Oh, oh, I'm sorry,' the guy apologised as he swayed back to his friends.

'Thanks for that,' Chris said when he was sure he was out of range.

'You gonna buy a girl a drink then?' came the reply.

'Yeah, sorry. I was just about to order for my mates. What can I get you?'

'A double vodka will do nicely, thanks,' she said as she looked at him like she was trying to read his mind.

'Thanks for getting me out of that tight spot just then.' He thanked her as he passed over the drink.

'Not a problem. He was all over me earlier and I told him to shove off. I told him my boyfriend was on his way. Obvs pinned you as him when I came over.'

'I'm not sure which one I should have been most afraid of, a detective inspector or your boyfriend.' The girl saw the funny side of it and laughed.

'Thanks for the drink. I'm gonna find my mates now. Have a good night.'

'You too.' And then she was gone, as quickly as she'd appeared. Should he have asked her for her number? Did he perhaps know her? It had been incredibly random for her to appear like that.

'Who were you chatting up at the bar?' Sally asked as Chris made his way back to them.

'Well, a guy clocked who I was, but then this girl appeared from nowhere and told him I was her boyfriend and he soon backed off.'

'You pulled then?' Clive asked in his loud booming voice, clearly wanting the whole bar to hear his mate had pulled.

'No. I bought her a drink, and she vanished into the night.'

'Did you check and see if she left a glass slipper? That could have been the woman of your dreams.'

'I'll make sure I check next time, because with the amount of people that are in here it would have been stood on and smashed if she had.' Chris felt proud to be up on all his Disney Princess references. 'Have you heard any more on Hannah or Harry's movements?' he asked, desperately trying to move the conversation on to what they should be doing.

'Nothing from Hannah, but from what I've last heard Harry has dropped his car and is now on foot in Nottingham. One of my guys is on his tail.'

Chris tried to relax, but he was too conscious of what other people were thinking, seeing him sat there with a guy and a girl who were practically all over each other. But in all of this, in the back of his mind, he was still thinking about the Garner family and Jen; away from home for another night.

It was a little past eleven o'clock when they entered Dioxide in the middle of the Lace Market. After paying a ridiculous amount to get in, Chris wasn't surprised to see the place packed with students. Did they not have lectures to attend in the morning? Or was he beginning to become old before his time, too used to sitting at home with a cup of cocoa? The music was loud, the drink prices were truly extortionate and he couldn't hear himself think. Plus, the one person who had wanted a tour of Nottingham hot spots hadn't even turned up!

Chris found a place to sit and planted himself on a stool overlooking the dancefloor. He'd sit here people-watching, give it another couple of hours and then make an excuse and leave.

At least that was his plan until he noticed Harry, or at least someone who looked like him. He was also acting really strangely but, then again, from an onlooker's perspective, so was Chris. He looked around and spotted Clive signalling him over.

'Have you heard from your guy? Is Harry here?' Chris asked, walking over to him.

'Just this second we bumped into each other in the entrance. Here take this,' Clive added, giving Chris a bottle of something random.

'I think he's over there.' Chris attempted to point without seeming too obvious.

'I'll get hold of my guy and get him to check. He should still be watching Harry. Leave it with me.' Chris looked around the club from his vantage point. No Hannah, no sign of Sally and now Clive had left him. How was he supposed to make an arrest now? He needed to catch Harry dealing first. Taking a gulp from his bottle of what tasted like beer, he returned to his stool. As he watched the dancefloor, he was aware of an attractive blonde coming to sit next to him. He couldn't help but wonder if someone was having a laugh at his expense. Two fit girls in one night, when he was lucky if he ever got approached by any?

'I'm sorry, I'm not interested,' Chris said as he turned to face the woman beside him. As he looked at her more closely, he couldn't help but wonder if it was the same girl from the bar. He recognised the twinkle in her eyes, the freckles on her face. Hang on ...

She stood up and moved in front of where Chris was sat. 'Play along,' she whispered seductively into his ear as her lips brushed towards his neck. He didn't have any choice but to play along as her tongue found its way into his mouth. All his primal urges were telling him to touch her, as their mouths continued to collide. Chris really had no idea what was going on when she pulled away from him, giggling.

'Come on Detective Inspector, you can do better than that.' Chris looked at the woman again, as she moved and straddled him. 'Care to dance, Inspector?' Chris was suddenly unsure what to do. This woman knew he was a detective and now she was willing him on to the dancefloor. Clive and Sally were nowhere to be seen, no doubt making out somewhere, so he couldn't signal anyone. As she brought his left hand up to her face something fizzled and sparked between them. He gently cupped her face and brought his closer to hers. Their mouths met again and his arms started to make their way around down her back towards her amazing arse. Chris was completely caught up in the moment as his body was beginning to react to the position he suddenly found himself in.

'Let's dance.' She dragged him onto the dancefloor and he suddenly became twenty-one again as this unbelievable woman continued to rub herself up against him. He needed to stay in control. The last thing he needed was to get a stonking great hard-on. As she manoeuvred her body away from him, he grabbed her close, kissing her and making sure he got a good feel of her body as an electric urge hit and rushed through his veins.

'Shall we go in for the kill?' she whispered after they had been dancing around each other for what seemed like a lifetime. As she took his hand, Chris wished he was being led away for something more physical. He knew in his heart where they were really going, and it wasn't to make out.

'After you,' he said, nibbling on her ear, as they moved

towards the edge of the dancefloor. As they stopped, he grabbed her again for good measure.

'Hey, you got anything?' the girl asked Chris' target.

The lad looked around and moved closer and almost whispered 'What are you after?' Everything that Chris had hoped wasn't true started to dawn on him as he realised he needed to lay it on thick, because they weren't just talking to anyone. They had just propositioned Harry.

'We're looking for something so we can continue the party back in the hotel room,' said the girl. Chris began to kiss the back of the woman's neck as his arousal started to go through the roof.

'It'll be fifty pounds. Get your bloke to follow me into the toilets in five.'

She turned to look at Chris and removed a rolled up fifty-pound note from her cleavage. As he turned to follow their suspect, she grabbed him again. Pulling himself away from her, Chris followed the guy into the men's loos, which seemed to have more light than the club itself. The sudden scent of urine brought Chris crashing back to earth. Walking over to the guy he exchanged the cash for a single pill in a small plastic bag and then left. Chris placed the bag between his body and the elastic of his boxers.

As he looked around, he was once again met by his accomplice. She pulled him close and nibbled on his ear, placing her hand into his left pocket and bringing out an identical small bag. She removed the pill and placed it into her mouth. She smiled at him and brought her mouth towards his as she transferred the pill into his mouth. Unsure what he was about to swallow he took the pill, pulled away and swallowed. Whatever that was, he was sure he would find out in about thirty minutes.

'Come on, let's go and make our own fun,' she said as she led Chris out of the club and into a taxi. Her hands were all over him as they drove the short distance between the club and a hotel.

'This isn't a good idea,' Chris said as she led him into the reception area of the hotel. 'I don't take random girls back from nightclubs.' She continued to lead him through the hotel reception. As the lift doors opened, she forcefully shoved him into the lift.

'We've got to put on a show for the cameras,' she whispered once more, as the magnetic charge, pulled them together again and their mouths met.

As they got to her floor, she kicked off her shoes. 'Come and get me,' she yelled, running down the hotel corridor and giggling as he did exactly what she told him to do. As she stopped, he pinned her up against her door, feeling for the handle that seconds later clicked. They were in the room.

Chris wasn't sure whether he was lucky or unlucky when his companion's personality changed.

'Well done, Inspector. I had my doubts, but you managed to pull through in the end,' she said as pulled off her wig, letting her natural hair fall from the hair net.

'Woah.' Chris stood back and looked at Hannah. 'Shouldn't we go and arrest that bloke who I assume was Harry?'

'Nah, leave it to the clean-up team. I'm sure he'll be waiting for you in the holding cells in the morning. Anyway, let's see the pill, assuming you've still got it?' Chris reached into the waistband of his boxers and pulled out the bag, inspecting the pill before passing it to Hannah.

'How did you know?' he asked, spotting the imprint.

'We knew Harry had headed into Dioxide and Clive said you had a good visual on the bloke, so we decided to reel him in.'

'And I was the perfect patsy.'

'I guess you could see it that way, but we got a result. What was your plan anyway? Sit and watch him all night then chase after him at the end? At least this way he did the transaction. We've got the pill and DI Manson can pick him up.'

'Was that you at the bar as well?'

'Afraid so. I got a bit worried when you were spotted and, not having a clue who we were looking for, I reacted the best I could to the situation.' Hannah continued to undress in front of Chris who was now totally sober from his experience and was wondering where he should be looking.

'I guess I'd better head off?'

'Nah, you need to leave it for a bit. Unless you're super quick in bed, then be my guest.'

Chris tried to laugh it off as Hannah took shots at his pride.

Just then a device Hannah had in the room beeped.

'They've just arrested him, with what they are expecting to be Ecstasy all marked up with our mystery imprint.'

'Quite a successful night then.'

'All in a day's work. At least you got to do the fun bit. Your colleague Sally isn't going to be too impressed with you in the morning.'

'How come?'

'Well, let's put it this way. She had already formed a bond with the DI. We couldn't then tell her to be all over you.'

'So, they sent you to me. What was that tablet you gave me by the way?'

'Nothing to worry about, Detective. It was just some chalk tablet we use. You're not going to be hallucinating anytime soon. You weren't that bad though. Who knows? When I get back to London, I might suggest they headhunt you. I'm gonna jump in the shower ... unless you want to join me?'

Chris laughed, knowing what answer he really wanted to give and where his primal instincts wanted to be. But this wasn't the time to be hit on by the naked detective in the shower.

Chapter Twenty-One

Jen had presided over Chloe's desk since she had arrived in the office. She didn't like the hours detectives worked; she much preferred the stay-at-home-mum timetable. She'd had such weird dreams overnight: she was running her usually route, but Chester was there waving at her. She wasn't sure what was going on her head and what it all meant, but she knew she hadn't run for days and that was usually how she cleared her mind. Unfortunately, there was no chance of that happening anytime soon. She'd been sat there daydreaming when Max appeared at the desk.

'Jen, there's been a turn of events over night. Grab Sam and come to the meeting room.'

'O ... kay,' Jen replied, unsure what her response was supposed to be as she turned and looked for Sam. Jen gathered her stuff and was about to head into the meeting when Sam appeared, looking all flustered.

'Sorry, sorry,' she said as she walked through the office.

'Max wants us in the meeting room,' Jen told her.

'Great, I'm running late and everything. I've not even had a chance to get a coffee.'

'Don't worry about it, Sam. I'll go and get the drinks, give you time to get sorted.'

'You sure?' Sam questioned as if Jen was pulling a great big prank on her. Jen just smiled and left Sam to get organised. Jen wondered if she had played the heartless bitch a bit too much. Who knew? One day, Sam might be the one person between her and a bullet.

By the time Jen made it to the meeting room with drinks in hand, Sam looked more composed and was waiting with Max.

'Right, there's no easy way to say this ...' Max began. 'Harry Greenidge was arrested last night dealing Ecstasy in a Nottingham club.'

Jen wasn't sure whether her mouth fell open or it just felt like it; this wasn't the Harry she knew. 'Hang on, what?' she questioned.

'His car was later found with more pills and they all bear the George Crawford logo. The car has now been moved to a secure location to be searched further.'

'Why on earth was Harry selling Class A drugs? Never mind the branded drugs? Was there anyone else with him? I mean, was James there as well?' The question left her mouth before she could stop it.

'From what Hannah said to me earlier, it sounds like he was arrested alone. He was tailed from his home into Nottingham and then on to the club.'

'So that means you were correct, Jen. The CCTV footage Chloe had collated did have Harry in. Given his arrest, this pretty much confirms his identity,' Sam said with some excitement.

'I don't like this. Have they had the chance to interview him yet?' Jen questioned.

'Hannah was on her way in when she phoned, but I doubt it. She also mentioned that the team down there had managed to work on the list of dealers on Chloe's spreadsheet. The majority of them are from the two rival gangs in Nottingham, but there are still some unknown.'

This was all getting a bit too close to home for Jen.

'Did either of you get anywhere with the visitor lists, Sam?' Max asked.

'Unfortunately not. Though Gwen and Tilly Adams visited George early on, they don't seem to have communicated any further with him while he was in prison,' Sam replied.

'What about Harry?' Jen asked as Sam began typing away on her spreadsheet.

'Nope.'

'So how is Harry connected to all of this, if we can't find a connection to George? Unless ...'

DI Chris Jackson

Chris arrived at the office just after 10 a.m. He'd got home, showered, shaved and had a stand-off with Fluff who clearly knew he had been elsewhere.

As he got out of the car, he was sure he heard a wolf whistle. He scanned the car park, looking for the culprit before entering the station. The mocking started before he had even removed his ID from his pocket to be swiped in.

'Did you have a good night, sir?'

'Was she good in bed?'

'Sally told us all about it and showed us the pictures.'

What pictures? he wondered, as he stood being continuously mocked by his team.

'At least one of us got it last night,' Chris shouted back at them, leaving them to whistle and jeer as he headed towards his office. He didn't mind being mocked. It came with the territory. Finally making it to the safety of his office, he took off his coat, dropped his bag and made his way to his desk. Someone had beaten him to it as he found a pair of lacy knickers on his chair. A slideshow of pictures from the night before played on a loop on his screen. Chris couldn't help but watch the footage which looked like it had come from the security cameras inside the club and hotel. Suddenly there was a knock on his door and the smell of perfume infiltrated his senses.

'Sir.'

'Sally, did you have a good night?'

'Not as good as yours.' She chuckled.

'Are you to thank for the slideshow?'

'Afraid I can't take credit for that. Sir, I'm going home for some sleep.'

'You okay?'

'Yeah, just a very long night that didn't go the way I was expecting.'

'I thought you said you'd got back?'

'Yeah, DI Manson dropped me home long enough to jump in the shower and then I came back to work.'

'You should have just stayed in bed.'

'There was work that needed doing, but now I just want to sleep.'

'Get yourself home. We can always give you a call if we need you.'

'Thanks, sir.'

Sally left his office and he was alone with his slideshow. He clicked the mouse, bringing his computer back to life with the reassurance of the police logo and blue background of his desktop. He logged in and clicked to open his emails before he heard the recognisable laughter of Clive Manson approaching his office.

'Good morning, Chris. Good night I hear?' he said with a wink. Either that or he had something in his eye.

'It ended rather unexpectedly.'

'I've seen the pictures of you in action.'

'The guy we picked up, I'm guessing it was Harry Greenidge?' Chris asked, desperately trying to steer the conversation in a different direction.

'Yes, he's at the holding cells, I was hoping we could have a debrief with Hannah and come up with a plan of action.' Clive winked again as Chris seriously started considering that there was something in his eye. 'I was just coming to check you'd made it in okay.'

'I'm guessing these belong to you, Clive,' Chris said, throwing the underwear towards him.

'No. Maybe someone left them here last night?' Clive said as he held them up to study before throwing them back.

* * *

After grabbing himself a strong coffee and a couple of biscuits, Chris made his way to the team's office. As he stood behind the door, he could hear Clive's distinctive booming voice.

Be professional, Chris told himself as he opened the door, ready for whatever ridicule he was about to face. The first person he saw was Hannah. Fighting flashbacks of the night before, he took a large gulp of coffee.

'Morning all.' Chris tried desperately hard not to make eye contact with Hannah and walked over to where everyone else was standing. 'Sally's gone home. I informed her that I'd call if she was needed back here.'

'Okay, well we can continue without her,' DI Manson replied.

Chris planted himself on the table at the front of the room. Every time he stole a glance at Hannah an electric urge ran through his body. Should he go and say something to her? If so, what? *Sorry for last night?* It wasn't like he had done anything wrong, had he? He was a grown man and a professional. Why was this woman, who he was likely never to see again after they'd cracked this case, having such an effect on him?

'Okay,' Clive said as he moved over to the incident board, pinning a new photo in the centre of it. 'This is Harry Greenidge who we arrested last night for dealing Class A drugs. When we searched him, he was carrying around ten Ecstasy tablets which all had this imprint.'

'Do you remember if Harry was on Chloe's original list?' Hannah asked as Chris moved across the room, pulling up the list on the main screen.

'I can't see Harry mentioned on here. Does that not imply that Chloe wasn't investigating him and there was someone further up the chain?' Chris asked.

'I think we can say that Harry wasn't involved with column A or C, right? So, in my mind it means he must be involved with someone in this middle column of names we didn't recognise,' Hannah responded, pushing that loose strand of hair from her face again.

'Didn't you say right at the beginning of all this, Clive, that tensions were high as there was someone trying to muscle into other dealers' patches?' Chris questioned.

'Yeah.'

'I might be making assumptions, but Chloe knew who she was tracking so why isn't Harry on this list?' Chris asked.

'We need to find out where he got the drugs from, then go from there,' Clive responded.

'There is also something else we need to consider. Harry is best friends with someone called James Garner whose wife Jennifer is still missing.'

'Do you think that Harry could be involved in Jennifer's disappearance?' Clive asked.

'I don't know. I really didn't want to believe it was domestic violence, but now we've got drugs involved and the commonality of the imprint ...' Chris caught Hannah's eye as she smiled at him.

'Was James Garner at the club last night?' Hannah questioned.

'I didn't see him, but that doesn't prove anything. I'd like to think he was tucked up at home looking after his family.'

'I must admit, it's a cause for concern,' Hannah began as she made eye contact with Chris. Could she sense the urges he was feeling? 'Has there been any progress made in the missing person's case?'

'I'm afraid not. Due to resources available and it not being a priority, the case has been scaled back,' Chris responded sourly.

'I'm not sure what you think, Clive. Our main priority right now needs to be to find out where our suspect got his batch of drugs from,' Hannah said.

'Chris, is there any cause for concern for Jennifer's wellbeing?' Clive asked.

'As of right now, we have no idea where she is. My gut feeling is, unless her husband is a super criminal mastermind, it's very unlikely that the drugs have come from that household.'

'Then let's concentrate on Harry and see where that leads us. Hannah, are you happy if Chris and I speak to our suspect? We can concentrate on where the drugs have come from, and see where the conversation goes from there.'

'I think that might be a good idea. Keep me out of it for now,' Hannah agreed.

'Chris, are you happy with that?' Clive asked.

Chris nodded and the plan was put into place.

Jen Garner

It was decided that Sam would try to trace Gwen and Tilly Adams, while Jen would look at the list of ports and lifeboat and police stations. All the ports listed ran along the Thames from the North Sea to the centre of London, but that seemed to be their only connection. The more she studied the list the more she wondered if Chloe knew the drugs were coming in from outside the UK.

'Jen, I think I've got something,' said Sam.

'Shoot.'

'From searching, I've got one Gwen Adams who had one child, Tilly. I've pulled up Tilly's birth certificate and the father is listed as unknown. This is Gwen now,' Sam said as a photo appeared on the screen of a, clearly, surgically enhanced blonde female.

'Is there anything she hasn't had surgery on?' Jen muttered.

'Now Tilly is the one we've got problems with. I can only trace her so far.'

'Name change possibly?' Jen wondered aloud.

'Not sure. Her national insurance code isn't being used, but that doesn't mean anything because she might not be working.'

'What have you found on Gwen Adams?'

'Gwen seems to be an interesting one. She's been linked to many minor celebrities and crime bosses.'

'Arm candy?'

'Possibly, but I also noticed she has a pretty nasty drug habit. She was caught up in a raid last year and, to cut a long story short, she was bailed to a Jessica Adams of 7 Oaks Drive, Clapton, which is the first time a Jessica Adams comes up on the system.'

Jen gasped as she heard Jess's name. 'Could Tilly have possibly changed her name to Jessica? Do we have a location for Gwen?' Jen started to fire questions at Sam, giving her little time to investigate.

'Afraid not, she seems to have vanished. Probably on some dealer's arm somewhere.'

'Okay, because I've got a really bad feeling about this, Harry is dating someone called Jess. I'm beginning to wonder if this is the same Jess who bailed Gwen last year, which would explain the drugs connection.' Sam just looked at Jen, unable to offer an explanation.

'Max!' Jen said, running into his office. 'Max, I think we've got something.'

'Give me a minute,' he said, looking up from whatever he was typing.

'Max, I think I know what Harry's connection is to George!' Jen said, not wanting to wait for Max to finish. 'I think Harry's girlfriend, Jess, is the same person who was visiting George Crawford as Tilly with her mum.'

'Isn't that a bit of a stretch?' he questioned giving up on whatever he was trying to type.

'Come through to the meeting room, and I'll get Sam to explain.'

Max got up and followed Jen back into the meeting room where he listened to the explanation. 'Great work, Sam. But with George behind bars, where are they getting the drugs from?'

'I think that's where these list of ports come in,' Jen replied. She knew she should be focusing on that, but she really wanted to work on the Harry and Jess issue.

'Could the drugs be coming in from outside of the UK?' Sam questioned.

'It would explain the list,' Jen responded.

'Do you need me to plot them for you? It'll take a couple of seconds,' Sam offered.

'Great. Thank you, Sam,' Jen watched as Sam pulled the map and started to highlight all the ports Chloe had listed.

'Okay, this is what we've got,' Sam said as she transferred them onto the main screen while Jen continued to look at it on the screen in front of her.

'There seems to be a lot of ports flagged in Gravesend. What was Chloe so interested in there?'

'I think I've got something,' Sam said, looking up.

'Go on,' Max prompted.

'I'm not sure. I'm wondering if someone is bringing drugs into the country via the Thames.'

'What makes you think that?' Jen questioned. It was beginning to look like she'd underestimated Sam all along.

'Chloe had listed all the lifeboat and police points along the Thames, especially in Gravesend, which is where the Thames meets the sea.'

'Okay, have we got a huge import issue then?' Max questioned as a look of grave concern fell across his face.

'She has noted that there's a lifeboat station in Gravesend, but then there is the Silverdale Gateway, which deals with large import and export goods and is closer to the sea,' Sam continued as Jen started to see the bigger picture.

'Okay, so why go there and not the port at Tilbury?'

'Looking at the map,' Jen said as she got up and moved to the main screen, 'the main port has stacks of containers that are waiting to be taken on to the next part of the journey. What if drugs are coming into the country in those containers?

Plus if they are coming in via Tilbury they've got to get past the police and lifeboat stations, and it's a smaller port.'

'A longer journey means more risks of being picked up. Plus, if they have someone on the inside at the Gateway ...' Sam added, picking the thread back up.

'I think we need to go and have a look round the Gateway and get a staff list,' Max concluded. 'Fancy a trip out again to the Silverdale Gateway with Jen, Sam?' he asked

'As long as we don't end up digging dead animals up.'

Jen laughed a bit too loudly at Sam's comment.

'Well, I'm not letting her go off on her own, so if you're free?' Max prompted.

'I'll get my coat,' Sam said, getting up.

'Is this really a good idea Max?' Jen questioned.

'She knows what she's doing. If there was any really danger, I wouldn't be letting you go either. Plus, hopefully, when you get back we'll have news from Hannah about these drugs.'

DI Chris Jackson

Arriving at the holding cells was now becoming a frequent occurrence for Chris. He wondered if the staff there all knew about his antics and he would be faced with more mocking. Clive had been full of questions about his night with Hannah on the way over. Wanting to play the gentleman, Chris had just said that he never kissed and told. But this just seemed to ignite further questions from Clive. Chris couldn't pretend he hadn't been attracted to Hannah; she had looked hot.

'You going to lead?' Chris asked, wanting to steer Clive away from the previous night.

'If you're okay with that.'

They were able to sail into the holding cells, with Clive being a regular, and were soon sitting in an interview room waiting for Harry.

'Good morning, Harry,' Clive said as the short, ginger-haired man made his way into the room followed by a young officer. Chris could see him more clearly now he was in the light and not the dark nightclub. The bruises from his run-in with James were still visible.

'So it's you that James had an altercation with?' Chris said as Harry sat down and Clive began to run over the procedural questions.

'Harry George Greenidge, I'm arresting you on suspicion of dealing a Class A drug with the intent to supply.' Chris watched as Harry just sat back in his chair and stretched his legs out, lightly kicking them both in the process. Arrogance and overconfidence oozed from him.

'Can you please confirm your name and date of birth for the tape?' Chris knew this was going to be a long and fun interview when Clive's questions continued to be met with silence.

'Harry, I must inform you that you have the right to request a solicitor at any time. Can you please acknowledge for the tape that you have declined one at this time?'

Silence.

'Harry, I was wondering if you knew what the imprint on the batch of drugs we arrested you with means?'

'No comment.' Well at least they had some response out of him, even if it was just a no comment.

'Harry, these drugs have been causing quite a stir on the streets of Nottingham. Some people even say there is a new kid on the block, but we know you're not at the top of the chain, Harry. You're just someone's lackey.'

'No comment.'

Chris couldn't see Clive getting any response out of Harry. He seemed not to care about what he was being charged with.

'Do you know how long the prison sentence is for dealing a Class A drug? Are you really going to sit there and take the fall for some else?'

'No comment.'

Chris knew they couldn't mention the dead detective. He still had the Jen card to play and, seeing as they weren't getting anywhere, it was time to try something else.

'Where is Jennifer Garner, Harry?' he asked. Chris noticed the hint of recognition cross Harry's face.

'What have you done with her, Harry?'

Harry fidgeted in his seat.

'On the night of Sunday the 17th October, I saw you leave the Garner household and you know what I think? I think you've done something to Jennifer, and you went to visit James to discuss what to do with her body.'

'Murder carries a life sentence, Harry,' Clive said as he picked up the thread.

'Was she getting too annoying? Did she find out about yours and James' drug network and tell you she was going to the police?' Chris asked. 'You see Harry, we're giving you the chance to talk first. We're giving you the chance to tell your side of the story before we bring James in,' Chris continued.

'No comment.'

'Those poor children. What were their names again, Chris?' Clive asked. 'Losing their mother and father in the space of a week.'

'James has nothing to do with this,' Harry said, suddenly sitting forward.

'Sorry, Harry. Did you say something?' Chris asked. A dent no smaller than a pinhole had been made in Harry's defences.

'I said James has got nothing to do with this!' Harry almost shouted.

'Oh, sorry. So it was just you? Why did you kill his wife, Harry?'

Chris and Clive continued to throw questions at Harry, giving him little time to think and respond. 'Were you jealous, Harry? Did she not find you attractive?'

'Would she not leave her husband, is that it? Were you two having an affair?'

'I know nothing about Jen's disappearance,' Harry growled at them both.

'You see Harry, you aren't giving us anything to go on here. You're sitting there and everything we ask you, you respond with "No comment". We have a missing person who you're connected to. You don't just wake up one morning and find these drugs on your doormat and start selling them,' Chris said.

'No comment.'

'You aren't making things very easy for yourself, Harry. You will speak up and deny having anything to do with Mrs Garner's disappearance, but when it comes to what you have been arrested for, you stonewall us. You can't blame us for making assumptions,' Clive said as Harry sat back in his chair again.

'I've nothing to do with Jen's disappearance. You're asking the wrong person.'

'Maybe James has done something to his wife, Clive, which is why Harry was over there on Sunday?'

'Ah, I can see where you're coming from. We'd better leave you Harry and go and arrest Mr Garner. Do you mind giving social services a call Chris, and I'll begin to make arrangements?' Clive said as he started to move from his seat.

'Wait a minute,' Harry shouted as he pushed his chair back.

'Yes, Harry?'

'Look, James has nothing to do with his wife's disappearance. Those two are two of the most solid people I know.'

'Thank you for your input, Harry. We will make sure we take note of that when we start questioning James shortly.'

They stood up and exited the interview room, asking the young officer who had been stationed outside the room to escort Harry back to his cell.

Chris and Clive went in search of a drink. The canteen wasn't much to get excited about. The holding cells were run by a small team of officers; everyone else who came to the cells was only ever passing through as they brought or collected their prisoners. They sat at a spare table, wrapping their hands around their polystyrene cups as if trying to harness their magic powers.

'What do you make of Harry?' Clive asked.

'There's no doubt he's a dealer as we caught him red-handed. But as for everything else?'

'I didn't think we were going to get anything out of him until you mentioned Jennifer Garner.'

'Do you think he's capable of murder? Because don't forget we've got a murder case which is undoubtedly connected to all of this,' Chris said.

'If pushed, people are capable of anything. Do you think Jen has got herself caught up in all of this and been killed?' Clive asked the question that had crossed Chris' mind so many times since the arrest. The domestic abuse angle was still hanging in the air. Just because they hadn't managed to locate Jen at one of the women's shelters, it didn't mean she wasn't on the run. He couldn't see James being involved in all this. He just didn't fit the profile of your typical dealer, just like he didn't fit the profile of a wife beater.

'Honestly Clive, it's all too much of a coincidence.' Chris sighed, stretching out his legs. 'So where do we go from here? I don't want to say anything about Chloe without Hannah's say so. Could we get a warrant for his home and go and turn that over?'

'I can make some phone calls,' Clive replied, grabbing his phone from his pocket as Chris stared absentmindedly at his drink. Up until recently, Jen had been at the forefront of his mind – but now she'd been forced out of the way and all he kept thinking about was Hannah and the night before.

'A search warrant is being issued as I speak,' said Clive, looking up from his phone.

'Great, I'll phone the station, get a team together, speak to Hannah and see how they want to play this.'

Chris looked around at the curtain twitchers as the white tent was erected in Harry's front garden. He felt like waving at them sometimes. 'Ready when you are,' Clive said as he climbed into his white overalls.

'Isn't this a bit over the top for a house search?' Chris questioned.

'If this is a murder scene we need to be prepared. You're not a fan of these suits either?'

'Not the first thing I pull out in the morning.'

As they entered Harry's house, Chris noticed how immaculate and clean it was. It was a proper bachelor pad, but this bachelor had money as well. They began to do their initial search of all the rooms for any signs of a body or any noticeable forensics, but everything seemed to look like a showroom. There wasn't so much as a sock on the floor.

'Detective Jackson.'

'Dr Walsh,' Chris greeted her as she entered through Harry's front door. 'From our initial searches of the property, there are no bodies or blood evidence,' Chris told her.

'Perfect, I'll get my team to do a sweep while you search out whatever you're looking for.'

'If something did happen here, someone has done a good job cleaning it all up,' Chris said as he ran his finger across the top of the television.

Harry's home was now an area of interest. Every inch of the house was searched for anything that would explain where the drugs were coming from or any sign of Jen.

'Chris, I've found something,' Clive shouted from above him.

Chris cautiously climbed the stairs, unsure of what he was about to be faced with.

'What have you found?' he asked as he entered the room

to find Clive crouched on the floor, trying to see something at the back of the desk.

'Help me move this,' Clive directed as Chris began to help him manoeuvre a ridiculously heavy desk out of the way. 'Bingo,' Clive said, victoriously holding up one of the bags he'd removed from a hidden compartment. Chris looked into the space and couldn't believe what he was seeing. He had never seen so many drugs in one place. He stood up and moved out of the way. 'And there is the imprint we're looking for. Harry has a lot of explaining to do,' Clive concluded as he congratulated himself.

'I'm going to see if the pathologist has found anything,' Chris said, leaving Clive and his team with the drugs.

'Found anything?' Chris asked Dr Walsh who was busy doing a fingerprint search in the kitchen.

'Most probably not, but I'll keep searching until something pops up.'

'Clive has just found his stash upstairs.'

'I heard the celebrations. I'll finish up in here and head up and see if there's anything I need to do before the drugs get moved,' Dr Walsh said as she continued to look around the immaculate kitchen.

'Any signs of blood?' Chris asked the nearest CSI who apologised and continued to spray items in search of something.

Chris felt exhausted, having not had a solid night's sleep. He hadn't dared mention his tiredness to anyone because he knew all too well what their response would be.

Chapter Twenty-Two

Jen Garner

As they travelled through to the Silverdale Gateway, Jen could feel the excitement radiating from Sam. She really hoped that she hadn't made a mistake bringing her along. Jen doubted she would be in any danger, but when she thought about the man who followed her, Chloe's death and George Crawford's warning, she realised it was best to have someone with her – even if it was the PA.

'What do you need me to do?' Sam suddenly broke into her thoughts.

'I phoned the management before we left and I told them we had some concern about their security and would like to take a look around.'

'Who did you say we were?'

'Oh, some government agency.'

'And they bought it?'

'People believe anything you say these days when it comes to national security.'

Sam smiled, clearly unsure how to respond to that statement.

'So, how did you find your way into the department?' Jen asked Sam, trying to make conversation.

'I'm not totally sure myself.'

'Yep, that seems to be the beginning of everyone's story.'

'When I was applying for just general secretarial work, I never imagined that I'd end up having to sign the Official Secrets Act. I was just looking for something to tide me over until I decided what I wanted to do with my life. Five years on, I'm still here doing my part in saving the world.'

'Do you ever see yourself training as a detective?' Jen asked curiously, to which Sam responded with a laugh.

'Maybe? Sometimes I fantasise about it. About how great it would be, but right now I like my uncomplicated life.'

The words stung Jen. *Uncomplicated life*. She used to have one of those; get up, take the kids to school, go for a run, do housework, pick the kids up. What the hell was she doing driving at forty miles an hour into the unknown?

They arrived at the Gateway just after lunch, parked up and began to walk towards the glass building.

'What do I do? What do I say?' Sam asked as her nerves began to push their way to the surface.

'Nothing, don't panic. You'll be ace, you're that kind of person.'

'What do you mean, "that kind of person"?'

'Sam, you're outgoing, friendly, confident and you have time for anyone.' Sam looked at Jen curiously. 'We'll probably be escorted on a tour of the facilities. All you need to do is follow them around and ask questions about the place, their security and procedures. Pretend that you're looking at storing your most prized possession there and you want to be assured it will be safe.'

'I can do that.'

'You'll be a pro at this Sam, I promise.'

They both entered the glass building and headed over to reception. Jen always wondered what it would be like to work in a glass building. Could everyone really see what you were doing? She thought about the buildings in Nottingham and tried to remember if she'd ever looked up from the street below.

'Good morning, we're here to see Mr Gregory,' Jen said as she approached the reception desk. She didn't dare turn and look at Sam, hoping that she appeared calm and collected. They were left waiting in reception until a highly attractive young man came to greet them both.

'Good morning.'

'Thank you for taking the time to see us, Mr Gregory. I'm sorry for the short notice.'

'Not a problem Miss ...'

'Klee and this is my colleague, Katharine.'

'Nice to meet you both,' Mr Gregory said, shaking both their hands. 'Shall we start with the tour and you can ask your questions when we get back to my office?'

Sam seemed to be holding herself together pretty well, though Jen still dreaded every moment she took a breath. She needed to trust her, right? They were both working on the same case, one way or another.

Mr Gregory escorted the girls around the site for well over an hour, and to Jen's surprise, Sam asked questions with a degree of confidence and keen interest. She also flirted, which undoubtedly got their tour guide on side.

'That completes our tour.'

'Thank you for your time, Mr Gregory,' Jen said as he led them both to his office.

'If you want to help yourself to a drink, I'll go and find where we are with the staff list,' he said as he left the room.

Sam reached over and poured herself a drink from the decanter, knocking it back straight away. 'Sorry mega thirsty,' Sam said, noticing Jen looking over at her.

'You did well,' Jen praised her as Mr Gregory reappeared with several sheets of paper.

'I've got this printed off. Can I ask what the security issue is?' he questioned.

'I'm afraid we are not at liberty to say, but I can assure you it's nothing to worry about. Do you have an electronic version of this at all? Save my colleague here having to input all the data twice.'

'Of course, my apologies. All our staff are vetted prior to working for us.'

'Please take my card, my address is printed below,' Sam said, holding out a business card she had been issued with before they'd left the office. 'Thank you for your time and we will be in touch.'

'I look forward to reading your report and recommendations.'

Jen and Sam left the building and headed towards the car.

'You did well. You okay?'

'I took your advice. My nan will be as safe as houses here.'

DI Chris Jackson

Chris found himself back in the office, watching Hannah. He was in his thirties; he was too old for schoolboy crushes ... wasn't he?

Chris hadn't been really paying much attention as Clive spoke excitedly about the raid on Harry's house and what they'd found. Having tried to call someone in forensics multiple times to see if they could give him an update, he decided to be patient. The days were beginning to get shorter as it got dark earlier and today had flown by, having spent the majority of it searching through Harry's spotlessly clean house.

'The drugs that you brought back from his house, did they all have this same imprint on?' he heard Hannah ask.

'Yes, the pills looked like they did, but it was hard to tell as they were all bagged up like Smarties,' Clive answered.

'Can I make a suggestion?' Chris asked, as he watched for that sparkle in Hannah's eyes. 'Why don't we go in and ask Harry about Chloe? We should say to him we've got a dead detective who was investigating this batch of drugs he has in his possession. Tell him that, as he's refusing to answer any questions as to where the drugs came from, we'll be charging him with the murder of the detective as well. We can always add in stuff about Jen and make connections between Jennifer and Chloe.'

They all sat around the table, taking in what Chris had just suggested.

'What if we still get nothing out of him?' Hannah asked.

'You take him back to London with you and do whatever you do with people who kill detectives.'

Hannah mulled it over for a second. 'Go in as you said earlier and refer to Chloe as a detective or simply as an officer. If you still get nowhere I suggest we scare him. I'll arrange for some armed guards to escort him back to London.'

'I get this feeling that he's a very small fish in a big pond. Just purely from the way we caught him. No criminal mastermind does their own dirty work and if they do, they don't get caught that easy.' As Chris finished his sentence, he looked towards Hannah who smiled at him from across the table which, to him, might as well have been the Great Wall of China between them.

'Harry, we've got a problem. You know we got a search warrant for your house, and we don't need to tell you what we found behind your desk. Is there anything you'd like to say about what we found?' Chris asked, setting things up for the kill.

'No comment.'

'Well the main thing we did find, I guess, is more pills. They all have this same imprint on.' Chris moved a picture towards Harry who momentarily glanced at it as a look of confusion washed over his face.

'When we spoke to you this morning, we asked you questions about these drugs. You didn't respond and as I'm a nice officer, unlike Clive here, I wanted to give you a chance to talk to us.'

Silence.

'Do you know what happens to people who kill police officers, Harry?' Clive asked as Harry continued his poker face. 'Well, once all the other officers in the station get wind of it …'

'Did you know Chloe Seaward?' Chris asked as confusion crossed Harry's face.

'No. Why, should I?' he asked, moving closer to the table.

'Well, this is her now,' Clive barked, as he showed the photo of Chloe from the morgue. 'One of our own was killed last week, Harry. One of our brightest was murdered.'

'I don't understand why you are telling me this?'

'You see Harry, unknown to us, Chloe was investigating these little pills you have been selling. It doesn't take much of an imagination to add two and two together.'

The realisation suddenly started to dawn on Harry's face. 'I had nothing to do with that woman's death.'

'We know you did, Harry. We've read extensive reports about these pills that Chloe had written and she was on to you.'

As Chris took a breath, Clive picked up the baton and laid it on thick. 'I think you killed her Harry and dumped her body. What did you do? Pick her up at some club. Invite her back to your house, rape her, beat her half to death and dump her?' As Clive began to rage, Harry's demeanour completely changed as he started to realise the gravity of the situation.

'I want to speak to a solicitor,' he shouted.

'That is in your right Harry, but they'll want to take you up to London first because you've killed a member of the police force. Plus Jennifer is still missing, so this is a very big case and needs to be handled by those at the top.'

'If you decided to speak to us now though, Harry, we could try to make it easier for you.' Chris spoke quietly, pretending he cared.

'I want to speak to a solicitor. You're not pinning the murder on me.'

'That's fine, Harry. I'll get someone to meet you once you get to London.' With that Clive and Chris left the interview room with smiles on their faces. They had broken the little shit and, hopefully, it would only be a matter of time before he talked.

'Well done, mate.' Clive said, turning to Chris and slapping him on the back. 'Mission accomplished.'

'Yeah, we certainly scared the crap out of him. Let's hope he wants to tell us something before they do transport him up to London.'

'Everything might return to normal now, no more tension on the streets,' Clive said, looking hopeful.

'I still think he is a very small fish trapped in a huge pond, and did you not see the look on his face when we showed him the pills?'

'But if he won't talk to us, there isn't anything we can do to help him.'

'Leave him to Hannah's team. I'm sure they'll break him one way or another.'

As Clive started to head back towards the car, Chris lagged behind and pulled his phone from his pocket. He was about to do something that in his heart he didn't want to, but his head was telling him differently. He had to do what was best, regardless of the consequences.

'Sir.' Julie answered within the first ring. 'Everything okay with Harry and the DI?'

'Julie, I need you to do something.'

'Anything, sir.'

'I need you to get over to the courts and get a search warrant for James Garner's place.'

'On what grounds?'

'The disappearance of his wife.' There was silence on the other end as Chris ended the call.

James Garner

They were all sat around the table about to start dinner when there was a loud knock on the door followed by the ringing of the doorbell.

'I'll go,' his mum said, excusing herself from the table and heading towards the hall.

'Detective Jackson, nice of you to come and visit us again.

Would you like a coffee? I'm afraid we're just sitting down to eat dinner. If I'd known you were coming, I'd have made sure there was enough for you.' James strained to hear who his mum was talking to.

'Hi, Mrs Garner. I'm afraid this isn't a social visit. We haven't got much time. Julie is waiting in my car just around the corner. I need you to grab the children and go and get in the car with Julie.'

'Why, what's happened?'

'I'm afraid a warrant has been issued in relation to Jen's disappearance and my colleagues are on their way over to conduct a search of the house.'

James could hear his mum's muffled voice as he struggled to work out what was going on. He knew he'd heard the words 'warrant' and 'children'. He turned and looked at his dad who returned the confused expression.

'Why on earth for?'

'Please, Mrs Garner. Julie will tell you more in the car. I've been afforded an extra ten minutes to get the kids out of the house because they don't need to see any of this.'

'Okay. Thank you, Detective. Alex, Melanie, I need you both to get your shoes,' his mum shouted as she headed back towards where the family were all sat for dinner.

'Rita, what's going on?' his dad asked as he got up from the table.

'The kids and I are just popping out. I need you to stay here with James,' his mum said as she passed both the kids their coats.

'Mum?' James questioned.

'Where we going, Gran? We've not even finished dinner yet.'

'Come on you two, I'll buy you both an ice cream sundae once we get where we're going, okay?'

His mum looked at his dad and then back at James and guided the now excited children through the conservatory and out of the house.

'I'll call you later,' she shouted back as she left.

'I'm going to go and see what's going on,' James said, standing up and pushing his chair back with some force.

'James?' his father warned but it didn't matter. He was off to investigate as he marched to the front door to be greeted, seconds later, by DI Jackson.

'Mr Garner, I am here to present you with a warrant for the search of the premises in relation to the disappearance of Mrs Jennifer Garner,' the DI said as he handed the piece of paper over to James. 'I suggest you let us come through, Mr Garner. It'll make things a lot easier.'

James automatically stood to the side as Chris was followed in by a procession of police officers.

'What the …?' James said as he heard the detective issue orders to his team.

The Detective paused in what he was doing and looked over towards to where James was now standing. 'We might be here for some time, so I suggest you go and sit with your father. I will ask someone to come and explain what's going on.'

' I don't understand!' he raged.

'Let's go and sit down, son,' his dad said as he appeared from the kitchen.

'What right do these officers have to storm in to my house whilst I'm eating dinner with my family?' James shouted, starting to square up to Chris.

'Mr Garner, I suggest you sit down and let us do our jobs. If you cannot remain seated or would rather not be present during this search, I can arrange for one of my officers to escort you to a waiting car outside,' Chris said, taking a step back.

'Please James,' his dad pleaded with him as he moved to get in between the Detective and his son.

'What right do you have?' James continued to rage, now at his dad as he tried to get closer to Chris.

'Mr Garner, I suggest you take a seat or I will have no choice but to remove you from this property.'

'Son, please.'

Just then a shout came from upstairs.

'Excuse me,' Chris said as he manoeuvred himself away from James and headed towards the shout.

'What are they shouting about?' James said, following Chris.

'Come on, son. Let's go and sit down.' His father tried to get his attention.

Detective Jackson stood in the doorway of the bedroom as James reached the top of the stairs. Though he'd tried to tidy things up and everything looked to be back in its right place, a lot of the furniture in the room had clearly sustained some damage. There was splatter on the walls from the make-up and perfume, and broken lipsticks and make-up palettes were scattered across the dressing table. In front of the dressing table, the paint looked darker than the rest of the room where the mirror had been.

'The en-suite is pretty much in the same state, boss,' another officer said.

'I can explain,' James shouted as he barged passed the Detective.

'Officer, I need you to stay stood exactly where you are,' Chris spoke, ignoring James' presence and heading back downstairs to find Derek.

'Mr Garner, can I suggest you get James to calm down, and I will try to make this as easy and painless as possible?' James overheard Detective Jackson speaking quietly to his dad.

James knew exactly what the room had looked like to anyone else looking in. He had removed the glass and the mirror so the kids wouldn't hurt themselves, but the room had taken the brunt of his anger and needed more than a quick tidy. How was he going to explain this on top of the fight he'd had with Harry?

* * *

James and his dad found themselves in paper suits sat next door on Jodie's sofa while a police officer made them all tea, their radio crackling in the background. The house was now a suspected murder scene and, as James sat with his head in his hands, he couldn't work out where everything had gone so wrong. A week ago everything had been perfect between him and Jen, and now here he was sat in paper overalls.

'Officer, do you know where my children are?' James slowly rose his head to ask.

'My colleague is with them and Mrs Garner at a hotel just outside of town.'

'Are they okay? Do you know when I will be able to speak to them?'

'I can assure you that they're fine. My colleague has them thinking they are on a great big adventure. I'm sure you will be able to speak to them first thing in the morning once we've got all of this cleared up.'

'Is there no way I can speak to them now?' James asked, as his temper started to rise again. It had taken him long enough to calm down after they were so rudely interrupted and made to strip to their boxers before being led next door to Jodie's house to sit and wait.

'I think it would be best for all concerned if you wait until morning.'

James' dad put his hand on his son's shoulder, clearly noticing he was starting to get angry again. The last thing they all needed was for James to lose his temper. It wouldn't help his case given the evidence that had greeted the officers when they'd arrived an hour earlier.

'At least the kids are safe and aren't here in the middle of this, son.'

'Hmmm.' James wasn't in the mood to talk. There was a reasonable explanation for all this; he just needed to be given the chance to talk to Detective Jackson. Every time he looked at his dad he could see the worry and concern etched on his face. He had been there when he trashed the room; he was a witness and knew that it had nothing to do with Jen.

'At least our nosey neighbour will have enough material to keep her happy for weeks,' James said as the police officer handed them both a drink.

'She'd better not say anything while I'm in earshot,' Jodie defended James and the scene that was unfolding behind the long draping curtains that hung just above the floor. 'Because I'll be putting her right, I can tell you that now.' James smiled over to where Jodie was sat.

'I just wish I knew what they were looking for?' James said. 'Because I'd quite happily go and point it out to them. I know the bedroom looks a state but I've been working on repairing stuff.' James dropped his head in shame as he thought back on his behaviour last time he'd had a visit from the DI. He'd promised his mum and dad that it'd been a one-off. He knew how it must have looked for the DI and the officers who had first arrived at the property. Hopefully some common sense would prevail and they would be back inside their home in a decent set of clothing before the night was out.

Just then the doorbell rang and the officer went to see who it was. They all sat in silence, trying to hear what was going on and who was at the door.

'Detective Jackson,' James spoke, standing up as the Detective entered the room. 'Please tell me this has all been a silly mistake and we can all go back home and get on with our evening.'

There was a moment's silence where you could have heard a pin drop as Chris took a breath.

'James Garner, I'm here to arrest you for the possession of a Class A drug.'

'What!' his dad was out of his seat as the Detective continued the caution

'I am also hereby arresting you on the suspicion of the murder of Officer Chloe Seaward.'

'*What?* I don't understand,' James said, also rising to his feet.

'... and the disappearance of Mrs Jennifer Garner.'

'Son, don't say a word. I'm calling a solicitor.'

'But I've done nothing wrong, Dad,' James said as disbelief washed over him, forcing him to sit back down again suddenly.

'Anything you do say may be given in evidence,' the Detective finished, and the room fell silent. 'Mr Garner, I'd rather not cuff you ...'

Everything was happening to fast around him; he had gone from loving father, to murdering drug taker in a space of an hour. Even in his shock, James knew there was no point getting into a fight with the Detective because that would just be another thing he'd done wrong and would no doubt be added to his caution. He sighed and stood up.

'Yeah, it's okay, I'm coming,' he said as he walked towards the Detective in total defeat.

'James, don't say anything, okay? Until I've got a solicitor,' his dad shouted after him as he was led out of the house to the waiting cars.

Jen Garner

'Max, we're back,' Jen told him as she poked her head around the door.

'Great. Successful trip?'

'I think so, all good here?'

'Possibly not.'

'Oh ...'

'Grab Sam and Tim and come to the meeting room.'

'Will do ... coffee?'

'No, I'm good, but you might need something a bit stronger.'

Jen was worried now as she returned to her desk to check if

an email had come through yet. 'Max wants us in the meeting room,' she told Sam.

'Shall I grab us some drinks?' Sam asked, automatically returning to her PA role.

'Max says we might need something strong, so I think we best get in there quick. Tim?'

'Be there in five,' he answered, sounding like he was as tired as she was. She could never work as a detective again at this level because this case was beginning to drain her. Or was it just because it was all too personal?

'Are we all here?' Max asked, looking around the room after they'd gathered. 'Great. I've just heard back from Hannah and following Harry Greenidge's arrest last night, they conducted a search on his house and found vast quantities of what they believe is Ecstasy, all with the Crawford logo on.' As Max pulled up on screen a photo of the drugs that had been found, Jen felt herself take an audible deep breath.

'We need to consider where we are with this case since this turn of events. Jen, I know you personally knew Harry, which is making this case even trickier.' Max put another photo on their screen that Jen was all too familiar with.

'This is James Garner, Jen's husband. James got into a fight with our suspect on Saturday and ended up in the holding cells with a drunk and disorderly fine.'

Things started to add up far too quickly in Jen's head as Max continued.

'We need to consider the idea that James Garner and Harry Greenidge are part of this bigger picture.'

Jen wanted to speak up to defend her husband but she couldn't find her voice.

'Do we need to consider that Jen has been part of some elaborate plan? Have these two been peddling the Crawford branded drugs on the street while keeping Jen out of the way?'

Now Jen found her voice. 'Max, I know I need to keep an objective head on, but this is my life we are talking about; the past ten years of it. I have slept with this bloke, I have had two adorable children with him. There is no way he could be part of this because I'd have known.'

'I hate to say it Jen, but would you have?' Tim suddenly perked up. 'Were you so blindsided by the perfect man he portrayed himself to be that you missed the signs?'

'There have been no god damn signs,' she shouted back. She never realised when she left home last week that this is where it would all end: being told her husband was a drug-pushing murderer. 'James was with me the weekend Chloe was killed. He couldn't have done it.'

'This is where Harry comes into the picture,' said Max.

Jen didn't have an answer for that one. All she could feel from around the table was sheer hate for the man she loved … *the man she thought she loved*. 'Where did Harry get the drugs from to sell in the first place? That's the obvious thing we need to investigate, before we go accusing my husband.' Jen wasn't even sure she believed what was coming out of her mouth. 'We've checked George's visitor log. Neither James or Harry visited him at all during his sentence. So how could they've been involved?' Jen knew she had to try and fight her husband's case.

'What about this Jessica or Tilly, or whatever?' Sam said quietly out of the blue, almost like she didn't dare say anything.

'Sorry, Sam?' Max asked

'It is probably nothing but Jen herself said that this Jessica we found has the same name as Harry's girlfriend. We have a Tilly who was visiting George with what we believe to be her mum for the first four years of his sentence and since we are unable to trace her we were thinking that maybe Tilly changed her name to Jessica. I know I might be going above my remit and should probably just keep quiet.'

'Sam, it's fine,' Max reassured her. 'I wanted your input into all of this.'

'But what if that is the same Jessica? And for want of a better phrase she took over her father's fallen empire?' Jen argued. She'd never liked the woman and always thought that there was something not quite right about her; maybe this was it.

'But she'd probably have been too young to even know about it when he was sent down, so how would she know there was something to take over?' Tim argued back again. Jen felt herself getting more and more annoyed at him. What was his problem with her and her family?

'What the fuck have you got against my family?' Jen couldn't hold it back any longer. 'Are you jealous or something, Timothy? That some of us have made something of our lives? While you're sat with your cock in one hand and playing *Minecraft*, or whatever the cool thing is now, with the other every night?'

'At least I know where mine have been. Anyone can see Jen, you've been duped into marrying a bullying, violent man.'

'I've slept with this guy and know his darkest secrets. Do you not think I'd know?'

'Well, come on. This isn't the first master criminal you've slept with, is it?'

Jen was up on her feet about to get in his face and ask him to repeat what he had just said when Max slammed a book on the table.

'Enough! I will not have my detectives fighting like this. We are in this together. We've all lost a colleague and I will not have everything falling apart because someone might have made the wrong life choices. Tim, I suggest you go back to your desk and see if you can find something to back up your theories. We need evidence that James is behind this, not mud that you are trying to make stick to a wall.'

Tim got up from his chair and gave Jen a look of sheer disgust. And then there was just her, Sam and Max and, at that moment in time, she really felt that everything she had built up was crumbling around her.

'I'm just going to look at something,' Sam said, excusing herself from the meeting room.

'I just want to go home, I don't want to play this game anymore,' she found herself saying as the tears finally began to fall. Had she really let herself get used in the name of love?

She hadn't been sure how long she'd been sat in the meeting room sobbing when Sam returned and placed a cup of tea down in front of her.

'Jen,' she whispered. 'I've brought you a drink and some biscuits, okay? I know you don't want to talk about it, but when this is all over I'm here for you, whichever way this turns out.'

'Thank you,' Jen said, wrapping her hand around the mug in front of her as she dried her face on the crumpled tissue Sam had also brought along. 'I'll be okay, I just need to see this case to the end, no matter what happens. I need to do this for Chloe. I promised her.'

'Can I ask you a question?' Sam said suddenly.

'Depends what it is, because I'm all out of answers when it comes to this case.'

'No. I noticed you keep rubbing your left wrist, and then I noticed the tattoo.'

Jen studied her wrist. 'I wouldn't be much good at poker, would I?' Jen laughed through her tears.

'I know that Chloe had one exactly the same on her ankle, though I only saw it a couple of times, usually when she was in the process of covering it up.'

'We were young and I don't think we thought it through properly at the time. You can't really be a highly trained undercover detective with an identifying mark such as a tattoo. We were both like naughty school girls, trying to hide it from our parents after we'd had them done. Max wasn't impressed.'

Sam laughed. 'I think Chloe used to use stage make-up to hide hers.'

'Mine faded not long after I had it done, then I met James so didn't need to worry as much.'

'You should get it re-inked when this is all over ... sort of as a tribute to your friendship.'

'Yeah maybe.' Jen wasn't convinced. She hadn't exactly been a great friend to Chloe recently, had she?

'You're going to solve this Jen, and your knight in shining armour will still be waiting for you.'

Sam left her alone again to gather her thoughts. When Jen had everything clear in her mind, she went over to Max's office, knocked on the door and walked in.

Chapter Twenty-Three

The previous evening's events played heavily on Chris' mind. He hadn't slept and spent the whole night either staring at the files on his computer or looking out towards the football stadium for inspiration. In all the years he'd been a detective he'd never been wrong about anyone. How had he missed all the signs with James? Would there have been more of a chance of finding Jen alive if he'd be quicker off the starting blocks, instead of messing around looking for CCTV footage that wouldn't help find her any quicker?

Chris was in a sullen mood as he swiped into the station. He headed for the kettle and a cup of coffee that would be needed before he could face anything.

It had been late before he'd left the Garner household. James had been arrested and taken back to the station to be booked in by DS Goodwin. Chris waited until every last inch of the house had been searched and secured. Once the house was cleared Chris escorted James' dad back into the house so he could find changes of clothing for them all. Derek was then taken to where his wife and grandchildren were. At least he'd managed to do one thing right by getting the kids clear before anything happened. Derek had thanked him for as much.

'DI Manson?'

'He's on his way in,' Sally shouted from the back of the room, leaving Chris wondering how she knew and he didn't.

'Sorry boss,' Julie said as she rushed past him. 'I've just been down to the cells to check on our inmates.'

'Inmates?' Chris questioned as he was sure there was only one he knew of.

'Ah yes, sorry. They decided not to transfer Harry to

London. They thought it might be best for the case going forward if we kept him close.'

'Great,' Chris said, taking a seat and wondering whether what he'd said had come out far more sarcastic than it was supposed to. 'Has anyone heard anything from Hannah about how she wants us to deal with James and the additional pills that we've found?' Chris was greeted by silence as he walked over towards the incident board and sat on the edge of one of the tables. 'Okay team, everyone want to grab themselves a drink and we'll talk through what we know?' There was a sudden movement as his colleagues left the office in search of a refill of some kind.

'You okay, boss?' Julie asked as she walked over towards where Chris was sat.

'In all honesty, I'm lost. I can't work out how I could have got someone so wrong.'

'But maybe you didn't, boss. You know, innocent until proven otherwise?'

'I'm all out of hope, Julie. I really am.'

'Morning, team,' Clive boomed as he walked through the office, closely followed by Sally on his heels. Chris couldn't work out what Clive was so happy about. Probably because someone else had done all the work for him and hopefully cleared a harmful drug from the streets of Nottingham? Chris nodded his acknowledgement as he waited for his team to return.

'Okay team. Can I have your attention?' Chris shouted, bringing an end to Clive's cheeriness that he was still failing to understand. 'Right, I'm sure you are all aware of the outcome of the Garner house search last night.'

'James' father has been sat in reception since first thing this morning, boss. Waiting to speak to his son,' Colin pitched in.

'The pills we found in the pockets of James' discarded jeans have been confirmed as a form of LSD. They both have the matching imprint that we know Chloe and her team had been investigating. This same imprint was also found on the drugs we discovered in Harry Greenidge's house. I don't think it's any coincidence that these two are also best friends.' Chris looked around the room, waiting for questions from his team who sat giving him their full attention. 'Let's look at the drug angle to start, Clive?'

'I've been speaking to Detective Littlefair, who has returned to London. Sorry, Chris.' Clive stopped, hoping for a reaction from the room but nothing came so he continued. 'She is very interested in what we found at the Garners'. They have asked us to continue our lines of enquiry regarding where the drugs have come from.'

'Okay, and the dead colleague?' Chris asked.

'They seem pretty sure Harry played a very big part in her death. They don't see James as a suspect, but I guess if we can link him with her death, then it'll be a big payday for us.'

That wasn't quite how Chris was thinking about it, but if that was the way Clive wanted to play it then who was he to stop him? He'd thought James was innocent, so what did he know?

'Okay, team. We also still have this woman missing,' Chris said, pointing to Jen's picture which was back in its rightful place at the top of the incident board. 'As you will all no doubt know, she hasn't been seen now for nearly a week. There are two sides to her disappearance, if we take a moment to refresh on where we were up to prior to today.' There was a shuffling of papers and pens clicked into action. 'We managed to track Jen all the way to Nottingham until she got off the bus. The council haven't yet been able to restore their CCTV footage, and this is now a criminal investigation.'

'Do we have any idea where she goes from there?' Greg asked.

'In short, no.'

'Has someone phoned around all the shelters in the area?' Clive asked.

'Yes, and they don't have anyone fitting Jen's description in a shelter or awaiting accommodation,' Julie answered.

'No doubt you are aware of the state of the master bedroom and the en-suite when we entered during the search?' Chris added.

'Are we now going down the avenue that James has done something to his wife?' Greg asked, clearly trying to hide his shock.

'You are all my team and, for that reason, I'm going to be honest with you.' Chris took a breath before continuing. 'Given the state of the master bedroom and traces of blood found in the en-suite, on top of James' D&D arrest which, may I add, was for fighting with Harry, I don't think we've any choice but to explore this avenue.' There was a silence that fell in the room that Chris struggled to fill before Clive butted in with some stupid, unhelpful comment. 'Hopefully there will be a perfectly good explanation to all of this and Jen will be fine, and as for the drugs—'Chris began to conclude.

'—but it's not looking good, is it boss?' Trudie questioned.

'Where are the children, boss?' Sally asked.

'They are currently in a hotel not far out of town with their grandparents and totally oblivious as to what is going on by all accounts.'

'Do we need to get Child Services involved?' Colin asked.

'They are both safe with their grandparents. Let's deal with the issues in front of us and worry about everything else later. I really don't want to cause any further undue distress to this family.' Everyone nodded in agreement. Those two kids were safe right now, and that was all that mattered. Child Services could come later when everything had been cleared up.

Clive stepped forward. 'Not wanting to bring an end to this touching moment but back to business. Can I suggest both Chris and myself interview James in the first instance?'

'Okay,' Chris agreed.

'Anybody got any questions?' Clive asked, but no one wanted to be the one to break the silence that had fallen across the room. Everyone was thinking about the family they were breaking apart.

'Chris.' Clive opened the office door. 'You okay, or do you need five?' he asked as Chris followed him towards the custody suite.

'No, I'm good. Let's do this.'

Chris walked into the interview room holding three large cups of coffee.

'I've brought you a coffee, I hope you don't mind,' Chris said to James.

'I'd prefer a whisky,' James responded. He sounded downbeat and broken.

'Ah, I'm afraid that's reserved for special occasions.' Chris tried his best to sound light-hearted. Just then Clive bounded into the room and handed Chris a note with instructions that had come directly from Hannah. Clive moved towards the recording equipment and started fiddling with everything, trying to get it all set up. Chris felt like he should at least try and make conversation with James. He just couldn't stop seeing him as a grieving husband, not a wife-beating drug addict. Finally, Clive sorted out everything and they both took their seats to start the formalities.

'James, please could you confirm that you have declined to have your solicitor present?' Clive asked.

'Yes, I've got nothing to hide.'

'Thank you, James.'

Chris really didn't know how he was going to play this. He needed to stop feeling sorry for James and focus on stopping these drugs flooding the streets of Nottingham.

'Okay. For the tape, I'm Detective Inspector Jackson and sat with me is Detective Inspector Manson.' A heavy silence fell over the room. They'd previously agreed that Chris was going to lead the interview but now, in the moments of silence, he wasn't sure whether he could.

'James, yesterday at approximately 7 p.m., we conducted a search of your house in relation to your missing wife, Jennifer Garner. We later arrested you based on the evidence we found in the master bedroom. James, could you tell me what these are please?' Chris finished, handing James a laminated sheet showing a photograph of a single packet holding two white pills.

'They look like Paracetamol,' James responded as he pushed the sheet back towards Chris.

'James, during the search of the master bedroom we found these pills in a pocket of your jeans. I wondered if you could tell me where they came from?'

James was quiet for a moment while he seemed to weigh up his options.

'I got it from a mate. It's for personal use.'

'Which mate, James?' Clive asked, clearly trying to up the tempo of the interview.

'Just a friend. No one important. Like I said, it's for personal use, plus I doubt you found any more to be able to charge me with anything.'

'Can I ask if you recognise this logo?' Chris asked, pushing another photo over towards James which showed the mystery imprint up close.

'Can't say I've seen it before,' James responded, pushing the photo back once again.

'Okay James, can I be honest with you here? I'm not sure if you're aware, but we arrested Harry Greenidge for intent to supply. Later when we searched his house we also found hundreds more of these tablets.'

James fell silent as he picked up his coffee and took a sip.

'I understand you and Harry are best friends, James?' Clive asked.

'Yeah, we sometimes meet up and go out together, when his girlfriend is back in London.'

'Do you go out with Harry with the intent to sell these drugs?'

'No!' James responded in horror. 'Before the other day, I'd never seen these tablets.'

'So why do you have them in your possession, James?'

'I was given the tablets. Someone said it would help things. You know, now my wife is missing and we're sat here talking about two pills you found in my jeans—'

'—We'll get to that James,' Clive interrupted.

'Harry has been refusing to tell us where these drugs have come from, James. Though seeing as you are now in possession of said drug, maybe you can tell us?' Chris asked.

'I told you. I got them from a friend.'

'Not Harry then?'

James didn't answer, Chris knew that was exactly where he'd got the drugs from. He'd probably even witnessed the deal taking place on the evening he'd seen Harry leaving the Garners' house.

'James, can you remember that body that was recently dumped in Long Eaton?'

'Yes, why? I thought that had all been sorted now.'

'Well, you see, here's the problem. She was a detective like myself and Clive and she was investigating the same batch of drugs you have in your possession.'

'Right.'

'Her name was Chloe Seaward if you're interested. From what she's left behind, we believe she was close to finding the source of the drugs before she was brutally murdered.' Chris emphasised the word brutally. 'I think James, Chloe had got too close to the operation Harry and you were running, so you killed her.'

A look of confusion swept across James' face,

'James, where's your wife? Did she get in the way of yours and Harry's enterprise too?' Clive asked.

James shot up from his chair and hammered the table.

'Sit down, James,' Clive warned.

'I won't have you sitting there accusing me of drug dealing, murder and now the disappearance of Jen.'

'Sit down,' Clive warned again, 'or I will get someone to take you back to your cell.'

James sat again and put his head in his hands.

'Where were you on the night of the Sunday before last?' Clive continued his questioning.

'I was at home in bed with my wife. Why?'

'Can anyone vouch for that?'

'What happened in your bedroom, James?' Chris cut in. 'Is that Jen's blood we found that you missed when you were clearing up?' Chris watched as James lifted his head again.

'What? No! I just … I just got frustrated with the lack of progress in finding my wife. So I pulled a couple of drawers out looking for some clue as to where she was, that's all.'

'And the pub? Was that out of frustration with Harry because he was messing stuff up?'

'No.'

'James, you put on this calm and collected persona, but you know I think underneath you have one hell of a temper and lose control quite easily,' Chris concluded.

'I haven't done anything to my wife. The so-called drugs you found are for personal use and it doesn't matter where I got them from. It's purely a coincidence that you found the same pills at Harry's house.'

'Did you find out Jen was planning to leave you?' Clive continued, 'and taking the kids? Was she running away from *you*? But you caught up with her, didn't you? Making sure she'd never do it again.'

'No? What? Even if I'd done something to her, I was at work all day until 4 p.m. when the kids' school phoned. You know that yourself.'

There was silence again in the interview room.

'See, the problem we have here James is that Harry had

exactly the same pills as these hidden in his house, but he won't tell us where they've come from. Harry, you claim, is your best friend but you ended up in a bar fight with him?' Chris stopped for a moment to let it all sink in. 'We have a murdered detective who was investigating these drugs coming into Nottingham. On top of that, you claim that your wife is missing but the state of your house is suspicious.'

'No, you've got it all wrong. I've got nothing to do with the mess Harry seems to have got himself into. As for Jen and the dead detective, I don't have the answers. I really don't know where Jen is. You're the ones who have been tracking her for God's sake!'

'So you deny the charges of the murder of Chloe Seaward and the disappearance of your wife?'

'Of course I do, this is ridiculous! I've not done anything wrong. Do you seriously think that if I'd done something to my wife I would have rung you guys when she failed to come home? Would I have not just covered it up?'

The three men sat there for a moment.

'Officers, I really haven't done anything wrong! Other than accepting a pick-me-up from a friend. If I'd realised it was a Class A drug, I'd have declined. Never mind this damn logo.'

'Your father seems very keen to see you, James. I wonder if he thinks you're guilty too?' Clive asked as the anger flashed in James' eyes.

'Leave him out of it. What have you done with my children anyway?'

'They're safe, James. Out of harm's way.' Clive smirked.

'Do I need to get a solicitor?' James asked. 'Are you accusing me of murder?

'If the hat fits,' Clive replied.

'I've done nothing wrong here, except accepted a pick-me-up from a friend,' James repeated.

'I think we'll end there for now,' Chris said as he pushed his chair out. 'Come on James, I'll walk you back to the cells.'

'How much longer are you keeping me for? Do I need a solicitor?' James bombarded Chris with questions on the journey back to his cell. Chris didn't have any of the answers James wanted.

'Look, I need you to give me something, James. Because, as of last night, you look guilty as hell,' Chris told him as he stepped out of the cell and closed the door, leaving James by himself.

Chris arrived back in the office ahead of Clive, who'd been busy flirting with the girls in custody suite. He'd just walked straight past them and headed back up to his team. While he'd been away someone had added both Harry and James to the list of names that weren't affiliated with the main dealers in Nottingham.

'Has anyone had the chance to look up the people that we still have listed as not in either gang in Nottingham?' he asked.

'Just looking at it now, boss. A lot of them have minor charges against their names, nothing on the Harry scale,' Colin responded.

'How did it go with James?' Julie asked as she came over to where Chris was standing.

'In all honesty, I don't know. He hasn't got enough on him for us to charge him with possession. As for the murder and disappearance of Jen, we both saw his temper and the only one who can alibi him for Sunday night is his wife,' Chris responded.

'Well, I may have some good news for you,' Sally said as she manoeuvred herself in front of them both. 'Dr Walsh has just phoned with the preliminary findings from the blood found at the Garners'.'

Chris didn't even know why, but he felt really nervous about these results. He was putting all his hopes on the blood evidence being linked back to James.

'So … the blood found in the master bedroom belongs to James.' Chris let out a sigh of relief. 'The blood found between the tiles on the en-suite floor shares markers with James' blood. Dr Walsh assumes that it's likely to belong to one of the kids.'

'So, James is off the hook,' Chris summarised.

'Unless he beat and killed her elsewhere,' Clive responded, bouncing back into the office and killing the conversation.

'Boss,' Julie interrupted them all. 'We still can't get hold of this solicitor that Harry has requested. The law firm aren't even answering my call now.'

'Okay, any ideas why?'

'When you asked me to contact them boss, I was quite taken aback by who he'd asked for. They are a very esteemed company and don't just represent anyone, if that makes sense …'

'So your low-life scum like Harry isn't even on their radar?' Clive asked.

'Can we get him a duty solicitor? So we can break the bad news to him and see if he gives up anything?' Julie suggested, obviously keen to try and break the dead-lock they were facing.

'If it means we can have another go at him, I think it'll be worth putting a call in. Clive?'

'I don't see a problem.'

'Great. Julie, are you okay to sort that? Once we have a duty solicitor we'll have another shot at him.'

'How are you feeling, Harry?' Chris asked as Julie sorted the recording equipment. 'This is my colleague, Detective Sergeant Julie Ryan, who is going to sit in on this one with us. I trust you've had time to consult with your appointed solicitor?'

Silence.

Chris was determined he would break the cocky shit by the end of this interview. With Julie here instead of Clive, it might just happen. Clive had decided he wanted to speak to Hannah about James and how to proceed.

'Harry, we seem to be having problems getting hold of the solicitor you've requested,' Julie informed him.

'No, I'm good. He'll be in touch as soon as he hears I'm in here.'

'Well, in the meantime, we need to ask you about James. Which is why the duty solicitor is in here with us now,' Chris told him.

'I have advised my client—' the duty solicitor began.

'—Look mate, I've told you I don't need you here. I don't want you here. I'll wait for my solicitor,' Harry cut him off before he finished his sentence.

'Harry, I don't think he's coming. You really should listen to the duty solicitor's advice,' Julie suggested.

'Look mate, you can skip back off to wherever you've come from and invoice the police for your time,' Harry told the solicitor.

'Harry, tell me about James and his relationship with his wife?' Chris asked, realising he needed to move things along.

'I've already told you, I've got nothing to do with Jen's disappearance.'

'So it's all James then, is it? He's the criminal mastermind in all this?'

'What?'

'We found some of those pills in James' possession that match the ones we've also found in your possession, and then with the blood evidence we also found in the house …'

'Blood evidence?' Harry questioned.

'Yeah, looks like it had been cleaned off the bathroom floor but you missed some,' Julie offered.

'Where's Jen's body, Harry? We've already got Detective Seaward as you know. Let's bring Jen home so her remaining family can mourn her loss,' Chris said.

'I had nothing to do with that detective's murder.'

'Was it all James' idea?'

'What? No. James had nothing to do with it.'

'So, James was just involved with the drugs?' Chris asked.

'No! You're just trying to confuse me and trip me up. This is exactly why I wanted MY solicitor.'

'Okay, I'll make all this a bit easier for you, Harry. We found a tablet from the same batch we found in your house during the raid at James' home. We also found some unexplained blood evidence, where an attempt had been made to clean it up. We also have a dead detective who was investigating the same drugs that were appearing on the Nottingham streets which, lest we forget, you sold me two days ago,' Chris updated him.

'Harry, you won't tell us where you got the drugs from, the same as James, so what do you expect us to think?' Julie added. 'Because right now, we think that you and James are the new players our dead colleague was investigating.'

'How many times do I need to tell you guys? James had nothing to do with this, the death of your detective or Jen's disappearance.'

'But you did.'

'Look, I'm not saying any more until my solicitor gets here.'

'We've provided you with a suitable replacement. So why not just tell us now Harry? Let's quit the messing around.'

Silence.

'Harry, tell me about James and these pills.'

Silence.

'I am going to keep asking these questions until you answer,' continued Chris.

'You get me my solicitor and I will answer all the questions you have.'

'Harry, your solicitor isn't coming. We've been on the phone to his office so much they've stopped taking our calls.'

'He'll come as soon as they find out.'

'Who's "they", Harry?'

Silence.

'Harry, did you give James a couple of those pills?'

No comment.

'Harry, as mentioned yesterday, we've arrested James and in his possession were these pills.'

Harry nodded his response.

'But, you see, James won't tell us where he got the pills from. Which leads us to a slight problem.'

No response.

'Harry I am appealing to your better nature. Think of Melanie and Alex in all of this. They've already lost their mum and are on the verge of losing their dad too. Did you or did you not give those pills to James?' Chris sat there as he watched the cogs turn in Harry's brain. As a heavy silence cloaked the interview room, Chris shuffled in his chair as he waited for a response.

'Okay,' Harry spoke. 'I gave James the pills to help him through while Jen is missing.'

'Did you ever give him any more?'

'No.'

'Where did you get them from?'

'No comment, stop trying to trip me up!'

'Thank you, Harry.' Chris got up, scraping his chair against the floor. There was no point staying there asking Harry more questions he clearly wasn't going to answer. He nodded acknowledgement to the officer outside the interview room and returned to his office. Harry had just answered the one question Chris had about James' innocence.

'Julie, will you get hold of the CPS? Let's get the paperwork in line to get Harry charged with possession and dealing.'

'Okay, boss.'

'Detective Jackson,' the Desk Sergeant called him as he walked through the custody suite back to his office. 'The man in cell four, James Garner, has asked to speak to you.'

'You might want to check with DI Manson, don't want to

go stepping on his toes,' Chris said before he dealt with his other inmate.

'Need me to come with you and see James?' Julie asked, overhearing the Desk Sergeant

'I'll be fine, thanks,' Chris said as he made his way over to the custody desk. 'Has he said what it's about?'

'No, just that he wanted to talk to you.'

'Can you let me into cell four then, please? I'll see what he has to say for himself.'

The Desk Sergeant moved over and headed along the corridor to the cells, opening the hatch to James' cell.

'James, Detective Jackson is here to speak to you,' she said as she started to unlock the door. 'Do I need to see if there is a spare interview room?' she asked Chris as the door was ready to open.

'No point taking up a room. This will be a quick one. How can I help you, James?' he asked as he stepped into the cell and the door was closed behind him.

'There's something I need to show you. You've asked me to give you something to prove my innocence. I found it under the floorboards when I was searching.'

'Okay, and where is this now?'

'Still at home. If you let me go back with you, I'll show you.'

Chris held open the door as he led James to the reception area where his dad was still waiting.

'Dad.' James went over to him and they embraced.

'Is everything okay?' Derek asked, looking over towards Chris.

'James has been bailed to his home address,' Chris answered.

'Did you speak to a solicitor?' Derek continued to question.

'No Dad, I don't need one. I've not done anything wrong,' James defended himself.

'I'm going to grab a pool car, James. Meet you outside in five,' Chris said, leaving James and his father to talk to each other. He didn't need to be privy to any of it.

He was intrigued, though, about the box James said he'd found under the floorboards and wondered why the search team hadn't picked it up. Maybe they hadn't been looking for boxes with random items in them …

Jen Garner

'Hannah, what the hell happened to you?' Jen asked as she noticed Hannah returning to the office, positively glowing. Jen had been busy looking over the list of employees at the Gateway, but she was happy to see Hannah back.

'I think I've met someone.' She giggled.

'So much for a drugs bust,' Jen teased.

'Oh, no, this is someone who's part of the investigation actually.'

'Hannah, glad to have you back.' Max's voice boomed from the other side of the office. 'Catch up in five? Jen, Tim, Sam, you joining us?'

Tim was the last person she wanted help from; he seemed to have her family blacklisted.

'It turns out that the lead detective who is chasing you is pretty hot,' Hannah continued. On hearing the word 'hot', Sam's ears pricked up.

'Gossip?' she asked, walking over to join the others.

'Well, as you know we arrested Harry, and the detective and I had to do a bit of role play to catch him red-handed.'

'What did you do, Hannah?' Sam asked, egging her on.

'Well put it this way, he was like a rabbit caught in the headlights until he realised who I was.'

As Hannah retold the tale of her and DI Jackson, Jen couldn't help but remember when this used to be Chloe and her giggling about what they had got up to the night before.

Or sat on the sofa at the flat, talking through what had happened on a case over a glass of wine and a chick flick.

'Anyway,' Jen heard Hannah conclude, 'I've definitely got some unfinished business with our lead detective.'

'I want to know everything.' Sam tried to make her continue, but the story was done for now. 'I'm going to grab some drinks for the meeting. Can I get you anything?' Sam asked, seeming to suddenly remember that it was her job to set up the meeting room.

'But everything at home seemed alright?' Jen asked Hannah when Sam had gone to fetch the drinks. She really needed to know that everything in her bubble was okay; that she had some form of life to return home to, even if it was just a shell.

'Yeah, I've heard the kids are fine. I've brought the necklace back, though I understand from Max that Chester Bennington meant something to you.'

'Yeah, Sam and I went and dug him up; the hamster, I mean,' she reassured Hannah. 'Chloe left me a USB stick, which is where the list of dealers came from.'

'You two coming?' Max asked from the office door.

'We'll talk later,' Jen said as she grabbed her notebook and headed towards the meeting room. She promised herself she wouldn't let Tim bait her any more than he already had the previous day.

'Everyone settled?' Max asked, looking around the room, Jen was happy to see Sam had provided her with her own personal plate of biscuits which made her chuckle to herself.

'Sam, where are we with Jessica and Gwen Adams?'

'I'm afraid I have limited information. Tilly drops off the planet after she stopped visiting with her mum. So I worked on the angle that she changed her name to Jessica and, as Jen suggested, she is now Harry's possible girlfriend.'

'Hannah, did the team in Nottingham get anything out of Harry regarding the drugs and where he'd got them from?'

'Last I heard from Clive, he wasn't saying anything other

than "no comment" and that he didn't kill anyone, you included Jen.'

'Me?' she questioned, forgetting she was a damn missing person in the police's eyes.

'I looked into Jessica following the information Jen gave me about her and Harry and I can't find anything. Jen did give me Jess' number plate and I've got the system looking for hits,' Sam offered.

'If only she'd known that the personalised number plates on her pink Beetle would get her into trouble,' Jen mused.

'Thank you, Sam.'

'I had thought I'd seen this Jess with James and the family while I was in Nottingham, but after looking over photos I'm pretty sure it wasn't her,' Hannah added.

Jen let out a small sigh of relief, hoping at least this was one point for her husband.

'Over night the Nottingham team did a house search on Jen's home and James was later arrested.'

'What for? No one told me this.' Jen spoke out in shock as she waited for Tim to make some unhelpful comment.

'I think we can all agree the Detective was following the evidence as, in his eyes, you're still a missing person, Jen,' Max answered her.

'Did they find anything that links him to this mess?'

'From what I last heard, two pills which they think are some form of LSD, certainly not Ecstasy. But they do carry the Crawford imprint.'

'Branching out.' Jen ignored Tim's comment and waited for Max to continue.

'What has not helped James is the state of the master bedroom. There was some evidence that he had made an effort to fix the damage but it is still obvious, as you can see in these pictures,' Max said, putting up the photo of the room Jen had shared with her husband for the past ten years. The bed where the children had been created was damaged and the mirror was no longer in front of the vanity table. She also noticed her perfume bottles and make-up were missing.

'What have I done?' Jen moaned to no one in particular.

'Married a drug dealing murderer,' came Tim's quiet response.

Had she?

'During the search they found blood splatter evidence, which the lab have confirmed belongs to James and one of the kids.'

'The kids?' Jen questioned.

'Tim, have you found any mud that will actually stick?' Max ignored her question.

'I'm waiting on a call back from a Sergeant Gillroy. He isn't a big fan of James and Harry. He's been suspicious of them for a while.'

'What the *fuck*?' Jen started to argue.

'Okay, Tim. Let me know when you find some actual evidence,' Max said, turning towards Jen. 'Regardless of the personalities involved, where are we in finding Chloe's killer?'

The room was silent as Hannah and Sam exchanged looks. No one wanted to say anything that would add fuel to the fire.

'Jen, you need to think about this the way Lisa Carter would have,' Max told her.

Jen knew he was right. *What would Lisa Carter do?* In this situation, Jen knew in her heart that Lisa needed to come back instead of peering in around the edges. As conversations were going on around her, she loaded up the photo of James and Harry. She needed to do this for Chloe ...

Chapter Twenty-Four

DI Chris Jackson

Chris entered the Garner household behind James and his dad.

'Thank you for the lift,' Derek said as he turned to face Chris.

'Not a problem.'

'I know James has made some mistakes, but we'll get him back on the straight and narrow in no time.'

Chris smiled at Derek, unsure of what to say.

'Has there been any news on Jen?' Derek asked.

'We're working on it,' Chris told him, not wanting to disclose that James or Harry were still in the frame for being responsible.

'Okay, here it is,' James said, coming down the stairs holding a box.

'Shall we go through to the kitchen?' Derek offered. 'I'll put the kettle on.'

'As I told you at the station, Detective.' He wasn't 'Chris' any more, Chris noticed. He'd obviously gone past that point after he'd arrested James. 'I found this under a floorboard in the bedroom.'

Chris took the battered box from James and placed it on the table.

'One thing that isn't in there now is Jen's wedding ring. I threw it somewhere in a fit of rage,' James said, looking like he regretted it.

'Okay.' Chris opened the box and inside was a photo of Jen and another woman he instantly recognised as well as a screwed up piece of paper with some address in Mansfield written on it. 'So, this is everything?'

'Yeah, I'm not sure what to think, Detective. Isn't that other girl the one who was found in the ditch recently?'

Chris didn't dare to admit it; he needed to work it out for himself before confirming James' suspicions.

'Do you mind if I take the photo with me? So we can compare it to what we have on the murder case?'

'Be my guest. No use for it now, if she's gone,' James said solemnly, handing over the photo.

'I promised you at the beginning of all this that I would bring Jen home, and my promise still stands. I'll be in touch.'

'Thank you, Detective Jackson,' Derek said, holding out his hand. Chris shook it and then headed away from the house with the photo in hand.

After queues of traffic and what seemed a lifetime parked on the M25, Chris arrived in Croydon. He'd known as soon as James had presented the photo of the much younger Jen and Chloe that he'd need to go to London and visit where Chloe had once lived to find out if Lisa Carter and Jen were one and the same person. He needed answers.

As he drove, he couldn't help but think back to Daisy and where she fitted into all of this. Had she been dealing the same batch of drugs they'd found Harry with?'

Had Jen run back to her old team when Chloe had been killed, instead of coming in to see the team who'd been running the investigation into Chloe's death to begin with? Was that why the CCTV footage had mysteriously disappeared? The connections were all there; he'd just not seen them until now. As he navigated his way into the car park of Chloe's former address, he decided he was going to get answers, whatever it took.

Chris climbed out of the car and looked around. There was no police presence; everything just seemed normal. Chris located the block Chloe had once lived in, made his way up the flat and was about to knock when a man dressed in a smart black suit opened the door. Had he been looking out for Chris or something? The man let himself out of Chloe's flat and closed the door behind him.

'I'm sorry sir, you can't enter this property.'

'I'm Detective Inspector Jackson. This property is part of an ongoing criminal investigation, and I need access to look for evidence connected to my case.'

'I'm sorry, but I cannot allow you to enter the property.'

'I am a member of the police force,' Chris said, getting his warrant card out. 'I need to search this property as part of an ongoing investigation.'

'I don't care who you are. You are not entering this property, sir.'

'You are obstructing a member of the police force by refusing me entry. I am within my rights to arrest you for obstruction and have you removed from the property.'

Chris was sure the response that came back was 'good luck with that' but he chose not to rise to it.

'I suggest you contact whoever is in charge and get them to grant me access,' he continued.

'As you wish,' the man in the black suit said. 'Wait here.' He went back into the flat, closing the door in Chris' face. There was no way Chris was going anywhere until he got access to the flat and had the answers he needed so he could bring Jen home to her family and lay the memory of Daisy to rest.

Chris hammered on the door again for good measure. 'I'm not going anywhere,' he shouted.

Jen Garner

'Team,' Max said, approaching them all sat round the conference table. 'I need to pop out. There's a meeting I need to attend. Let me know if anything happens. I'll be on my mobile.'

'Okay, boss,' they echoed. Tim had left them all to it as he went in search for more evidence that Jen's husband was involved in the death of their colleague, while Jen, Sam and Hannah were cross referencing lists to try to find some form of match between those working at the Gateway and those who'd visited George. Right now, they were coming up with nothing. All they had were names of people with no connections between them.

'I've just emailed my contact at Scotland Yard and asked them to put up an alert for Jessica's car. All being well, if she enters London we can get a tail on her and see where it leads,' Hannah told them both as she looked up from her computer.

'Great,' said Jen absent-mindedly. She was too busy looking at the photos from Chloe's memory stick. She knew it didn't hold any answers, but she felt herself drawn to the photo of James and Harry together, both seemingly oblivious to the camera, unaware that the moment in time had been captured.

'Jen, do you recognise any of the backgrounds in these photos?' Sam asked, noticing her looking at them.

'I wish I did,' was the only reply Jen could muster. She was so busy going back through the last ten years of her life, looking for clues. Had James ever been away for days on end? Had she ever felt so out of it she'd wondered if her drink had been spiked? Was there even a way out of this mess? Every scene she tried to pick holes in, every holiday memory, every surprise night away. She had drawn a blank. James had been the perfect gentleman from the beginning and continued to be until the day she'd walked out on him. If anything, she'd been the one who was too rough and controlling. The question that hurt the most was would she ever see Melanie and Alex again? She missed their innocence, which would be ruined if James was the master criminal Tim painted him as.

Hannah excused herself and Jen suddenly noticed the commotion outside of the meeting room. Sam tried to ask her if she was okay, but she was too busy watching what was going on.

'I'm sorry, Sam,' Jen said, getting up from her chair and walking out from the room.

'Hannah?' Jen asked, noticing that Hannah was stood

with a phone to one ear and typing away at the same time. 'Hannah, what's happened? What's all the excitement about?'

'We've just got a hit on the ANPR camera on Jessica's pink Beetle going over the Dartford Crossing,' Hannah answered.

'Great, get me a car. I'm going after her.'

'Jen, you can't go anywhere. You know what Max would say if I let you out of the office.'

'This woman might have killed my best friend and I'm not having you or anyone else standing in the way of answers.'

'Jen, calm down. Go back in the meeting room for a second.'

'No, Hannah, you listen. Before you came along I used to run the team here and if I said we were all go, then we were all go.'

'I understand, Jen. Just go to the meeting room and I'll be there in five, okay? I need to make sure we get a tail on her.'

'How are we going to lose a pink Beetle on the M25?'

'You'd be surprised. Jen, please,' Hannah pleaded with her. 'Just five minutes.'

Jen knew she shouldn't have given in the way she did when she returned to the meeting room and sat next to Sam.

'What's happened?' Sam quizzed her as soon as she sat down.

'They've picked up Jessica on the Dartford Crossing,' Jen answered as she began to scroll through the notes on the system, searching for something to occupy her for the five minutes she was willing to give Hannah before she demanded answers.

Chapter Twenty-Five

DI Chris Jackson

'Detective Inspector Jackson.' Chris turned to the sound of his name as he noticed another man heading in his direction. He had been stood outside the door for the past hour, waiting for someone to come along and let him into the flat. The man who had called his name was much older than the one he'd encountered when he first arrived. He was in no doubt that this was someone else coming to stop him in his quest. 'Detective Chief Inspector Collins,' he said holding his hand out towards Chris. He immediately shook it. Chris couldn't help but wonder if he'd used his title in order to make Chris aware that he outranked him.

'I've heard a lot about you,' the DCI told him.

'Good things, I hope?'

'Mostly I'd say, yes. Can we walk and talk? I know a nice little café down the road from here.'

'I would rather have access to this flat if that's okay, sir?'

'I can assure you there is nothing to see here. My team has already been in and cleared up the mess that had been left.'

'If it's all the same?'

'As you wish.' The DCI knocked on the door and exchanged words with the guy from earlier and Chris was given access to the flat. Which was, as he'd been told, completely empty.

'Can I ask, did Chloe Seaward reside here prior to her death? I assume this is why we are both standing here.'

'She did indeed, Detective. As I'm sure you're aware, she used to live here with another one of my team, Lisa Carter.'

The dots were beginning to connect at last.

'And Jennifer Garner?'

'Jen is fine. She is back at the office now helping with the investigation.'

'Can I see her? Because I know three people who are missing her.'

'Chris … can I call you Chris?'

'I'm happy to drop the formalities as I'm hoping we are all on the same team.'

'Max,' the DCI introduced himself.

'Great.'

'Chris, this operation that you have found yourself in the middle of has been running for over fifteen years. Thanks to another victim, who you are no doubt aware of, it was brought back onto our radar last year.'

'Daisy,' Chris found himself saying.

'I'd offer you a seat but as you can see we are a little limited on furniture. Do you need to look around some more or are you happy? We can continue our conversation in that café I mentioned earlier.'

Chris nodded his acknowledgement as he followed Max from the flat. The doors were well and truly opened and everything Chris had been searching for in the last week was about to be revealed to him.

Jen Garner

'How on earth did you manage to secure these?' Jen asked as she jumped into the car with Hannah.

'I'm just hoping you remember how to fire a gun, seeing as I've just handed you one.'

'I'm not too sure. I might need a demonstration, as well as for this pesky thing you've made me put in my ear.'

'The latest communication equipment between ourselves and the office. It's a bit like the one you wore when you walked me through your house, but better.'

Hannah had returned to the meeting room as promised and filled Jen in on Jess' whereabouts, then she had asked Jen if she really wanted to go back out into the field. Hannah had told her that she would totally understand if she opted to stay in the office and that she wouldn't judge her. But Jen knew if she didn't go out there and see this thing to the end she'd regret it. All she wanted to do was look Jessica in the eyes and ask her why. Why now? Why Chloe? And how had she found her?

'You've got to let me lead this though, please Jen. If Jess is involved in this, which I think we both know she is, we need a clean conviction.' Jen nodded her agreement, but she knew in her head she wouldn't think twice about bringing Jess down.

'So, where are we going?' Jen asked eagerly.

'We have a trace on Jess and she is heading along the A13 into Basildon.'

'How far are we away from there?'

'Normal driving, I'd say an hour or so but you're in the car with a pro,' Hannah said, putting her foot down on the accelerator. Jen grabbed hold of the handle above the door.

'So, what's the plan?' Jen questioned, unsure whether this was the end game.

'Tail Jess and see where we end up, unless there is anywhere else you'd rather be?'

'Home,' Jen found herself saying before she thought about it. Hannah turned towards her and smiled.

'Yeah, I'd rather be in DI Jackson's bed, but the things we must do.'

Jen laughed. 'I hope he is all you're expecting him to be.'

'Pft. I learnt from the best. Except I may have slipped up somewhere and not given him a fake name. Oh, and he also knows who I work for so I think I've failed already on that one,' Hannah said, trying to lighten the mood a little.

'Well, I can say from personal experience you're doing better than me. I possibly married a drug lord who killed my best friend.'

'Come on, Jen. You don't think that. We train our butts off to get where we are. Do you really think you'd have been so blindsided by love that you missed the signs? Ten years is a bloody long game to be playing if he just wanted to murder your best friend. He could have done it after nine, possibly?' Jen knew that Hannah was trying to reassure her about James, but that seed of doubt had been planted.

'Hannah, Jen,' the voice suddenly came into Jen's ear, making her jump.

'Go ahead, Sam,' Hannah said.

'Our target has just stopped at number 38 Grange Road, Basildon, current occupant a David Freedman. I'm running his name as we speak.'

'Thank you, Sam. We're about thirty minutes away. Can you send through the postcode and we'll get ourselves over there?'

'Will do. I'll ask the team to keep an eye on any further movements.'

'Thank you, Sam.'

'Well, that's a turn up for the books. I hope Harry isn't the jealous type, if she's going to see other men?' Hannah said as the car's display flashed up a number and postcode.

'Maybe perfect Jess isn't so perfect after all,' Jen mused to herself.

'I'm sorry you two.' Sam's voice came again in their ears. 'David Freedman is showing up as an employee at the Silverdale Gateway and has been for the past five years.'

'Shit,' Jen responded. 'I thought I recognised his name.'

'Thanks, Sam,' Hannah said before turning to her. 'I hope you've remembered your training Jen, because I think you might just need it.'

'It's been a long time, but don't they say it's like riding a bike, once you've done it the once?'

'Are we going to get matching tattoos when it's all over?' Hannah turned away from the road to look at her for a second.

'Sorry?' Jen was totally confused about what Hannah was

talking about, then she realised she was rubbing her wrist again. 'What about "bad girls for life"? On our lower backs?'

'A slag tat? Yeah, I'm sure I'll be able to hide that without a problem.' Hannah smiled, returning her attention to the road.

'Sam tells me stage make-up is a god-send.' They both laughed and the tension they were both feeling was momentarily lifted.

Chapter Twenty-Six

DI Chris Jackson

Chris let Max direct him to a small café not far from the flats where he'd left his car.

'Can I get you a drink or anything?' Max asked as they took a seat at the back of the café next to a painting of the Battle of Waterloo, which Chris briefly thought was a strange thing to have up in a café in Croydon.

'Coffee would be good, thank you.'

'Two coffees please, miss,' Max said to the waitress when she appeared.

'Can I get either of you gentleman a bite to eat?'

'No. I'm good, thank you. Chris?'

'No, I ate on the way,' Chris lied. He'd eat when this was all over.

'So where would you like me to start?' Max asked.

'I guess the beginning?'

'I recruited Lisa Carter or, as I think you have probably realised by now, Jen Garner, straight from Hendon. She'd shown such potential and was street savvy, which is what we needed in the team at the time. In the same year I also recruited Chloe Seaward and through advanced training, these two became inseparable, and to their credit they worked great together.'

Chris nodded. He had suspected as much when he'd looked at the photo of Jen and Chloe that James had given him. 'So, who are your team? I mean where do you fit in? What do you do exactly?'

'We're simply another division of the police force. We just work on the more risky cases that are too big for a local police force to handle but not big enough for MI5. So drug gangs, trafficking, anything that falls on my desk that I think the team can handle.'

'But there's no trace of you anywhere. Chloe and Lisa's police records are both restricted access.'

'We don't like to make a big scene about the stuff that we do, and I try to keep my officers as anonymous as possible. A case fell on my desk that was hitting London pretty hard; believe it or not it all stemmed from a vacant yard not far away from here, actually.' The coffees arrived, so Max stopped talking while the waitress came and then left again.

'Lisa and Chloe both went undercover and managed to infiltrate gangs run by the head guy George Crawford, who had his hand in everything – and I mean everything. After years and years of work we finally caught him and Lisa and Chloe both had a big part to play in bringing him down.'

'So, when did Lisa become Jen?' Chris questioned.

'I always knew both the girls worked hard and played harder. Who could blame them with what they went through on a weekly basis bringing George Crawford down? They would go out to clubs, sleep around and then go back to work, but Lisa fell in love.'

'With James.'

'Yes. I'd always known that I would end up losing her. The thrill of the chase wasn't enough for Lisa anymore. When the case ended and she put her papers in to leave, I let her go.'

'Did you know about James?'

'I suspected as much. She was changing and there was only one thing I knew of that could make a girl like Lisa change: love. The case ended and Lisa left me to start her new life. It wasn't until much later I found out she had met someone and changed her name.'

'So is James clean?' Chris asked.

'When I looked into him originally, yes. Though there are those on my team who believe that he is this big drug lord.'

'I know the guy's in bits about Jen being missing; admittedly he hasn't made good choices in the last week. But there is certainly something there.'

'Good. I just hope that after all this they can make it work.' Chris looked at his coffee.

'Go on. Ask me the other question you are dying to ask?'

'Huh?' Chris was unsure about what Max was getting at. Was he talking about Hannah or …?

'Daisy,' as soon as Max said her name, Chris knew she was the last piece in the puzzle.

'I'm guessing your team had something to do with her death too?'

'Chloe had come across Daisy during some other work she was doing for us. In fact, I hate to say it, but Daisy is where the second half of this story begins.'

'She had the drugs, didn't she? With the imprint?'

'Yes, and just as Chloe was getting close to encouraging Daisy to tell us where she had obtained the drugs from, she got herself arrested with that stupid footballer.'

'So, who killed her? And, more importantly, why wasn't I allowed to investigate?'

'Daisy was connected to something bigger and the powers that be didn't want some small-town cop ruining the bigger picture.'

'So I was taken off the case and led down a black hole?'

'Afraid so. I can tell you this though and leave you to join up the dots. Due to similarities between Chloe and Daisy's murders, we believe that the same people were responsible.'

Chris took another sip from his coffee as he felt his phone vibrating in his pocket. 'So where is Jen now? Is she planning to return home?'

'Jen is at my office looking into Chloe's death, but I will send her home when all this is done. I promise.'

Just then Max's phone started to ring.

'Excuse me, Chris,' he said, going to answer it. 'She did what? She went where?' was all Chris could hear as he tried to listen in. 'I want an armed response team on their way to Silverdale Gateway and I want her bringing back in. One

260

second … I'm sorry Chris, I'm going to have to take a rain check.'

'I hope everything is okay?' Chris questioned.

'I'm sorry, I've got to go. I'll be in touch,' Max said as he threw some money down on the table. 'Who the fuck let them out of the office?' Max barked into his phone as Chris watched him leave the café and run back in the direction they had just come from.

Chris sat back in his chair, trying to take in everything that Max had just told him. He wished that Jen hadn't just upped and left her family behind, but then he would have still been pissed about the Chloe Seaward case being taken from him. He'd have got over it, eventually. At least he now had closure on the Daisy case if nothing else. Taking his phone out of his pocket he noticed the message from Julie asking him where he was and if everything had gone okay with James. He typed out a quick message telling her he'd call later and headed back in the same direction as Max.

Jen Garner

Jen and Hannah had been parked outside the property on Grange Road for the past hour and a half. The gloom of the evening was beginning to fall all round them. They'd secured a tracking device to the bottom of Jess's car so she wasn't going anywhere without them knowing, but now everything was quiet.

'Maybe she just has another man on the go and it's a coincidence that he works at the Gateway?' she speculated as she sat there and watched the same scene as Hannah. Hannah had surveyed the area and there was no other direction that Jess was leaving in but this one. As they watched a black cat dart across the road, a voice came into their ears.

'Hannah, Jen, I want a full status report.'

They'd been busted.

'Max, we are sitting outside a house that our suspect, Jessica Adams, is currently residing in.'

'Why on earth didn't either of you ring me?'

'Because you were busy?' Jen answered for the first time.

'Bullshit.'

'Max, there is movement from the house. Are we okay to proceed?'

'Does it even matter what I say?' Max asked them.

'We are taking that as okay to proceed,' Hannah said as they watched Jess and David get into a second car that was parked outside the house.

'Can we get a trace on the number plate hotel, whisky, zero, two, echo, foxtrot, X-ray?'

'The owner is one Mavis Fry,' Sam's voice came back to them. She sounded like she'd lost some of the bravado she'd discovered when the girls had left her in charge.

'That'll be why we haven't got a bloody tracker on it.' Hannah cursed. 'I'm following a silver Volvo heading towards the Pitsea roundabout. They're taking the fourth exit on to the A13,' Hannah relayed.

'We both know where they're going,' Jen turned and said to Hannah as they continued to follow at a distance. The talking in their ears went silent as Hannah continued to relay their journey until it was clear where the car was heading.

'This is a direct order, do not engage with the suspects. Wait for back-up.'

Hannah pulled the car to the side of the road and looked over towards Jen. 'I'm sorry, Max. We didn't quite get your last message. We are proceeding into the Gateway in pursuit of the suspects,' Hannah answered as she smiled over towards Jen. 'Let's go and bring Chloe's killer in.'

Jen followed Hannah into the Gateway. 'This is a big ass place, Hannah.'

'Are you okay to proceed?' Hannah asked in return.

'I'll clear left if you're happy to clear the right?' Jen said, feeling the buzz kicking in.

'Watch your back. We don't know who else is here with them.'

'Wait for back-up, do not proceed,' Jen could hear Max shouting through her earpiece.

'Max, we can't wait. If we lose them now, we're likely to lose everything,' Jen responded.

'Okay, ready when you are,' Hannah said as she started off to the right.

'Stay safe,' Jen told her as they walked away from each other. They were both doing the one thing they shouldn't in situations like this, but what choice did they have? They had a large space that they needed to cover before Jess could make her escape.

Jen removed the gun from the holster and held it with both hands as she headed towards the east of the lines of containers. It was cold and she could feel her feet turning into blocks of ice. She wiggled them, hoping to bring them to life and keep the blood circulating. She was now alone with her thoughts as she tried desperately to keep on the task.

As Jen held the gun up, she could feel the coolness of the barrel against her face. She started to creep down the first row of containers. Passing each one, she looked at the labelling and the colouring, wondering what was inside ... or who. As she crept, she could hear voices in the distance, talking loudly between themselves.

'Row one cleared,' she whispered into her earpiece and seconds later got a reply from Hannah that her first row was clear.

'I can hear voices, one male and a female. Proceed with caution.' Hannah broke the silence in Jen's ear.

'Back-up is on its way. Please remain at your current positions,' Max responded, but Jen had other ideas as she started to clear one row at the time, heading towards the chatter. She'd been trained using many scenarios just like this. She knew what to do and how to clear the scene.

As Jen continued with only the sound of the distant traffic for company, she tried her hardest not to think of home. There was an eerie silence from her earpiece that she didn't dare disrupt. She couldn't tell them which rows she had cleared because she knew the response she would get back.

As the voices became clearer, she was sure she'd heard one of them before. Her mind attempted to place the voice as she continued on her travels, then suddenly coming to a halt.

'We just found this one creeping around the other containers.' Jen began to pray that it hadn't been Hannah they'd just caught as she braced herself for gunfire.

She continued up the row and heard something hit the ground with a thump.

'Who have we got here?' the female voice asked.

'We caught her near the second container. She was carrying ...' There was a clang as something metal hit the ground. Then the voice came again in her ear.

'Hold position. Back-up is three minutes out.' *Three minutes.* So much could change in three minutes. Jen heard a second thud followed by a cry. She was getting close, but she couldn't tell exactly where the noises were coming from.

'I see we've caught ourselves a police officer.'

'How do you know?' a male voice responded.

'Just call it intuition. I didn't think it would be long before they started tracking us, but it looks like they've come on the wrong day.'

The wrong day? Wrong day for what? Why else were they having a meeting at a port full of containers? There was suddenly a yelp and the female started to shout. 'Where's Detective Garner?'

'I don't know who you're talking about.' A second female spluttered. The voice returned as it seemed to be attempting to talk and spit at the same time. Having not heard from her in a while, Jen had no doubt in her mind that they'd caught Hannah.

'Come out, come out wherever you are,' the first female taunted her. 'I know she's here somewhere. David, go and find her.'

Jen had seconds to decide. She knew she hadn't cleared all the rows and it would be a rookie mistake. Hannah was in trouble and there was only one way she was going to end this on her terms.

'Get her trousers down and I'll give her a taste of what we gave that last detective.' Jen knew she couldn't let Hannah suffer the same fate as Chloe. Taking a deep breath, she shouted.

'I'm here.'

James Garner

'Dad, I'm going out,' James shouted to his father who had been busy cooking dinner for the arrival of the rest of the family. 'I won't be long, there's something I need to do.'

'Okay son,' his father responded.

There was somewhere that James hadn't searched; a number that had never responded when he'd phoned it. The address and phone number on the scrap of paper was his last-ditch effort to try and bring his wife home safely. James drove off the drive and headed towards the motorway as he programmed the address into his sat-nav. He'd never been to Mansfield so hoped it would be an easy journey given his time limits. He wanted to be home for when the kids arrived. He let his mind wander as he drove, trying Jen's number again, even though the police still had all her electronics. He also tried Detective Jackson's number which also went to answer phone. The Detective must have known what was going on by now; he had the photo and the missing link to the dead body. Jen had known the woman who'd died, which explained her strange behaviour before she left. He just hoped that he wouldn't be too late to bring her home safely.

The street hadn't been hard to find and, to James' relief, there was plenty of parking. He just had to find number 25, having already driven up the street once to make sure he was getting the right place. He climbed out of his car, went up the steps and rang the doorbell. He didn't have to wait long before a grey-haired lady answered the door.

'Hello. I wonder if you can help me?' James asked the old lady. 'I'm looking for my wife. Let me show you a photo.'

'No need, James. Come in, I've been expecting you.' James was mystified but had no choice but to follow her inside.

'My name's Isabelle. Can I get you a drink of tea or something stronger?' James was taken aback. Maybe this was just an old lady who was glad of a bit of company ... but she knew his name? As he sat on the sofa, he watched the carriage clock on the mantlepiece, remembering the one his mum had owned just like it when he was little.

'Now then, James,' Isabelle said as she returned with a tray of drinks that James was sure he'd declined. 'You're here about Jen, aren't you? I've been expecting you for a while actually ...'

Chapter Twenty-Seven

Jen Garner

'I caught her snooping around one of the containers,' David told Jess triumphantly as he pushed her into the open space.

'The place is surrounded, you've got nowhere to go,' Jen said as she was hauled into the light. 'Jess?'

'Nice for you to join us Jen, or should I call you by your official title, Detective Jennifer Garner? Now drop your gun on the floor and kick it over here nice and slow.' Jen didn't move, keeping her eye on Jess.

'Okay, play it your way,' Jess said as she moved over towards Hannah and pulled her head back by her hair, pressing a gun to the side of her face. 'I'll tell you what I might have let Chloe suffer, but I liked Chloe. She was fun.'

Jen knew what was coming and there was no way she was going to let Hannah suffer because of her.

'Here,' Jen said as she dropped her gun on the floor and kicked it towards Jess then pulled out the device that had been safely fastened into her ear; she was sick of having other people's voices in her head. She took in her surroundings as, to her relief, Jess let go of Hannah's head and it returned to the gravel floor with a crunch. There was another male who was standing not far from Hannah who looked to be unbuckling his trousers. She knew him from somewhere, but she couldn't quite place where he fitted into all of this.

'Let her go,' Jen shouted as she locked eyes with Jess, who was clearly the one in charge of this little meeting. 'I'm the one you want, let her go and you can have me in her place.'

'If only, Jen. Did you like the gifts I sent you?'

Jen held her position as she looked at where her gun had landed and moved towards Hannah whose face was now turned towards her. She could feel her whole world crashing down, but she needed to stay in control.

'Don't worry. You can have both of them later, though I'm informed once you've had one detective, you've had them all,' Jess informed the second male while laughing at her own joke. 'So Jennifer, have you figured it all out? Oh, and how's the family doing? Those two adorable children of yours and the handsome hubby? I hope you don't mind but I deleted the touching message you left for them while I was comforting James. I'll make sure I'm the first to offer him my condolences and a shoulder to cry on,' Jess taunted.

Jen took a bold step forward, positioning herself between the mystery male and Hannah. Though she was unarmed and David had a gun pointed at her, she knew there was a way out of this. There had to be.

'This whole place is surrounded, Jess. The game's up.' Jen could actually hear her heart racing as she kept her eyes on Jess.

'Oh come on Jen, you don't expect me to believe that? You may have fooled my father all those years ago, but I'm not as foolish as he was.'

Jess could give her all the answers she needed, but she had to concentrate on getting her and Hannah out of this situation safely. She could hear a helicopter in the distance and prayed it was the cavalry.

'So, it's you who's been re-manufacturing those drugs, and it was you who set Harry up to take the blame?'

'Ah yes, Harry, stupid boy. All he had to do was sell a couple of pills in the odd nightclub while I was away, but he couldn't even do that could he!' Jess's foot made contact with Hannah again with a thud. 'But I made sure there were insurances in place. I bet he nearly died when he saw the amount of drugs I had stashed at his house.'

'Why did you have to kill Chloe? If this was all about drug distribution you could have just set up again without killing her?' Jen was playing for time, hoping someone was on their way.

'I met up with one of dad's old friends and we were sat talking about dad's network and how I could just walk in where he left off. One day I took my dad's friend to one of my little parties, and you know what? The funniest thing happened; he recognised Chloe.'

'So, you killed her?'

'Slow down, Jennifer. I've not got to the best bit. I kept her close and fed her my plans. Dad's friend brought me some photos, and who did I see in one of the photos along with Chloe? I saw you! I saw Little Miss Perfect. Everyone was always gushing about how perfect you were. Harry was always "Jen does this, Jen does that" so I left you a gift.'

'I bet your dad is proud of you, continuing his legacy.'

'I've no idea I've not seen him since … well, years ago. Mother dearest used to get drunk and she'd tell me all about the glory days.'

Jen took another step forward. She was almost standing close enough to Hannah to feel the heat from her body.

'Slow down, Detective. You're missing something. You've met Oliver here? He's been following you for ages. It's a shame you took so long to notice. Do you want to know the best bit? Oliver knows all about your life in Long Eaton. Your darling children. He's been watching you, Jen. He's even been getting close to your husband's work colleagues. They all think Oliver is great and is going to be the perfect asset to the company. He was *that* close to making sure your world came crashing down. But I wanted the last laugh.'

'So, you killed Chloe to get back at me?'

'Oh dear, Jennifer. I sent you some flowers and a card. What more did you want?'

'And the picture?'

'Oh yeah I forgot about that one. Did you like it? I thought it was very artistic. It captures Chloe's last breath perfectly.'

'What have you gained in all this, Jess? Has it all really been worth it? Here we are in the middle of nowhere in the freezing cold. You've got nowhere to run, it's over.'

'But I'm a survivor, Jen. I always have a backup plan and powerful friends in the right places. Chloe wasn't the first person I've had to dispense with and certainly won't be the last.' Just then a helicopter hovered overhead and Jessica momentarily took her eyes off Jen. She knew she just needed to take a couple more steps and she'd have the gun. She locked eyes with Hannah who faintly nodded her acknowledgement.

'Oh, look. Here's my ride out of here. Nice knowing you, Oliver,' Jess said as she took aim at him and fired, just missing Jen's left arm. 'It's a shame you got caught, I'd have had more use for you if you hadn't.'

Jen heard Oliver hit the floor as Jess's attention turned to David. 'And I won't be needing you either where I'm going.' David looked at her with an open mouth as she fired and he fell. At that moment Jen hit the deck and rolled, gun in hand. She pointed it towards Jess.

'Give yourself up, Jess. You're not going anywhere.'

'Say goodbye to Harry for me.' Jess turned and ran and Jen needed to make a decision. She stood up and fired the gun in the direction Jess had gone. As the sound of the gun shot filled the air, Jen began to run in the same direction as Jess. With her gun posed to take the shot, it wasn't long before several excitable dogs and people dressed in black gave chase.

'Stand down, Officer. We'll take over from here,' another officer told her as they caught up with her, but she wasn't listening. Hannah would be safe now. She had to end this for Chloe's sake, so she continued to run. Following the black-cladded armed response figures into the night, the next thing she heard was a short exchange of gun fire and then everything fell silent.

'Stand down, Jen. It's over,' someone said as they placed their hand on her arm. Jen attempted to blink away the gloom in front of her as she turned and looked at the stranger next to her.

DI Chris Jackson

Chris hadn't been sure what he was doing when he'd got back in his car. Something was clearly going on, from what he'd heard from Max's phone call and also his abrupt departure. Though he hadn't heard much, he was sure the name the 'Silverdale Gateway' had been mentioned and, if Max's reaction was anything to go by, maybe he should be getting himself there too. His sat-nav had told him it would take about fifty minutes. Chris promised himself that if he got to the Gateway and there was nothing going on, he'd turn around and go straight back to Nottingham.

As Chris arrived, he noticed several tactical units and dogs being held back by their handlers. He took his warrant card from his jacket pocket and approached the Officer who looked to be in charge.

'Detective Inspector Jackson,' he said, flashing his badge. 'Can I ask what's going on here?'

'We have a suspected situation going on inside the vicinities involving firearms and suspected casualties.'

'Is there anything I can do to help?'

'Excuse me.' The Officer turned away and spoke into his earpiece as a helicopter passed overhead. 'I'm sorry, sir. Can I ask you to please return to your car?'

Chris was about to respond when he heard the first gun shot, followed by a second. Then everyone started to run into the Gateway as a further shot was fired out.

'Please stay back, sir,' one of the armed officers barked at him as Chris began to sprint along with them. He wasn't going anywhere. He very much doubted these people were going to stop and arrest him when something bigger was clearly happening.

'Have it your way,' the same Officer shouted at him as he too sprinted off. Chris wasn't sure where he was planning to head once he was inside the dock but decided he would just follow everyone else and wing it.

As he turned a second corner he came face to face with the one person he had just spent the last week tracking. The panic was spread across her face, her eyes wide with adrenaline.

'Stand down, Officer. We'll take it from here.' It was the same Officer who had told him to stay back speaking to her but, like him, she ignored him and kept running until more gun shots echoed around the surroundings and she suddenly stopped dead. He reached out and put his hand on her arm.

'Stand down, Jen. It's over.'

Epilogue

THURSDAY
Jen Garner

Jen sat in the chair opposite Max's desk as the sun started to rise over London. Everything ached, and she was beyond tired.

'While you were out in the field, Sam worked out how George knew about your family.'

'Oh?'

'A pen-pal.'

'I don't understand.'

'George had a prison pen-pal. It turns out it was one of the mums from the school your kids attend.'

'Shit... and I bet I know exactly who he was communicating with,' Jen said, remembering Helen's excitement only a week ago. She had been so concerned about hiding from the past the most innocent thing had caught her out.

'She sent him some photos, telling him about a school event she'd been to and guess who was in the pictures?'

'My family?'

'Yup, the prison staff didn't think anything of the photos, so they weren't confiscated.'

'And Jess?'

'I don't think she knows who you are either. Both you and Hannah reported that she called you Jennifer on several occasions.'

'Where is Hannah now? Is she okay?'

'She's fine. No major injuries, just some bruising but we sent her straight to A&E to get checked over after we debriefed.'

'I'm hoping you're about to tell me Jess is dead, but I'm guessing I haven't got that lucky.'

'Her heart stopped a couple of times during surgery, but she'll make it through. Once she does she'll be locked up, awaiting trial for the murder of Chloe Seaward amongst other charges.'

Jen sighed. It had been a long night. 'So after all that, no one knows my real identity then?'

'It's looking that way. So, what do you want to do now, Detective?' Max asked as Jen slouched further down in the chair in front of him.

'I want to go home,' Jen said, as she once again studied Max's office walls.

'You are an amazing officer, Jen. One of the best.'

'I want to go home, Max. I want to see my family again.' She fell silent before adding 'if they'll have me.'

'I'm not going to make you choose, Jen. But it's got to be different this time.'

'I know, I know. I need to tell James everything, but our marriage vows were for better, for worse, right?'

'There will always be a home here for you, whatever happens.'

Jen noticed how the emotion that Max never showed was now appearing across his face as he struggled to fight back the tears. Standing up, she moved over towards him. 'I want you to meet James, I want the kids to know you.' Jen fought back the tears herself as she hugged Max.

'Goodbye, Lisa.'

Jen wiped her eyes and took a deep breath as she left Max's office for one last time. As she moved across the office, she felt that all eyes were on her, just like on the day she'd arrived. She walked over towards where Sam was sat, busy typing away.

'If you need any references for that application form, Max will know how to find me,' Jen told her as she turned towards Hannah's desk, which was piled high with files. Hannah would never replace Chloe but when she'd been working alongside her, at times she could have sworn blind she was working with Chloe.

Chloe's ghost had been laid to rest. Jen knew she could

finally move on from her past. Who knew what the future held? Hopefully, she could keep in touch with Max this time. He had always been a father figure to her, and she knew how much the kids would love him.

But right now, there was a car waiting to take her home.

DI Chris Jackson

Chris had been back from London since the early hours and found himself drifting in and out of sleep with Fluff curled up on his knee whilst catching up on rubbish television. He hadn't hung around at the scene once it was all over. He'd done his job and then walked away. He was unsure what was going to happen with Jen and the double life she had created for herself, but it wasn't his problem anymore. He had played his part and now she needed to play hers.

He hadn't made an effort to pack away the files he'd stolen. He needed to return them and no doubt attempt to explain why he had them at home. As for the memory stick, he'd keep that for now, just in case. If they knew he'd transferred files onto a USB, he'd tell them he'd destroyed it. He'd deal with the situation when it arrived. Right now, he was planning to unwind and hopefully visit the doctors about the headaches and focusing issues.

He had exchanged messages with Julie and learnt that Harry was just being charged with the drug offences and bailed on the murder charges. She had told him that Hannah's team had decided it was unlikely that he had been involved in the murder of Chloe but wanted to keep their options open until Jess could confirm otherwise.

The last week had been crazy; the busiest he'd ever seen the office. But he knew that once he went back, it would be like nothing ever happened and the budget cuts would keep on coming, no matter how many cases were solved and the manpower needed to solve them.

Though he knew he hadn't been able to fulfil the promise he'd made to James, he was content enough to know that Jen … Lisa …. whatever her name was, was safe. He just hoped that once James knew the truth, they would still be able to make their marriage work. Who would have ever believed that a highly trained officer lived on his patch in Long Eaton? One thing he couldn't stop thinking about was Hannah and that night at the club. He'd forgotten the last time a woman had made him feel that alive.

As he reached for his cup of tea, whilst trying not to disturb Fluff, there was a loud knock on his door. No one had buzzed up from downstairs asking to be let in ; maybe it was one of his neighbours or something? Moving Fluff carefully onto the chair, he made his way towards the front door.

Someone forced themselves into his flat as he opened the door, colliding with him and pinning him to the wall. The adrenaline pulsed through his body as he felt soft lips against his own. He tried to break free as he felt them brush across his cheek and move up to his ear.

'Come on, Detective Inspector. Put some effort in.'

He managed to free himself before pushing her up hard against the closed front door. She laughed as their lips met and his hands started to trail her body. He knew exactly who this was. He would no longer be left with what-ifs and regrets.

Because right now he had Officer Littlefair pinned against his front door and there was no reason to stop this time.

James Garner

'Right come on you two, we need to get you both back to school for this play,' James told Alex and Melanie as they attempted to run rings around him while he was trying to get them ready to go out. 'Come on, you promised Gran you'd help me out.'

James was about to shout at the children to get their shoes

on when there was a loud knock on the front door. James was tempted to ignore it; they needed to get out of the house if they were going to make it to the school on time, not be caught up by some salesman.

'Right, I expect you two to have your shoes and coats on by the time I've answered the door,' James shouted, heading to the hallway. He stood there for a second and studied the figure through the glass panel. Unlocking the door and opening it, he looked at the person in front of him.

'Hi.'

'Hi,' James responded, not sure what else to say, as they both stood there looking at each other.

'Mummy's home!' Melanie let out a loud squeal, making them both jump. Seconds later, Alex was also there as he flung himself at her.

'Mummy, where have you been?' Alex asked as the tears started to stream down his face. She knelt down as Melanie joined the embrace.

'Mummy, we've missed you,' Melanie sobbed.

'But you're home in time to come and see the school play,' Alex excitedly reminded her.

'I wouldn't miss it for the world, silly.'

So many thoughts entered James' mind, he didn't know what to do. He hadn't ever expected this day to happen after what Isabelle had told him. He'd never expected to see his wife and the mother of his children there in front of him ever again. As the children danced around excitedly and hugged their mum, he began to feel a lump forming in his throat.

'You coming now, or later when Dad picks Gran and Grandad up?' Melanie questioned, clearly wanting to get the car sharing organised in her mind.

'Come on you two, out of the way or Mummy won't be going anywhere,' James told them both as he stepped aside to let his wife back into the house they shared.

'Where have you been, Mummy?' Melanie asked.

'Did you buy us a present?' Alex jumped up and down.

The questions started as the kids freed themselves from her. Jen slowly stood up as the tears continued to trickle down her face. James stood gazing at her; she looked as beautiful as the first time he'd seen her. As the children ran back inside, James took a step back, unsure how to approach his wife as she slowly entered the house. He suddenly forgot everything that had happened over the week; all the hurt and pain didn't matter any more. As Jen took a step over the threshold, he couldn't stop himself as he held open his arms and his wife fell straight back into them where she belonged.

'I'm so sorry James, I can explain everything.' He didn't know how to respond as he felt his own tears falling into her hair. None of that mattered right now, all that mattered was his wife and the mother to his two children was home safe.

Thank You

Dear Reader

Thank you for reading my debut novel! I really do hope you've enjoyed it.

I was brought up on a mixture of *The Bill* and later *Spooks*. I always wanted to join the police service but life took me in a total different direction. I used to daydream about secret service officers and kick-ass females saving the day.

Though this is my first published novel I have plenty of teenage angst novels sat in my bottom drawer at home.

This won't be the end for Jen, Chris and some of the other characters in *Perfect Lie* and they will return in the next book.

If you enjoyed *Perfect Lie* please consider leaving me a review on Goodreads or the website where you bought the book.

And make sure you tell your friends ☺

Until next time,
Claire

About the Author

Claire lives in Nottingham with her family, a cat called Whiskers and a dog called Podrick.

She suffers from Multiple Sclerosis and as a result of the disease had to reduce her hours working in insurance for an Insolvency Insurer. This spare time enabled her to study a creative writing course which inspired her to write her debut, *Perfect Lie*.

When Claire isn't working she enjoys reading crime novels and listening to music – the band Jimmy Eat World is her biggest muse! Claire is also an avid reader and book blogger. The inspiration for her novels comes from the hours spent watching *The Bill* with her grandparents and auntie; then later, *Spooks* and other detective programmes like *Inspector Morse*, *A Touch of Frost* and *Midsomer Murders*.

To find out more about Claire,
follow her on social media:
Twitter: @ClaireEESheldon
Facebook: https://www.facebook.com/clairesheldonauthor

More Ruby Fiction

From Claire Sheldon

A Silent Child

Book 2 – Lisa Carter Files

The streets are no place for a child …

After a traumatic event that almost ripped Jen Garner's family apart, life is finally starting to get back to normal.

Then a woman's body is found in the river. Shortly afterwards, a young boy is discovered wandering the streets. He refuses to speak to anyone, just repeats one name over and over, to the confusion of most of the local authorities – but Jen knows exactly who he's asking for, and it's enough to make her blood run cold …

Visit www.rubyfiction.com for details.

Introducing Ruby Fiction

Ruby Fiction is an imprint of Choc Lit Publishing.
We're an award-winning independent publisher,
creating a delicious selection of fiction.

See our selection here:
www.rubyfiction.com

Ruby Fiction brings you stories that inspire emotions.

We'd love to hear how you enjoyed *Perfect Lie*. Please
visit www.rubyfiction.com and give your feedback or
leave a review where you purchased this novel.

Ruby novels are selected by genuine readers like yourself.
We only publish stories our Tasting Panel want to see in
print. Our reviews and awards speak for themselves.

Could you be a Star Selector and join our Tasting Panel?
Would you like to play a role in choosing which novels
we decide to publish? Do you enjoy reading women's
fiction? Then you could be perfect for our Tasting Panel.

Visit here for more details …
www.choc-lit.com/join-the-choc-lit-tasting-panel

Keep in touch:
Sign up for our monthly newsletter Spread for all the latest
news and offers: www.spread.choc-lit.com. Follow us on
Twitter: @RubyFiction and Facebook: RubyFiction.

Stories that inspire emotions!